Saved from the Sea

W. H. G. Kingston

"Saved from the Sea"

By

W.H.G. Kingston

1876

Saved from the Sea

Chapter One.

The wonderful linguist—I study Arabic—My first voyage to sea—We sail for the coast of Africa—The brig capsized—Saved on a raft.

"Never throw away a piece of string, a screw, or a nail, or neglect an opportunity, when it offers, of gaining knowledge or learning how to do a thing," my father used to say; and as I respected him, I followed his advice,—and have, through life, on many occasions had reason to be thankful that I did so.

In the town near which we resided lived a tailor, Andrew Spurling by name. He was a remarkable man, though a mere botcher at his trade; for he could never manage to make his customers' clothes fit their bodies. For fat men he invariably made tight coats, and for thin people loose ones. Few, therefore, except those who were indifferent on that point, went a second time to him for new ones. He repaired clothes, however, to perfection, and never refused to attempt renovating the most threadbare or tattered of garments. He had evidently mistaken his vocation; or rather, his friends had committed a great error when they made him a tailor. Yet perhaps he succeeded as well in it as he would have done at any handicraft. He possessed, in fact, a mind which might have raised him to a respectable, if not a high position, in the walks of literature or science. As it was, however, it was concentrated on one object—the acquisition of languages. Andrew had been sent to the grammar-school in our town, where he gained the rudiments of education, and a certain amount of Latin and Greek; and where he might, possibly, have become well-educated, had he not—his father dying insolvent—been taken from school, and, much to his grief, apprenticed to the trade he was now following.

Instead of perfecting himself in the languages of which he already knew a little, and without a friend to guide him,—having saved up money enough to buy a grammar and dictionary,—he commenced the study of another; after mastering the chief difficulties of which he began still another; and so he had gone on through life, with the most determined perseverance, gaining even more than a smattering of the tongues not only of Europe but of the Eastern world, though he could make no practical use of his acquisitions.

Apparently slight circumstances produce important results. Coming out of school one day, and while playing, as usual, in our somewhat rough fashion, my class-mate, Richard Halliday, tore my jacket from the collar downwards.

"That is too bad," I exclaimed. "A pretty figure I will make, going through the streets in this state."

"Never mind, Charlie," he answered. "Come into old Spurling's shop; he will sew it up in a trice. He always mends our things; and I will pay for it."

I at once accepted my school-fellow's offer; and we made our way to the narrow lane in which Andrew's small shop was situated. I had never before been there, though I had occasionally seen his tall, gaunt figure as he wended his way to church on Sunday; for on no other day in the week did he appear out of doors.

"Here's Charlie Blore, who wants to have his jacket mended, Mr Spurling," said Dick, introducing me.

"A grammar-school boy?" asked the tailor, looking at me.

"Yes; and in my class," answered Dick.

"Oh! then you are reading Xenophon and Horace," observed the tailor; and he quoted a passage from each author, both of which I was able to translate, greatly to his satisfaction. "You will soon be turning to other languages, I hope," he observed, not having as yet touched my jacket, which I had taken off and handed to him.

"I should like to know a good many," I answered: "French, German, and Italian."

"Very well in their way," observed Andrew; "but there are many I prefer which open up new worlds to our view: for every language we learn, we obtain further power of obtaining information and communicating our thoughts to others. Hebrew, for instance: where can we go without finding some of the ancient people? or Arabic, current over the whole Eastern world, from the Atlantic shores of Africa to the banks of the Indus? Have you ever read the 'Arabian Nights'?" asked Andrew.

"Yes, part of it," I answered.

"Then think how delightful it would be to read it in the language in which it is written, and still more to visit the scenes therein described. I began six years ago—and I wish that some great man would invite me to accompany him to Syria, or Morocco, or Egypt, or other Eastern lands; though that is not likely." And Andrew sighed. "However, my young friends, as you may have a chance of visiting those regions, take my advice: Study Arabic; you will find it of more use than Greek or Latin, which no one speaks nowadays— more's the pity. I will instruct you. Come here whenever you can. I will lend you my books, or tell you where you may purchase others. I won't say how soon you will master the language; that depends on capacity,"—and Andrew gave a self-satisfied smile; "but the sooner you begin, the better."

"But, Mr Spurling, I should like much to have my jacket mended," I observed.

"So you shall; I will do it while you take your first lesson in Arabic." And Andrew, without rising from his seat, shuffled along in a curious fashion to a bookcase hanging against the wall, from which he drew forth a well-thumbed volume. "It's as precious as gold," he observed. "Don't be daunted by the strange characters," he added, as he gave the book into my hands. "Now, you and Master Halliday stand there; while I stitch, you shall learn the first principles of the language."

Then taking my jacket on his knee, and needle and thread in hand, he commenced a lecture, from which, as Dick and I listened attentively, we really gained a considerable amount of information. It was, I afterwards discovered, in the first pages of the book, which he knew by heart; so he had not to draw his eyes from his work. I grew so interested, that I was quite sorry when my jacket was mended.

From that day onward, Dick and I became constant visitors at Andrew's shop after school-hours, and really made considerable progress in Arabic. I believe, indeed, that we should before long have advanced almost as far as our master had done, — for he had three or four languages in hand at the same time, to which he added a new one every year or so. My school-days, however, came suddenly to an end. I had always had a hankering for the navy, though I did not talk much about it. An old friend of my father, who had just been appointed to the command of a frigate destined for the Mediterranean, called before starting for Portsmouth.

"I will take one of your boys, Blore, as an offering to Neptune."

My father looked at me. "Charlie is rather too old, I fear, to enter the navy," he observed.

"Oh no! Lord Dundonald was much older," I exclaimed. "Let me go."

"He will do; I will take him," said the captain. "He must work hard and make up for lost time. He had better accompany me, and see the ship fitted out."

My father was an old soldier; and my mother being a strong-minded, active woman, directly my future captain left us all hands in the house were set to work, down to the nursery-maid, to prepare my kit; while I ran into the town to get my measure taken by Andrew Spurling, who promised to have a "nautical cut" suit ready for me by the next day. I had, in an impulse of gratitude, begged that he might make my clothes. It was fatal to my appearance as a trim midshipman; and I had to discard some, and get others altered, before I was fit to present myself on the quarter-deck.

As I was leaving his shop, Andrew took down a volume from his bookcase. "Receive this as a parting gift from one who wishes you well, and who, although his body is chained to his counter, will accompany you in spirit to those far-off Eastern lands it may be your happy destiny to visit," he said, as he handed the book to me, with a kind look which showed the sincerity of his feelings.

It was a grammar and vocabulary, with a portion of the "Arabian Nights" in Arabic. I promised to keep up the study of the language in which he had initiated me, and to add others as I might find opportunity.

The next night I set off with the captain to Portsmouth. As he had promised to make me a sailor, and I wished to become one, I soon picked up a fair amount of nautical knowledge; and by the time the ship was ready for sea, I could not only knot and splice, but had acquainted myself with every portion of her from "truck to keelson."

We had gone out to Spithead, and were expecting to sail in a few days, when who should come up the side but my old school-fellow, Dick Halliday.

"When I found that you had actually gone, I could not bear the thought of remaining behind; and I so worked upon my guardians to let me go to sea, by telling them that I should be miserable if I didn't, and fit for nothing else, that I succeeded. Moreover, at my urgent request, they, as you see, got me appointed to your frigate," he exclaimed in a tone of triumph. "I have my chest in the boat; what am I to do with it?" he asked, after I had expressed my pleasure at seeing him.

"We will soon hoist it on board," I answered.

The first lieutenant cast an angry glance at the chest, for it was unusually large; and before many hours were over, its owner, to his great dismay, saw it cut down into much smaller proportions.

We were at length at sea, running down Channel with a strong north-easterly breeze. I had the start of Halliday, and felt myself already a sailor, while he knew nothing about a ship; but I found that I had still a good deal to learn. I managed to keep well ahead of him while the ship remained in commission. Our captain, one of the best officers in the service, wished his midshipmen to see as much as possible of the places the ship visited, so as to gain all the information they could; and we, accordingly, had opportunities offered us of going on shore and making excursions into the interior. We visited Jerusalem, Cairo, Algiers, Athens, and many other places of interest. Halliday and I found our acquirements as linguists of very considerable value.

I cannot stop, however, to describe our adventures. Three years passed rapidly away, and we returned home nearly full-grown men, with a greatly increased stock of nautical and general knowledge.

We went, during our brief stay on shore, to visit Andrew Spurling; who listened eagerly to our accounts of what we had seen, and was delighted when I presented him with several really valuable volumes which I had picked up at Cairo. "You have amply repaid me, Mr Blore," he exclaimed, fondly clutching the books. "I knew you would find an immense advantage from your knowledge of the chief language of the East, and let me now advise you to study Spanish; it is spoken over a large portion of the globe, and you are sure to find a use for it."

I so far followed his advice as to send for a Spanish grammar and dictionary, which I intended to use as soon as I had leisure. My stay on shore, however, was short; for in a couple of weeks I was appointed to the *Viper*, a ten-gun brig destined for the coast of Africa. Her commander knew my family, and had offered to take me. And I found Halliday on board, he having been appointed to her by the Admiralty.

She was a very different craft from the fine frigate to which I had before belonged. She was of narrow beam, and carried taunt masts and square yards; indeed, we all saw that she would require careful handling to avoid being capsized. But she was a new, tidy, fast little craft, and no one on board allowed forebodings of evil to trouble his mind. The commander did not express his opinion till we were clear of the Channel, when he addressed the crew.

"You will have to be smart in shortening sail, my lads," he said, after making some other observations. "The last man off the lower deck when the hands are turned up must look out for the consequences."

They all knew what that meant, — a "black listing," "six water grog," or walking the deck with a shot in each hand during a watch. Still, though they did not like it, they knew it was for the good of all. And besides, we were continually exercised in shortening and making sail, to get the crew into proper discipline.

One day — the commander being on deck — a sudden squall struck the brig and heeled her over till the water rushed through her lee-scuppers. "All hands save ship!" he shouted. The men came springing up from below, some through the fore-hatchway, but a greater number through the main. The commander himself was standing near the companion-hatch — intended only for his own and the gun-room officers' use. Our tall, thin commander had just turned round to take his spy-glass from the beckets in which it hung, when a petty officer, — a knowing fellow, who had slipped through the gun-room passage in order to take advantage of the other men, — springing on deck, butted right into the pit of his stomach. The blow, doubling him up, sent him sprawling over on his back, with his legs in the air. But, without waiting to apologise, the seaman sprang up the rigging like lightning, and was laying out among the others on the main-topsail-yard before the commander could open his eyes to ascertain who had capsized him. He was, naturally, excessively angry, but probably did not like to shout out, "You fellow, who knocked me over, come down from aloft." And just then, indeed, all hands were really required for shortening sail. Few of the officers had seen the man upset the commander, and those who had could

7

not say positively who he was. I had my suspicions; having caught sight of an old shipmate—Ben Blewett—running up the main rigging over the heads of several others in a way which showed he had some reason for so doing. All the efforts of the officers to discover the culprit, however, were unavailing; and I thought it wisest to say nothing about the matter. The commander could not justly have punished the man for knocking him down, as it was done unintentionally, though he might have done so for coming up the officers' passage. And so we enjoyed a hearty laugh in the berth at the whole affair.

I should have said that the caterer for our mess was a steady old mate, Reuben Boxall; a most excellent fellow, for whom I entertained a great regard. He followed the principle my father had advised me to adopt, and never threw away a piece of string—that is to say, when an opportunity occurred of acquiring knowledge he never neglected it. His chief fancy, however, was for doctoring—that is to say, the kindness of his heart made him wish to be able to relieve the sufferings of his fellow-creatures; and he could bleed, and bind up broken limbs, and dress wounds, as well as the surgeon himself, while he had a good knowledge of the use of all the drugs in the medicine-chest. Boxall had indeed a good head on his shoulders, and was respected by all.

Many of us were still laughing at the commander's capsize, some declaring that it served him right for being in such a hurry.

"Let me tell you youngsters that we must be in a hurry on board this craft," observed Boxall. "Do you know the name given to ten-gun brigs such as ours? I will tell you: 'Sea-Coffins.' And the *Viper* will prove *our* coffin, if we do not keep very wide-awake, let me warn you."

Most of the mess thought that old Boxall was trying to frighten them; but I cannot say that I was comfortable, as we had already discovered that the brig, to say the best of her, was excessively crank. The two lieutenants and the master had served chiefly on board line-of-battle ships and frigates before they got their promotion, and were inclined to sneer at the commander's caution, and I know that during their watch they carried on much longer than he would have approved of.

We were somewhere in the latitude of Madeira, when we encountered a heavy gale which severely tried the brig. Though we saved our spars by shortening sail in time, two of our boats were lost and the rest damaged, our weather-bulwarks were stove in, and we were in other respects handled very roughly.

We had got somewhat to rights, and were running down the African coast, keeping closer in-shore than usual. It was night, and the second lieutenant's watch. Boxall and I—who had the first watch—having been relieved, went into the berth to take a glass of "swizzel" and some biscuit and cheese, after which we sat talking for some minutes before turning in. The rest of the watch were below fast asleep. We were standing by our hammocks, about to undress, when we felt the brig heel over on her beam-ends.

"I advised him to shorten sail before he let the watch go below," exclaimed Boxall. "It's too late now. Stick by me, Charlie, whatever happens."

"Turn out there, and save ship!" he shouted, as we sprang on deck; and together we made our way up to the starboard hammock-nettings, on which we found several people clinging, but in the darkness could not make out who they were. The water was rushing in fast through the hatches, and the brig was evidently sinking. Shrieks and cries for help came from the lee side, to which most of those on deck had been thrown; but the greater number of the watch had, I judged, been aloft at that moment, about to shorten sail, and were already struggling in the water.

"Now, my lads, the brig is going down, and we must find something to cling to if we don't want to go down with her," sung out Boxall. "Who is there will try and make a struggle for life?"

"I will," cried a voice, which I recognised as Halliday's.

"And I," said Ben Blewett, who worked his way up to us with an axe in his hand.

The boats which had escaped the previous gale were under repair; so we could not trust to one of them. Making our way to the booms, Blewett cut several away; and, providentially, some planks had been left by the carpenters, which we got hold of, together with a few fathoms of rope. The planks and spars, under Boxall's directions, we rapidly lashed together, and Halliday and I each got hold of a small piece of board. Launching our roughly-constructed raft abaft the mainmast, we threw ourselves on it and paddled away from the wreck for our lives. The officer of the watch must have been thrown to leeward when the brig went over; neither the commander nor any of the other officers had time to make their escape from their cabins. We heard several men, however, who were forward, crying out for help; but it was impossible for us to go to their assistance, and we could only hope that they were attempting to save their lives by constructing a raft, as we had done.

Scarcely had we got clear of the brig when her masts rose as she righted, and down she went, dragging with her all those on board, as well as the men clinging to the rigging.

The dark clouds passed away, and the moon shone forth brightly on the sparkling waters, revealing to us a few floating planks and spars—all that remained of our brig. Not a human being was to be seen; every one of our shipmates had been engulfed by the hungry sea. We paddled back, and getting hold of such spars and planks as we could find, placed them crosswise under our raft to prevent it from upsetting, though it was even thus a ticklish affair. Ben had taken his seat forward, I sat astride at the other end, Boxall and Halliday occupied the middle. How far we were off the coast of Africa we could not exactly tell, but we judged that we should have fifteen or twenty leagues to paddle before we could reach it. This would take us two or three days at least; and, without food or water, how could we expect to hold out? Our prospects were indeed miserable in the extreme; still, we had reason to be thankful that we had escaped the fate which had overtaken our shipmates.

"TRUST IN GOD," EXCLAIMED BOXALL, POINTING UPWARDS

On and on we paddled, till our arms began to ache. "We are making no way, I've a notion; and as for reaching the shore, that is more than we can do," exclaimed Ben at length, as he placed under him the piece of board with which he had been paddling. "Our best chance is to be picked up by some passing vessel; and I hope one will heave in sight when a breeze gets up."

"I fear there is but little chance of that," said Halliday in a desponding tone; "a vessel may pass close by and not see us, seated as we are scarcely above the surface."

"Trust in God," exclaimed Boxall, pointing upwards. "See! the morning is breaking—the clouds overhead are already tinged with the sun's rays; a breeze, too, has sprung up: let us hope that before long one of our own cruisers or some African trader may sight us and take us on board."

Fortunately Boxall and I had had supper, and could hold out longer than our companions. Halliday said that he was not hungry; but I knew that he would be before long, when he would be singing out for food.

"When you are, sir, say so," said Ben. "I shoved a biscuit into my pocket at tea-time last night; and I have got three or four quids in my baccy-box, so that I shall not want it."

"Thank you, but I cannot take it from you," answered Halliday.

"Do you think, sir, that I could munch it up and see you starving," answered Ben. "Come, that would be a good joke. I shan't get hungry, for you must know that I have more than once been three days without putting a morsel of food between my teeth—and wasn't much the worse for it, either. I shouldn't mind a drop of grog, I will allow; but what we can't get we must do without—and, as Mr Boxall says, 'Trust in God.'"

I was thankful that we had so right-minded a man as the old mate with us; still, I could not help thinking about the fearful probability there was that we should perish. We were already in the latitude in which sharks abound; and should those foes of the seaman find us out, they would certainly attack us,—tempted, as they would be, by our feet hanging in the water. I said nothing, however, as I did not wish to impart my uncomfortable feelings to my companions—especially to Halliday, who was already downcast.

At length the sun rose, and we eagerly looked out for a sail; but not a speck could be seen above the horizon. Eastward was a haze, which Ben asserted indicated land; and Boxall, who had before been on the coast, agreed with him, though he said it was a long way off. No remark was made about the non-appearance of a vessel; we could not trust ourselves to speak on the subject.

Slowly the sun got higher in the sky, and the outline of the land, as his rays dissipated the mist, became more distinct. This encouraged us once more to attempt gaining it. Boxall and Halliday took their turn at the paddles; but as we could not venture to shift places, they were unable to make so much use of the pieces of wood as Ben and I were, who were seated at either end. As we were paddling on we caught sight of some spars floating at a little distance on one side. We made towards them, and found an oar and boat-hook.

"These may serve us as a mast and yard; we must manage to make a sail with our handkerchiefs and shirts, and then, when the sea-breeze sets in, we shall make more progress," said Boxall.

Having secured the boat-hook and oar, we soon fastened our handkerchiefs and shirts together; and the breeze setting in shortly afterwards, we went skimming along at a much greater rate than at first. It again fell calm, however, and we were left as before, scarcely moving unless we used our paddles. The heat, as may be supposed, was very great; and what would we not have given for a few pints of water! We should have infinitely preferred that precious fluid to the choicest of wines.

Chapter Two.

Cast on a sand-bank—Our sufferings from thirst—A happy discovery.

Boxall did his uttermost, by his cheerful conversation, to keep up our spirits; but we were little inclined to talk, and sometimes we sat for an hour together without speaking, when his remarks would arouse us. Boxall was one of those quiet, unpretending men who can dare and do great things without making a boast of it, and at the same time endure trial and suffering without complaining. He did not tell us his thoughts, but we might have supposed that he felt certain of being preserved, so calm and even cheerful did he appear.

Halliday was an excellent fellow, who had never, that I know of, done an unworthy action; but he was apt to take things as he found them, and not to look far beyond the present. When with merry companions, he was as merry and happy as any of them; but if in sedate society, he was quiet and sedate.

Ben was, like many other British seamen, indifferent to danger, of a cheerful disposition, and generous and self-sacrificing; always ready to take a glass with an old messmate whenever an opportunity offered,—though he seldom if ever got intoxicated, even on shore, and never on duty.

I may be excused if I say but little about myself. I felt our position, and could not hide from myself the fearful danger we were in, although I did not altogether despair of escaping.

We had been silent for some time, when Halliday exclaimed,—"I could stand the hunger, but this thirst is terrible. I must take a gulp of the water alongside."

"On no account, my dear fellow, as you value your life," cried Boxall; "it will only increase your thirst, and very probably bring on delirium. Numbers have died in consequence of doing as you propose. Bear it manfully. Providence may save us when we least expect it."

"You had better take a bite of my biscuit, sir," said Ben, turning round; "it will give your mouth something to do. Chew it well, though. I and four companions were once in the Pacific in a whale-boat for three days, under the line, without a drop of water to cool our tongues; and all we had to eat were some flying-fish which came aboard of their own accord—or rather, it's my belief that Heaven sent them. Three of us who stuck to the fish were taken aboard by our own ship on the fourth day; and two who would drink the salt water sprang overboard raving mad just before she hove in sight. It has been a lesson to me ever since."

"Thank you, Ben; we will profit by it," said Boxall.

We were paddling along as at first, all this time,—though, as we made but slow progress towards the shore, Boxall began to suspect that the current was carrying us to the southward. Still, we hoped that a breeze would again spring up and send us along faster; at all events, should a vessel appear in sight, our mast and sail, such as they were, would afford us a better chance of being seen than would otherwise have been the case. But hour after hour passed away, and still no sail hove in sight; indeed, while the calm lasted we could not expect to see one.

"What sort of people are we likely to meet with on yonder shore, should we ever get there?" asked Halliday. "Charlie, do you know?"

"Moors or Arabs; I don't suppose any black fellows are to be found so far north," I answered.

"I would rather land among blacks than Moors, from what I have heard of the latter," said Boxall. "However, we may, I hope, be picked up by some European vessel."

It was the first time Boxall had made any remark calculated to increase our anxiety, and his words had apparently slipped out unintentionally. I remembered having read an account of the barbarous way in which the wild Arabs of the African Desert had treated some European sailors wrecked on the coast; and I could not help reflecting that the most abject slavery might be our lot, should we fall into their hands. A discussion as to the character of the natives we were likely to meet with, should we reach the shore, occupied us for some time. Again Halliday complained of fearful thirst, when Ben succeeded at length in persuading him to munch a piece of his biscuit; but he declared that without a drop of moisture he could not get a morsel down. Just then Ben sang out that he saw some round things floating in the water a short way ahead.

"It may be sea-weed—though I have a notion it is something else," he added, as we paddled eagerly forward.

"They are oranges!" he soon shouted out; "and whether they have come from our vessel or some other, there they are."

We strained every nerve to urge on the raft, as if they would sink before we could reach the spot. How eagerly we picked them up! There were two dozen altogether. Directly Ben got hold of one he handed it to Halliday, who began sucking away at it with the greatest eagerness. They were all perfectly ripe; and even had they been green, they would have been most welcome.

"Providence has sent this fruit for our relief," said Boxall. "Let us be thankful to the Giver."

There were six apiece. We stowed them away in our pockets, for we had nowhere else to put them. They might be, we thought—as indeed they were—the means of preserving our lives. By Boxall's advice we ate only one each, reserving the others till hunger and thirst might press us more than at present. I suspect that otherwise Halliday would have consumed all of his share—as perhaps might the rest of us.

All day we were on the look-out for a sail; but the calm continuing, no vessel could approach us. We had reason, however, to be thankful that a strong wind and heavy sea did not get up, as our frail raft, on which we could with difficulty balance ourselves, would speedily have been overwhelmed. On we paddled; but, as before, we made but little progress. A light breeze springing up towards evening, we hoisted our sail; and steering as well as we could with our paddles, or rather the pieces of board which served as such, we glided on towards the still far-distant shore. Had we known more about the coast and the dangers which fringed it, we should probably have endeavoured to gain the offing, where we might possibly be seen by a vessel passing either to the north or south—which none was likely to do closer in with the shore. Still, we all agreed that if we remained at sea and no vessel should come near us for a couple of days, we must, without food and water, inevitably perish.

We were all greatly overpowered with a desire to sleep, which even the fear of falling off into the water could scarcely conquer. I know that, though I was steering, I frequently saw the stars dancing before my eyes and shining in a confused manner on the mirrorlike surface of the water, while I scarcely recollected where I was or what had happened. At last I could stand it no longer, and was compelled to tell Boxall how I felt. Though there was great risk in changing our position, he insisted on taking my place; and as he was next to me, he told me to stoop down while he crept over my head. The centre part of the raft was more secure. Halliday, who had, I found, been sleeping for some time, was being held on by Boxall, who undertook to help me in the same way. In a moment after I had got into my new position I was fast asleep; and though the wind had been increasing, and the sea was consequently rougher than before, even the tossing of the raft did not awake me.

We had been running on for some time, when suddenly I was aroused by a violent shock.

"What has happened?" I exclaimed, opening my eyes.

"We have run on a reef!" exclaimed Ben; "and it will be a job for us to get over it."

The mast had been unshipped, and fell over Ben; but being only an oar, it did not hurt him. We found ourselves on the top of a level rock, with the water quite shoal all round us.

"What is to be done now?" asked Halliday.

"We will take our sail to pieces, and resume our shirts and handkerchiefs," said Boxall calmly. "If the tide is at present at its height, the rock will be dry shortly, and we can remain and stretch our legs till we ascertain how far we are off the coast."

"But had we not better drag the raft over to the other side, into deeper water?" asked Ben; "we may then be able to continue our voyage."

"We must first ascertain where the deep water is," answered Boxall.

"I will soon learn that," said Ben, taking the boat-hook in his hand to feel his way. He went forward carefully for some distance. At last he shouted out,—"The reef is higher here than where we struck it, and I am pretty sure I see a sand-bank at no great distance. I will go ahead and let you know."

Halliday was so stiff and worn out that he was unable to move, and neither Boxall nor I liked to leave him. As Ben was strong, and a good swimmer, we felt sure that he could manage by himself.

We now refreshed ourselves with another orange; and I felt that I had still some strength left for any further exertions we might have to make.

After waiting for some time, we thought we heard Ben shouting to us.

"Yes, I am sure that is Ben's voice," said Boxall. "Come, Halliday, are you able to move?"

A SAND-BANK IN SIGHT.

"I will do my best," was the answer; and getting up, we made our way over the rocks in the direction from which Ben's voice proceeded. After passing over a dry ledge we found the water again deepening; but I took Halliday's hand, and together we waded on, followed by Boxall—who was ready to give either of us assistance, should we require it. The water was growing deeper and deeper, till it almost reached our chests.

"We shall have to swim for it," I said; "but I don't think it will be far." Just then we again heard Ben's voice. "He would not call to us if there was any danger to be encountered," I observed. The next instant we all had to strike out; but we had not gone twenty fathoms when we found our feet touching the bottom, and once more we waded on.

"I see him," I cried out, as my eye caught sight of a figure standing, apparently on dry land. "It may be the coast itself which we have reached—sooner than we expected."

We had still some distance to go, but the water gradually became shallower. Halliday, overcome with fatigue, cried out that he could go no further; but Boxall, overtaking us, made him rest on his shoulder. The water being now no higher than our knees, we advanced more easily; and we soon caught sight of Ben, who had gone some distance over the sand, running to meet us. When at length we reached the dry land, we all three sank down exhausted.

"But have we really reached the coast of Africa?" eagerly asked Boxall of Ben.

"I am sorry to say we have not, sir; we are on a sand-bank ever so far from it, for not a glimpse have I been able to get of the coast—though we may perhaps see whereabouts it is when the sun rises."

This was disappointing intelligence.

"Still, we ought to be thankful that we have a spot of dry land on which to put our feet," said Boxall. "As we have been preserved hitherto, we ought not to despair, or fear that we shall be allowed to perish. At daylight, when we shall ascertain our position better than we can do now, we may be able to judge what we ought to do."

Of course, we all agreed with him, and at once made our way up to the highest part of the bank, which was covered with grass and such plants as usually grow on saline ground seldom or never covered by the sea. Exposed as it was, it afforded us space on which to rest our weary limbs. Led by Boxall, we returned thanks to Heaven for our preservation, and offered up a prayer for protection in the future; and then we stretched ourselves out on the ground. Having no fear of being attacked by savage beasts or equally savage men, in a few minutes we were all fast asleep.

The sun had risen when we awoke. We all felt ravenously hungry, and were burning with thirst. Our thirst we slightly quenched with another orange apiece; but as we gazed around the barren sand-bank, we had no hopes of satisfying our hunger. Unless we could quickly reach the land, we felt we must perish. Standing up, we looked eagerly towards the east; a mist, however, which the sun had not yet dispelled, hung over that part of the horizon. The sand-bank, we judged, was a mile or more long, but very much narrower. It had apparently been thrown up by a current which swept round it inside the reef; while the reef itself appeared to extend further than our eyes could reach to the southward, and we supposed that we were somewhere near its northern end.

Halliday and I sat down again, not feeling inclined to walk about. We asked Boxall what he proposed doing.

"We must return to our raft, and try and get her round the reef," he answered. "The weather promises still to be moderate, and I think we shall have no difficulty in doing so."

"But how are we to get on without food?" asked Halliday. "If Ben would give me another piece of biscuit I might pick up a little; but I never could stand hunger."

We looked round for Ben, but we found he had walked away, and was, as it seemed, sauntering idly along the beach. The tide had by this time gone out, and a considerable space of rocky ground was uncovered. We none of us felt inclined to move, but at the same time

21

we knew that we must exert ourselves or perish; we wanted water more than anything else.

"We have no chance of finding it on this barren sand-bank," I observed with a sigh.

"I am not so certain of that," said Boxall. "I have heard that in the driest sand, provided the sea does not wash over it, drinkable water may be procured by digging deep down. Let us try, at all events."

Agreeing to do as he proposed, we got up and walked along till we saw some tufts of grass; they were thin, and burned brown by the sun.

"Let us try here," said Boxall. "This grass would not grow without some moisture; and possibly, by digging down, we shall find it at the roots."

We set to work with our knives, but soon found that we could throw out the sand more rapidly with our hands than with these. We worked away, eagerly scraping out the sand. The roots ran very deep. "This is a most encouraging sign," said Boxall. "Observe how much cooler the sand is here than at the top." It continued, however, to roll down almost as fast as we threw it up, and we had to enlarge the circumference of the hole. Still no appearance of water; but the roots extended even further down than we had yet gone, and we persevered. We had got down nearly three feet, when we saw that some of the particles of sand glistened more than those at the top, and were of a brighter hue.

"See—see! they are wet!" exclaimed Halliday, digging away frantically.

We now got down into the hole, and threw the sand up behind us. Halliday at length brought up a handful which was moist, and pressed it to his lips. "It is free from salt!" he cried out; and again we all plunged down, till we came to a patch of wet sand. By keeping our hands in it, a little water at length began to trickle into them, which we eagerly drank. But this process appeared a very slow one. Had we possessed a cup of any sort to sink in the sand, we might have filled it; as it was, we were compelled to wait till we could get a few drops at a time in the hollow of our hands. Slow as was the proceeding, however, we at length somewhat overcame the burning thirst from which we had been suffering.

"Why should we not try to fill our shoes?" I exclaimed, as the thought struck me.

"We might try it; but it will take a long time to fill *one* of them," said Boxall; "and I am afraid that the water will leak out as fast as it runs in."

"I am ready to devote mine to the purpose, at all events," I said, taking them off and working them down into the sand—though it was evident that a long time must elapse before water could flow into them.

"But what has become of Ben?" I asked; "we must let him know, as probably he is as thirsty as we were."

We looked round, and at last caught sight of him stooping down, as if picking up something at the edge of the water. We shouted to him, but he was so busily engaged that he did not hear us.

"He has found some mussels or other shell-fish," exclaimed Halliday, setting off to run; "I am desperately hungry."

"Depend on it, Ben will give us a due share of whatever he has found," said Boxall, as we followed our companion.

"Have you found any mussels?" Halliday was asking as we drew near.

"Better than mussels—oysters," answered Ben. "It's a very hard job, however, to get them off the rock. I intended to surprise you, thinking you were all still asleep, and so I waited till I could get enough for all of us."

BEN'S DISCOVERY

He showed us his ample pockets already full; and, hungry as he was, I am certain that the honest fellow had not touched one of them. We retired to the dry sand, and sitting down, eagerly opened the oysters with our knives. How delicious they were! meat and drink in one, as Ben observed—for we could scarcely have swallowed any dry food just then. We found our strength greatly restored after our meal.

Having told Ben of the means we had taken to find water, we advised him to come back with us and get a drink.

"No, no, gentlemen," he said; "it will be wiser first to collect as many oysters as we can secure before the tide comes back, for we shall not then be able to get them."

So we all set to work to collect oysters, filling our pockets and then carrying them on shore, and there piling them up beyond high-water mark. We knew that we should require a large number: indeed, Boxall reminded us that we could not expect to live long upon them and keep up our strength. It was tantalising, also, to reflect that we could not carry any quantity on our intended voyage.

Boxall then proposed that we should return to our water-hole. "Though I am afraid, Charlie, we shall not find your shoes very full," he observed.

"Perhaps not; but if we take a few of the deepest of these oyster-shells, we may get water more quickly," I answered. The thought that they would be of use had just struck me.

Away we went, our pockets loaded with as many oysters as we could carry. When we got to the hole I was disappointed to find that Boxall was right, and that there was only just sufficient water in my shoes to enable Ben partly to quench his thirst. By further increasing the hole, however, and putting down our oyster-shells, we found that we could obtain a much larger quantity of the precious liquid than by means of the shoes. Still there was only just enough to quench our thirst; and even had we possessed a bottle, it would have required some hours to fill it.

The tide had already begun to rise, and we agreed that no time was to be lost in crossing the channel to our raft, as we should now have the advantage of shallow water; whereas, if we waited, we should have to carry the raft a considerable distance over the rocks to launch it.

"I won't disguise from you that I consider our expedition a dangerous one," said Boxall. "Heavy weather may come on before we reach the shore; or a current may sweep us either to the north or south on to another reef. And when we do gain the shore, we cannot tell how we shall support life, or what treatment we may receive from the inhabitants, should we fall in with any, in that desert region. We can, however, trust to One above to take care of us. Let us pray to Him for protection."

We knelt down, and Boxall offered up a heart felt, earnest prayer, in which we all joined. Then we rose from our knees, with strong hearts to encounter the dangers before us.

Chapter Three.

We quit the sand-bank—A sail! a sail!—Saved—Don Lopez's indignation—The ship strikes—Fire! fire!—Cruelly deserted—The wreck blows up.

We had marked the spot where we had landed on the sand-bank, and we hoped therefore without difficulty to find our raft on the top of the reef. Before starting, we swallowed as much water as we could collect, and filled our handkerchiefs and pockets with oysters— which we took out of the shells, for otherwise we could have carried but few. It was not a time to be particular, but the oysters *did* feel somewhat slimy, and did not look very nice. How much we wished for a bottle in which we could carry water!—but all our ingenuity could devise no means of securing any for the future. We had an orange apiece remaining, and that was all on which we could depend for quenching our thirst till we could reach the shore; and perhaps even then we might be unable to find water.

"Cheer up, cheer up!" cried Boxall. "We have thought sufficiently over the dangers before us, now let us face them bravely." Saying this, he led the way across the channel; Halliday and I followed, and Ben brought up the rear. We were able to wade the whole distance, though in the deeper part the water was up to our shoulders. We found the raft as we had left it, for the tide, even at its height, did not reach the top of the reef. At Boxall's suggestion, we took it apart and dragged the pieces down to the edge of the water, so that when put together again it might float as the tide came in. We also lashed it together more securely and balanced it better than before, while from one of the boards we cut out two fresh paddles; thus all hands were able to urge on the raft. Judging as far as we were able—by throwing a piece of wood into the water—that the current was setting to the southward, while we wished to go round the north end of the reef, we determined to wait till the tide slackened, which it would soon do; indeed, our raft was not yet completely afloat. The water rising higher and higher, however, we at last got on the raft and sat down. And while Boxall took the boat-hook to shove off, the rest of us paddled with all our might.

"Away she goes!" cried Boxall; and we were fairly afloat.

Just at that instant Ben cried out, "A sail! a sail! away to the north-west."

We looked in the direction indicated, and clearly made out the top-gallant-sails and part of the royals of what was apparently a large ship, standing almost directly towards us. Our hearts leaped with joy. Instead of the weary paddling towards the arid coast, parched with thirst and suffering from hunger, we might soon be safe on board ship, with the prospect of returning to our friends and country.

"We shall easily cut her off, if we steer to the westward and make good way," cried Ben. "But there is no time to lose, in case she should alter her course."

"I cannot understand why she is standing in this direction," observed Boxall. "Her commander can scarcely be aware of the existence of this reef, or he would be giving it a wider berth."

The wind was against us, and the send of the sea drove us back almost as much as we went ahead; so that we made but slow progress. The ship, however, approached nearer and nearer, till we could see nearly to the foot of her courses. When at length her hull came in sight, both Boxall and Ben were of opinion that she was foreign,—either French or Spanish. Boxall thought that she was the latter; and indeed we soon clearly made out the Spanish ensign flying from her peak.

"I will get a signal ready," said Ben, taking off his shirt and fastening it to the end of the oar which had served as a mast. It was still too evident, however, that we were not seen.

"If that ship were to stand on an hour longer, or even less, she would run right on the reef not far to the southward of this," observed Boxall. "It will be a mercy if those on board see us, as we will be able to warn them of their danger. Let us, at all events, do our best to get up to her."

Cheering each other on, we paddled away as vigorously as we could.

"I think she will see us now. Let us hoist our signal," cried Ben; and taking up the oar which lay along the raft, he waved it, with his shirt at the end, as high as he could. Some minutes more passed. The ship had got so far to the southward that we were directly on her beam. Ben waved the signal frantically; and uniting our voices, we shouted as loudly as we could.

"I am afraid our voices don't reach her in the teeth of the wind," observed Boxall.

"But our signal is seen, though," cried Ben; and as he spoke the ship's head was turned towards us, while we energetically paddled on to meet her.

In a short time she was up to us, and we got alongside; ropes were hove to us (one of which Ben made fast to the raft), and several men came down the side to assist us in climbing up. Among the most active were two negroes—one a tall, powerful man, but about as ugly a mortal as I ever set eyes on; the other, a young, pleasant-looking lad, though his skin was as black as jet. The two seized me by the arms and dragged me up, though I could have scrambled on deck without their help.

"Muchas gracias," (Many thanks), I said.

"I thought you English officer," said the young black.

"So I am," I answered. "How is it that you speak English?"

"I served aboard English man-of-war, and knew that you were English officer directly I saw you," he answered.

This was said almost before I placed my feet on the deck—where we were all soon standing, looking around us. The ship was apparently a man-of-war; but there were a number of soldiers and people of all ranks, evidently passengers, walking the deck, besides the officers.

"I say, Charlie, as you speak Spanish, you had better tell the captain that he will be hard and fast on shore in a few minutes if he does not alter his course," said Boxall to me.

Followed by my companions, I accordingly stepped aft to an officer whom I took to be the commander, and told him that we had only just before left a reef which ran north and south, and that he would soon be upon it unless he steered more to the westward; also that, if he kept a sharp look-out, he would see the sand-bank behind it. He seemed very much astonished, and at once gave orders to port the helm and trim the sails so as to stand off from the dangerous neighbourhood. I observed that our raft was towing astern. "We will hoist it on board by-and-by," said the captain; "it will serve for firewood, of which we have not too large a supply."

I heard several people talking about the reef. One very consequential-looking gentleman declared that we had not spoken the truth, and that the reef must be much further off than we had said. I took no notice of this; indeed, I thought that I might possibly be mistaken, especially as I was not accustomed to hear Spanish spoken, although, thanks to honest Andrew, I was able to express myself with tolerable clearness on simple subjects. We convinced the captain, however, that my account was true, by showing him the oysters with which our pockets were filled, and which we were very glad to get rid of. Being about to throw them overboard, the young negro stopped us and begged to have them, as they would be very welcome at the mess to which he belonged. "We no get too much food here," he observed; "very different to English man-of-war."

I asked the young black his name.

"They call me Pedro aboard here; but I got many names, according to the people I live among," he answered with a laugh. "The English sailors call me Black Jack; and when I once lived with the Moors, my name was Selim; and in my own country, Quasho Tumbo Popo."

"And what is the name of the big black man who helped me up the side?" I asked.

"Him called Antonio here," answered Pedro, glancing round to ascertain that the person we were speaking of was not near. "Take care of him, massa; him no good. Once got flogging aboard man-of-war, and no love English officers, depend on that. He pretend to be great friend to you, but you see what he do."

I thanked Pedro for his caution, feeling certain from the tone in which he spoke that he was sincere.

The captain seemed really grateful for the service we had rendered him by preventing him from running on the reef. He invited us down to his cabin, and asked us if we would like to turn in and rest while our clothes were drying.

"Will you tell him that we are dying of thirst," exclaimed Halliday, "and that we should not object to have something to eat first?"

I explained that we had had no food except oysters since the previous evening, and that we should be grateful if he would order us some supper—for the Spanish dinner-hour had long passed.

"Of course," he observed; "I forgot that,"—and he immediately ordered some water and light wine to be placed on the table. He seemed amused at the quantity we drank; having, I suspect, had very little experience of the way men feel who have been exposed to hunger and thirst, as we had been, for so many hours. Some light food was then brought in, to which we did ample justice.

On my mentioning Ben to him, he observed,—"He will be taken good care of by the black Antonio; he understands your language."

The captain appeared to be a quiet, gentlemanly man; but it struck me at once that he was not the sort of person to keep a disorderly crew and a number of troops and passengers in order. He again expressed himself deeply obliged to us for the service we had rendered him; and taking a small telescope in a case from the side-cabin, begged I would accept it as a mark of his gratitude. "There are some aboard here who pretend to understand better than I do how the ship should be managed; and it was by their advice that I was steering the course I was doing when I fell in with you," he observed.

I told Boxall what the captain had said.

"A pretty sort of commander he must be, to allow civilians, even though they may be scientific men, to interfere with the navigation of the ship," he observed. "For my part, I should tell them to keep as sharp a look-out as they liked upon the spars and ship, but to let me steer the course I considered the best."

After supper we thankfully turned in—the captain politely giving his berth to Boxall, while two of the lieutenants begged that Halliday and I would occupy theirs. When we left the deck I observed that the wind had completely fallen, and I could not help wishing that we had been further off from the reef. The frigate, I should have said, had come through the Straits of Gibraltar, from Malaga or some other port on the south of Spain, and was bound out to Manilla in the Philippine Islands, carrying a number of official persons, with some settlers of lower grade. But having told the captain of the danger near him, we hoped that he would do his best to avoid it, and so ceased to let the matter trouble us.

As may be supposed, we slept soundly, worn out as we were with our exertions; and it was daylight next morning when we awoke. I apologised to those whom we had kept out of their berths; but they were very civil, and replied that they had slept on sofas, and that we evidently required all the rest we could obtain.

On going on deck we found that the calm still continued, and the ship lay on the glass-like surface, her sails idly hanging down against the masts. I observed that a hand was in the chains, heaving the lead; and on going into the mizzen-top, I made out the reef and the sand-bank behind it,—although, had I not known it was there, I might not have been certain what it was. Going forward, I found Ben, and asked him how he had fared.

"Pretty well, thank you, sir; owing to the black Antonio, who looked after me," he answered. "He is a rum sort of a chap, though; and I shouldn't wish to have many such aboard a ship with me. He is civil enough, to be sure, as far as I am concerned; but he is bitter as olives against all above him: and it's my opinion he would work you, and Mr Boxall, and Mr Halliday a mischief, if he had the power, though you never did him any harm. I see clearly enough what he is about: he wants to gain me over to side with him—and that's the reason he's so terribly civil. Depend on it, Mr Blore, there'll be a mutiny aboard before long; and when it comes there'll be murder and fighting, and we shall fare ill among the villains. I cannot say much for the discipline of this ship, either; she is more like a privateer than a man-of-war. It's a wonder she has got as far as she has without meeting with some misfortune; and I only hope that we shall touch at a port before long, where we can get clear of her."

"What you say is not pleasant; and, from certain things I have observed, I am afraid it is true," I answered. "If we don't touch anywhere, we may fall in with an English vessel; and I am sure Mr Boxall will agree with me, that we had better go on board her, even though she may be a merchant-man. But if we meet with a man-of-war, we shall be all right."

"I hope we shall, sir," said Ben. "Antonio tells me, too, that the ship was on fire two nights ago, through the carelessness of some of the men, when more than half of the crew went down on their knees and cried for help to their saints, instead of trying to put out the flames; and if he and a few others had not set to work with buckets and wet blankets, the ship, to a certainty, would have been burned."

"Well, Ben, keep your weather-eye open; and if anything of the kind occurs again, we must show them what British discipline and courage can do," I said.

Going aft, I told Boxall what I had heard; and he agreed with me that it would be well to leave the ship as soon as we could, though we ought to be thankful that we had reached her, instead of having to make our way to land on our frail raft.

We had certainly no reason to complain of want of civility from the officers of the ship; but the civilians, some of whom rejoiced in high-sounding titles, treated us with marked contempt, as beings altogether inferior to themselves. We agreed, however, to take no notice of this, and made ourselves as happy as we could. Halliday, after two or three substantial meals, recovered his spirits; and I jokingly told him that it would be wise to keep his pockets, in future, well stored with provisions, in case a similar accident might occur — though I little thought at the time that he would take my advice in earnest, and follow it.

A breeze at last sprung up, and the huge galleon began once more to glide through the water. The officers had again politely offered us their berths, but we positively refused to accept them, — saying that, as our clothes were dry, we could sleep perfectly well on sofas, or on the deck of the cabin, for that matter. The captain then begged that we would occupy the main cabin, which was only used in the daytime.

After supper, we all three walked the deck till the great men had retired to their berths. It was a lovely night; the sea was smooth, and the moon shone brightly; a light air filled the sails, while the tall ship glided calmly onward. It was indeed such a night as one might have thought it impossible any accident could happen to a ship in. While we were walking the deck, Boxall stepped up to the binnacle and glanced at the compass. On returning to us, he observed —

"It seems extraordinary that, notwithstanding the warning we gave the captain, the ship is being kept more to the eastward of south than otherwise. I should say that south or south-south-west would be a safer course."

"I have a great mind to tell the captain," I said. "I suspect that he does not believe we are so close in with the coast as is really the case. He seems a sensible man, and will, at all events, be obliged to me."

I entered the cabin, but found that the captain had gone to bed. I then went up to the raised poop, on which the officer of the watch was standing, and, in as polite a way as I could, reminded him of the dangerous reef on our larboard beam. "Or rather, I may say, on our larboard bow," I added; "and if we stand on much longer on the course we are now keeping, we shall strike on it to a certainty."

"If there is a reef where you say, we must have passed it long ago," answered the lieutenant carelessly. "My directions are to steer the course we are now on; and I am surprised that a stranger should venture to interfere with the navigation of the ship."

"I beg your pardon, Don Lopez," I answered. "I have given you what my brother officers and I consider sound advice; and we, sir, should be as sorry as you would be to see the ship cast away."

"Really, Mr Englishman, we Spaniards understand navigation as well as you do!" exclaimed the lieutenant in an angry tone. "You seem to forget that we discovered the New World, and had explored a large portion of the globe before your countrymen even pretended to be a maritime people, as you now call yourselves."

I saw that it was useless saying more, and so rejoined my companions. Boxall was becoming more and more anxious. "We shall, to a certainty, be on the reef before many hours are over, if the ship's course is not altered," he said. "I suspect that the lieutenant has mistaken east for west, and that the captain really directed him to steer south-south-west."

I again went up to the lieutenant, and, as politely as I could, inquired if he did not think it possible that some mistake might have been made as to the course to be steered, and suggesting that he should alter it to south-west. This made him very indignant, and he hinted that if I again interfered with him he should order me under arrest. Making him a polite bow, I returned to Boxall, and we continued our walk. The air, after the heat of the day, was comparatively cool and pleasant, and neither of us felt any inclination to turn in. No one interfered with us; and we were talking eagerly about the probability of falling in with an English man-of-war, or of making our way home on board a merchant-man, when we suddenly felt a shock, but not of sufficient force to throw us off our feet.

"The ship has struck!" exclaimed Boxall. "What are the fellows about? They ought to clew up everything, and she might be got off."

In spite of the manner in which the officer of the watch had treated me, I ran aft to him, and urged him to do as Boxall advised, "The reef, do you say!" he exclaimed; "that was no reef, but a sunken vessel. See! we are gliding on as smoothly as before."

Scarcely had he said this when the ship again struck, and with far greater violence than before. The tall masts quivered, and seemed ready to fall. The captain, and most of the officers and crew who were below, came rushing on deck; the lead was hove, and shallow water found on either side. The captain immediately ordered the sails to be clewed up, and the boats to be lowered, that anchors might be carried astern, to haul off the ship.

"If it's high-water her fate is sealed," observed Boxall; "but if low, she might possibly be hauled off: and she has not, I hope, received much damage."

I ran to the chains, and observed that the lead-line was up and down—the ship was evidently not moving. By this time the civilians and other passengers had come on deck, and great confusion prevailed. Everyone wanted to know what had happened, and what was to be done. Several came to me. "We must first try to heave the ship off," was my answer to all.

The capstan was manned, and the crew commenced heaving; but not an inch did the ship move. The first anchor earned out, not holding, came home, and had with great labour to be lifted; the second held, though the strain on the cable was tremendous.

Boxall had carefully sounded the water alongside.

"She is moving!" he exclaimed at length. "Hurrah! work away, my fine lads!" he could not help crying out, though the men could not understand him. The water continued to rise, the ship moved faster and faster, and there appeared every probability of our getting off.

While the crew were thus busily engaged, several soldiers and passengers came rushing up the fore-hatchway shouting out, "Fire! fire! fire!" Halliday and I, who were standing together, hurried forward, hoping that it might be a false alarm, though I could not help recollecting what Ben had told me the previous day. Though no flames were visible, I discovered, even in the gloom of night, that the atmosphere was peculiarly thick, while I could smell an odour of burning wood. More people rushing up with the same fearful shouts, the alarm soon became general. Halliday and I cried out to the men nearest us to get buckets and blankets, and that we would try to discover from whence the fire proceeded, and endeavour to put it out; but no one listened to us. Some of the soldiers and passengers were rushing about the deck like madmen; others were on their knees calling to the saints to assist them; while a number of the seamen rushed below, returned with axes, and began hacking at the shrouds and stays—as if, having made up their minds that the ship would be lost, they intended to cut away the masts. Some of the officers were endeavouring to recall the men to their duty, but others seemed to have lost their senses; while the civilians were as frantic as the rest: indeed, a panic had too evidently seized the greater part of those on board.

Finding that we could do nothing, Halliday and I made our way aft to look for Boxall, and to ask what he advised we should do—feeling that it would be wise, at all events, to keep together. On our way we met with Ben. "I find, sir, that the careless Spaniards have forgotten to hoist our raft on board, as they intended doing, and she is still alongside," he said. "Now, as I see that these fellows are not likely to help themselves, it's our business, I have a notion, to look after number one; so I will just slip down on the raft and try what I can do to improve it, if you will send me over all the planks and spars you can lay hands on."

Fortunately, just then Boxall found us out, and approved of Ben's proposal. The officers, in the meantime, were lowering the boats which remained on board, the larger ones being already in the water. We offered to assist some of them who were trying to lower the starboard quarter boat; but even those who had before been civil to us now rudely pushed us aside; and we felt sure that, even should they succeed in launching her, they would refuse to take us on board.

Ben having got on the raft, had hauled it under the main chains. There was no lack of spars—the deck was piled up with a number, not only for the use of the ship, but for other vessels on the station; and there was also the framework and rigging complete of a small vessel. We quickly took from these spars and ropes sufficient to enable Ben to complete the raft—and had just sent him down the ship's fore-royal and its yard, with a couple of oars which we found on the booms, when a number of the crew discovered what we were about, and made a rush to get on the raft. We shouted to Ben to shove off,—telling him to come back for us, or we would swim to him. Before he was clear of the vessel's side, however, a Spanish seaman sprang on the raft; and having, as he thought, secured his own safety, he showed no inclination, notwithstanding the shouts of his countrymen, of returning to the ship.

The example we had set was immediately followed by such of the crew as had retained their senses—the boatswain and two or three more of the inferior officers taking the lead.

All this time no attempt had been made to put out the fire, which, from the slow progress it made, might, I felt sure, have easily been done. But the people now showed more energy in forming the proposed raft than they had hitherto done. It seemed surprising that the undisciplined crew did not take possession of the boats; but they were somewhat kept in awe by a party of marines or soldiers drawn up on the quarter-deck; and they had, besides, been assured by their officers that they should be taken on board when all was ready. The boats, which had in the meantime kept off from the ship, under the command of the lieutenants and other officers, were called up one by one. The barge being first summoned, the governor and his family, with several other civilians, ladies and children, embarked in her, with some provisions, and a few casks of water; more order and regularity being displayed on this occasion than on any other. The barge immediately shoved off; and then most of the civilians and naval officers hurriedly embarked in the other boats. I asked the captain if he would take us into his boat; but he replied, with a shrug of his shoulders, that it was impossible, as the Spaniards would not allow foreigners to embark while their countrymen remained on board. On hearing this, Boxall proposed to the boatswain that we should assist in building the large raft; and, as a considerable number of seamen on whom he could depend had already embarked in the boats, he thankfully accepted our offer.

Before letting ourselves over the stern, where the raft was being formed, I looked out for Ben. At length I observed him, some way off, with his companion, apparently busied in finishing the small raft. Boxall agreed with me that we should be better off with him than on the larger raft, so we hoped that as soon as he could he would come back to the ship. In the meantime we set to work energetically to assist the boatswain; while two or three of the officers remained on board, and, with the few men to help them whom they could get to work, continued heaving over all the planks and spars they could find, together with some empty water-casks and hen-coops, through the ports. We had already formed a good-sized raft, when an officer, who had hitherto been labouring on deck, slipped down and joined us, together with a number of people who were afraid of being abandoned should they not secure a place upon it.

THE END OF THE GALLEON.

Among the last articles sent down to us had been a top-gallant-sail, which Boxall, Halliday, and I at once got ready for hoisting on a long spar set up as a mast in the fore-part of the raft, that we might, should it be necessary, get clear of the ship; for although we were anxious to save as many people as possible, we knew that all would be lost should too many get upon it.

I had gone to the after-part of the raft, to suggest to the boatswain that we should fix a rudder, when I caught sight of the captain's boat pulling away from the ship, leaving a number of the marines on the quarter-deck. They were shouting to the captain, asking him to come back for them. His reply was, "I will directly; but I go to call the other boats to take you on board." This reply evidently did not satisfy the soldiers. Several of them shouted out, "We will fire, if you do not return immediately;" but no notice was taken of this threat, and the crew of the boat gave way with redoubled energy. I was expecting, the next instant, to hear the rattle of musketry, when a fearful report, like the sound of a hundred guns going off at once, rang in my ears; the deck of the ship appeared to lift, her masts and spars trembled, and bright flames burst forth from every side. It seemed impossible that any of those remaining on deck could have survived.

Chapter Four.

Meeting on the raft—an atrocious deed—A desperate fight—
Swimming for life—A terrible doom.

The people on the raft, overwhelmed with horror at the fearful
catastrophe which had occurred, were for a time unable to exert
themselves, and had we not been astern of the ship a large portion of
our party would probably have perished; but as it was, no one was
hurt. The boats, instead of returning to our assistance, continued to
pull away to the southward; they did not even stop to take on board
Ben and his companion, who, by the light of the burning ship, could
be seen at some distance.

As soon as those on the raft began somewhat to recover from their
consternation, they rose to their feet, uttering the most fearful
imprecations on the heads of those who, it was very evident, were so
cruelly deserting them. The brave boatswain was the only one
among the Spaniards who retained his presence of mind. He and I,
with Boxall and Halliday, managed to hoist a sail; when a light
breeze enabled us to get sufficiently clear of the burning wreck to
avoid the masts and spars which came falling down, hissing, into the
water. Several of the people shouted out, urging us to sail in chase of
the boats; but even had we attempted it with a strong breeze in our
favour, they would of course soon have got far ahead of us. As it
was, the wind again fell, and we lay on the calm ocean unable to
impel our raft either towards the shore or in any other direction,
while we gazed with sad eyes at the burning ship.

I looked round for Antonio and young Pedro, but could discover
neither of them on the raft. The friendly disposition the latter had
exhibited towards us made me hope that he had escaped in one of
the boats. Boxall said that he had seen Antonio not long before he
himself had got on the raft, and that he was nearly certain he had
been left on the burning wreck. Notwithstanding the bad opinion
Ben had formed of him, we agreed that we should have been glad
had he been with us, as he was certainly one of the most intelligent

and active seamen on board. Boxall, Halliday, and I sat near the mast with the boatswain, who tried in vain to arouse his companions to exertion,—urging them to secure the raft more firmly, and to endeavour to pick up anything which might be floating by. Those who had at first obeyed him willingly, now only grumbled; and from words I heard spoken, I was afraid that, should he attempt to enforce his orders, a mutiny would break out. On mentioning my fears to Boxall,—"We must try and defend him then," he answered. "I trust that some will remain faithful, and rally round us."

The night continued calm. This was the time when, if active, we might possibly have obtained some provisions, and might certainly have improved the raft. We three did what we could, but the people would not move out of our way, and no one would lend a hand. We succeeded, however, in picking up several articles: a boat-hook, some oars, and two casks—but whether they contained water or spirits we could not be certain. Boxall said that as they floated light he believed they were spirit-casks, and suggested that it might be wiser to let them go, in case the people should get drunk with their contents; still, as there was a doubt on the subject, and we were unable at once to examine them, we secured them to the raft.

The calmness of the sea alone saved many of the people sleeping near the edge from slipping overboard, or getting their limbs jammed between the openings in the spars. It was easy, however, to foretell what would happen should a strong wind and heavy sea get up: even should the raft hold together, many of those on it must be washed away; while if all hands had exerted themselves, it might have been greatly strengthened, and made secure against the dangers it would in all probability have to encounter.

Weary with our exertions, we at length agreed to go back to the mast and rest till daylight; but on reaching the spot where we had before taken our post, near the boatswain, we found it occupied, and were compelled to content ourselves with a less secure place at some distance from him. Not trusting those around us, we agreed that one should keep awake and watch over the other two. It fell to my lot to keep the first watch; and so, while Boxall and Halliday stretched themselves lengthways on a plank, I sat by their side.

I had not been there long when some men began talking near me (probably unaware that I understood Spanish). One of the men was, I made out, the boatswain's mate, and the others were ordinary seamen. They were speaking of the boatswain, and abusing him for what they called his tyranny. Each one had some grievance to complain of.

"We have him now in our power," said the boatswain's mate; "let us revenge ourselves on him."

"But who is to take command of the raft and guide us to the shore?" asked one of the men.

"I will do that," was the answer; "I am as good a seaman as he is. And when we get to land we will build huts and live at our ease, instead of setting off, as he will certainly wish to do, to find some port where we can start for Spain, where most of you will be sent back to the galleys."

A good deal more was said to the same effect; and my immediate impression was that the men he was addressing were emancipated convicts, and capable of any atrocity. I longed to warn the boatswain at once of the plot hatching for his destruction; but I knew that if I moved I should be suspected. I hoped, however, that at all events the wretches would not attempt to carry their nefarious plan out that night, and I resolved to take the first opportunity of telling the boatswain what I had heard. Growing very sleepy, I was compelled at last to awake Halliday and get him to keep watch. I told him to arouse me should the men make any movement, or show that they were about to carry out their treacherous project.

I went to sleep with the thought on my mind of the boatswain's danger; and I suppose this caused me to awake suddenly. Starting up, I found that Halliday had dropped off to sleep by my side. The raft had drifted to some distance from the ship, which was, however, still burning, the glare falling on the figures of my companions in misfortune,—some lying down, others sleeping in sitting postures. I looked around towards the spot where the boatswain's mate and his associates had been; they were not there. I crept towards the place where I had left the boatswain; but could not distinguish him. Happening to look to the further end of the raft, I saw a hand lifted up holding a dagger, which gleamed in the light of the burning ship. I shouted to Boxall and Halliday, who sprang to their feet; while I, followed by them, rushed towards the spot where I had seen the weapon raised.

"Stop! stop!" I shouted in Spanish. "Commit no murder." My voice aroused most of the other sleeping occupants of the raft; but before my friends and I could reach the spot the dagger had descended, and we were met by the glaring eyes of the boatswain's mate and his convict associates.

"You have killed the brave boatswain," I could not help exclaiming.

"You shall share his fate, whatever that is," growled out the murderer. "Who are you, who dares to interfere with me and my friends?"

I made no answer. The man held the still reeking dagger in his hand, and I could not help fearing that, should I get within his reach, he would plunge it into me.

The people on the raft were now shouting and talking together— some arranging themselves on our side, while others appeared inclined to take part with the boatswain's mate and his vile associates.

"Where is the boatswain? where is the boatswain? Pedro Alvez!" cried out some of the petty officers. No answer came. All the officers had their swords, and Halliday and I had got hold of two of the axes which had been taken to form the raft. Boxall told me to urge the carpenter, who seemed to be the chief in rank, to cut down the mutineers at once, and either xheave them overboard or lash them to the raft, as he was certain they would otherwise take an early opportunity of attacking us when unprepared, and would put us all to death. He hesitated, however, observing that most of them had their knives, and that it would be no easy matter to overcome them.

Again voices shouted, "Where is Pedro Alvez? Let him show himself."

"He went overboard and was drowned; and many more will follow him, if we are interfered with," answered some one from the end of the raft occupied by the mutineers.

This answer evidently alarmed the carpenter, who was a very different sort of man from the brave boatswain.

"We will remain quiet till we are attacked, and then, of course, we will defend ourselves," he observed in a low voice.

"Our only chance will be to keep together and be constantly on the watch," observed Boxall. "I wish he would let me have his sword; I suspect that I should make a better use of it than he will."

The carpenter declined to give up his own weapon, but promised to try and get one—as he was sure that the English officer would make good use of it.

Boxall had hitherto been able to arm himself only with a heavy piece of wood, but which his strong arm was likely to use with good effect. In a short time, however, the gunner brought him a sword.

"Tell your brother officer that I am sure he will fight well with it, and do his best to maintain order."

"Thank him," answered Boxall. "He may trust me."

Something like order was at length restored; and the mutineers held their post on the after-part of the raft, while we kept ours round the mast. Thus the remainder of the night passed away.

46

THE END OF THE GALLEON.

The sun rose at last hot and red over the calm ocean; the heat became intense, and every one was crying out for food and water. Halliday whispered to me that he had taken my advice, and had filled his pockets with biscuits and sausages—which he invited Boxall and me to partake of. We agreed that they would be nothing among so many; still we did not like to eat them in the presence of others.

"I ate as much as I wanted during the night," said Halliday; "and I think if you were to sit down behind me, you might be able to get some food into your mouth without being observed. I should like to give the carpenter some, though."

I undertook to convey a small portion to him. He was very grateful for it, and did not even ask if we had any more. I then told him of the casks. He called several men whom he could trust; who went to the side and, with our assistance, got the casks on the raft. The larger one contained spirits, the other water. On discovering this, a number of the people made a rush towards them, afraid of losing their share,— and we were compelled to keep them at bay with our weapons.

"The water and spirits shall be served out so that each shall have a due share," cried the carpenter. Some small cups were found which served as measures; and the people, awed by the bold front we exhibited, waited patiently till each person had received his proper portion. Very nearly half the cask of water was thus exhausted; and we should have acted more wisely had we waited till the people's thirst had become greater. Some of them had apparently a few biscuits and other eatable things in their pockets; but besides this, a cask of pork, which had been thrown overboard, and hauled up on the raft before it left the ship, was the only food we possessed. Our only hope of escaping starvation was by speedily reaching the shore.

"How soon shall we get there?" asked Halliday of Boxall.

"Never—unless a breeze springs up, and these fellows act like rational beings instead of madmen," he answered, in a more gloomy tone than I had ever yet heard him use. "We must not conceal from ourselves the fearful position in which we are placed. These ruffians will probably try to destroy the gunner and the other officers as they did the boatswain; and watchful as we may be, we shall scarcely be able to guard ourselves against them."

"I wish we had Ben with us," said Halliday. "A stout, brave fellow such as he is would have been of great help, and with the assistance of the better disposed we might have kept the villains at bay. I wonder what can have become of him!"

"He and his companion have probably paddled towards the shore," answered Boxall. "Self-preservation is the first thing a man thinks of; and though he might not, under other circumstances, have deserted us, he probably thought himself much better off on his light raft than he would be on this large one, — and was afraid, if he came near us, that others would attempt to gain a footing on it, and thus overload it."

"No, no; I do not think that Ben would willingly have deserted us," I observed. "I am very certain that he would have done his best to help us. He probably lost sight of our raft during the night, and could not find it again; or one of the boats might have returned, and taken him and his companion on board."

"Little chance of that," answered Boxall. "There is no excuse for their cowardly desertion of us, and they are not likely to have come back for the sake of rescuing any one."

This style of conversation, more of which I need not repeat, served to pass away the time. While the calm continued, our condition did not change for the better, as we could not move, and no sail could approach to our assistance. The Spaniards around us were talking in even a more gloomy strain, — uttering curses, not loud but deep, on the heads of those who had basely deserted them; while the mutineers sat together at the end of the raft muttering to each other, and, as we suspected, hatching mischief.

The day wore on, and the sun struck down on our unprotected heads with intense force; while the bright glare on the water affected our eyes, and compelled us to shield them with our hands, — for the sail, though hoisted, afforded us only a partial shade. The mutineers now began to cry out that they wanted more food and water.

"It is not time yet to serve it out," answered the carpenter, who had assumed the command. "If we use it up now, we shall have none for to-morrow."

"Better eat and drink while we are hungry and thirsty, and let to-morrow take care of itself," exclaimed one of the mutineers.

The carpenter took no notice of the remark, and the mutineers remained quiet for some minutes, apparently not having made up their minds how to act.

"Depend upon it, these fellows will attack us before long," observed Boxall; "we must be prepared. Tell the carpenter what I say." The latter agreed with Boxall, and spoke to the few around him whom he could trust.

Boxall now suggested that we should place the three casks and some loose planks so as to form a barricade in front of us, by which means we might better resist an attack. We were engaged doing this, when the leader of the mutineers cried out,—"What are you about? Let these things remain as they are. We want food and water: if it's not given to us, we will come and take it."

The carpenter, instead of boldly adhering to what he knew was wise, was advised by his more timid companions, and replied that he would give them a little pork and water provided they should remain quiet. I told Boxall; who desired me to warn him that he was acting very imprudently, as they would be sure to ask for more. He persisted, however; and telling the men to come for their rations, he gave each a small measure of water and a piece of pork. On this, several who had remained neutral joined them, and also insisted on receiving their rations. Being supported by the mutineers, the rest of the people very naturally cried out that they must have their share,— fearing that otherwise the mutineers would get the whole of it.

Scarcely had the distribution been made, when the mutineers again demanded another supply.

"We must be firm, or, finding that they can overawe us, they will insist on doing whatever they please," said Boxall.

The carpenter could not fail to see the wisdom of this advice, and replied that not another drop of water or particle of food would be served out till the next morning. The mutineers received the answer in sullen silence, making at the time no movement; and we began to hope that they would remain quiet. As, however, they soon again felt the gnawings of hunger, they began to talk together in low voices; and, influenced by the instincts of savage beasts, they seemed determined to take by force what they wanted.

Their leader, starting up, cried out, — "It's time to have more food; come, Mr Carpenter, give it to us at once."

"Be quiet, friends; you know that is impossible," was the mild reply.

It failed to influence them, however; and drawing their knives, with which most of them were armed, they sprang towards us. Just at that moment some one at the other end of the raft shouted out, — "A sail! a sail!" The welcome sound arrested even the savage wretches, and, sheathing their knives, they looked round in the direction in which the man was pointing. We cast our eyes towards the spot. There could be no doubt that there was a sail, but I saw at once that it must be a very small vessel, or a boat. I thought it best, however, not to tell the Spaniards this.

The mutineers sat down, looking out towards the sail. Though the prospect of relief was sufficient, one might have supposed, to arouse every one, yet so weak and dispirited were many of the Spaniards, that they scarcely moved from their positions, but sat, as before, with their heads resting on their knees. One thing was certain — that the craft, whatever she was, was standing towards us, bringing up a breeze; yet she approached very slowly.

"I suspected from the first what she was," observed Boxall. "Let me have your glass, Charlie, that I may be certain." I gave him my telescope, which I had kept slung at my back. "As I thought: it is a small raft—probably Ben's. Honest fellow, I wronged him. He calculated the direction in which we were likely to have drifted, and is coming to our assistance."

In a short time the carpenter also observed to me that it was a raft, with our countryman on it.

"We will not tell the mutineers so—let them find it out for themselves; as they may form a plan for taking possession of it, if they think that it would serve them better than this one," I observed.

How anxiously we waited the arrival of the raft! It came on very slowly, for the breeze was light. Our own sail remained hoisted, but as one of the sheets had been let go it remained partly furled round the mast, and did not move the raft. Looking through my glass, I made out Ben and another man. It was evident, then, that they had not succeeded in saving any people from the burning wreck; probably, therefore, all had perished.

The raft was soon visible to the dullest eyes of all on board. As she approached, Boxall shouted to Ben, and advised him not to approach too near—telling him of the disorderly state of those with us, and that they would certainly attempt to take from him any water or provisions he might have. Ben on this hauled down his sail, and we saw him apparently endeavouring to make his companion understand the warning he had received.

"We will do as you advise, sir," he shouted in return. "We have got food and water enough on board for three or four people; and knowing that you were likely to be short of both, we came to look for you. My mate here is the brother of the boatswain, and is a very good fellow. As you say, it will be dangerous for us to come alongside; but if Mr Boxall, Mr Halliday, and you will swim off to us, we will run in closer and take you aboard."

"A SAIL! A SAIL!"

"No, no! don't come any nearer; we can all easily reach you,"
answered Boxall. He did not wish to let the Spaniard know of his

brother's death, in case he might be less willing to remain faithful to us.

The mutineers, as well as the other people, suspected from this conversation what we were about to do, and also from seeing that the raft did not come nearer. It struck me that, since the poor boatswain was dead, we ought to invite the carpenter to accompany us. Boxall agreed with me; I therefore asked him in a low voice if he could swim, and was willing to try and get on board the small raft.

"I cannot swim," he answered; "and if I could, I would not desert these poor people who are trusting to me, for the mutineers would very soon put them to death. But as you are not bound to remain, I will help you to escape."

Thanking him heartily, I said that we would leap overboard suddenly, in order that no one might attempt to stop us. We were all very sorry to leave the carpenter, for we could not help fearing that when we should be gone the mutineers would attack him, and in all probability treat him as they had done the boatswain. We were still talking to him, when once more the ruffians at the other end of the raft shouted out that they must have water and provisions served out to them immediately.

"Ask them to wait patiently till the evening, and say that you will then do as they wish; you will have fewer mouths to feed by that time."

I little thought at the moment how truly I spoke; for scarcely had the carpenter uttered the words when the mutineers rose in a body, and, drawing their knives, made a desperate rush at us. We had only time to spring to our feet and defend ourselves. Though we might have leaped overboard and escaped, we felt that it would be cowardly to desert the carpenter and those who sided with him. As it was, three of the unfortunate people who remained neutral, and were without weapons to defend themselves, being nearest to the savages, were stabbed before we could help them. We fought with the greatest desperation. Boxall cut down one of the fellows, and the carpenter and I wounded two others. Still they came on, as if resolved to overpower us. I observed, also, that Ben was near enough to see what was taking place, and was hoisting his sail, unable to resist his desire to come to our assistance. Should he come near enough to enable any of the people on our raft to leap on to his, I felt sure that our chance of escape would be lost.

"Are we bound to sacrifice our lives for these people?" I asked Boxall.

"Not when we have lost all hope of assisting them," he answered. "Ask the carpenter again if he will accompany us."

I was on the point of putting the question, when the ruffians—who seemed resolved on his destruction, believing that then they could have everything their own way—made a desperate rush at him. He cut down one of them, and would have treated the others in the same way, when his foot slipped, and he fell into an opening between the spars. They immediately, before he could regain his feet, threw themselves upon him, and plunged their knives into his body.

"It is useless further to contend with the villains. Now is our time!" cried Boxall; and driving back the fellows who were attacking us, we made our way to the side of the raft.

"Now, Halliday, leap!" shouted Boxall, while he kept those who were attempting to stop us at bay. Halliday plunged into the water, letting go his axe as he did so, and struck out towards Ben's raft.

"Keep hold of your sword, Charlie," said Boxall; "I will defend you from these fellows." I did as he advised me; and putting the sword in my mouth, where I held it fast between my teeth, I leaped into the water, and struck out with all my might towards the small raft. With a sweep of his weapon my brave friend drove back the ruffians, who had now turned their fury on him, and were pressing him hard; then springing overboard, he followed close at my heels. Happily, none of the savages could swim,—or, at all events, they dared not trust themselves in the water, fearing that if they did so Boxall might have attacked them with his sword; though some, in their rage, threw large pieces of wood and other articles, which came very near us; and one of the most furious flung his knife, which happily passed between Boxall's legs. Shrieks, cries, and shouts for us to come back, were uttered by our enemies, with threats of vengeance; but these, of course, only made us strike out the faster.

Ben and his companion, in spite of the warning we had given them, had hoisted their sail, and urging on the raft at the same time with a couple of oars, were approaching us rapidly.

"Shorten sail!" cried Boxall; "don't come nearer; we can easily reach you."

Ben obeyed; and we had the satisfaction of seeing Halliday—who, having no weapon in his mouth, had kept well ahead of us—helped on to the raft. Just then Ben cast a look of dismay towards us. "Strike with all your might, and splash with your feet! Make haste! make haste!" he shouted frantically. At the same time seizing a lump of wood, he flung it into the water on one side of us; while he called to his companion, who had been steering the raft, to put in his oar to help us. The thought of the cause of his excitement flashed into my mind: he had seen close to us a huge shark, which he dreaded every instant would seize our legs. I had, I may say, less fear for myself than for Boxall, who was a little behind me; and I had made but a few more strokes when Ben and the Spaniard seized me by the hands, almost jerking off my arms as they hoisted me on board. The moment my feet were on the raft, my first impulse was to take my sword in my hand, ready to attack the shark should it approach.

In a few seconds, greatly to my relief, I saw Boxall hauled up likewise. Scarcely were his feet out of the water when the hideous monster made a dash at the raft, his jaws closing on a projecting part of it, which trembled with the blow. A stroke which I dealt with right good will at its throat,—for a moment exposed to me as it turned on its back to bite,—made it relinquish its hold; and it darted away.

Frail as was the structure on which we now found ourselves, we felt in comparative safety; but the impulse which had been given to the raft before the sail was lowered sent it dangerously near the big one. Judging from the attitudes of the people on it, we could make out that several were preparing to swim off to us; with the intention, in all likelihood, of making us prisoners, and taking possession of the provisions and water on the raft. On this Boxall called to Ben to work one of the oars, and Halliday and I assisted the Spaniard at the other. While we did our utmost to increase our distance from those whom we were now compelled to look upon as our enemies, they were all shouting and shrieking; some ordering us to come back, others entreating us not to leave them.

As we had to pull against the wind, we made but slow progress; and at length three of the boldest of the mutineers, urged by their companions, — probably because they were good swimmers, — leaped into the sea with their knives in their mouths, and made towards us. The attempt was a mad one, as with our swords and axes we could easily have prevented them from getting on our raft. As they evidently had not seen the monster shark which had so nearly caught us, I shouted to them, telling them of their danger, and advising them to go back; but, believing that it was merely to prevent them from attacking us, they disregarded my warning.

On they came, swimming with long powerful strokes, and threatened quickly to overtake us. Unwilling to injure them, we continued to row away as fast as we could — now and then turning our heads to watch them. They had got about half-way when a piercing shriek rent the air, and one of them, throwing up his arms, disappeared beneath the surface: a shark had seized him. His companions, seeing what had happened, turned round and endeavoured to regain the raft. We watched them anxiously, for we had no desire for their destruction, and gladly would we have saved them if we could. They had got some way back, and we hoped that they would succeed in reaching the raft; but when about a dozen fathoms from it, another huge shark rose to the surface, and dragged down a second shrieking victim. The third swam on frantically, crying out to his companions for assistance. They stretched out their arms to him, and we were thankful to see that he at length gained the raft in safety.

What the fate of those miserable wretches would be, with no one to command them, to maintain discipline, or to direct them how to gain the land, we dared not think. As for ourselves, we felt in comparative safety on our small but well-constructed raft.

Boxall consulted with Ben whether we could take off any of the unfortunate people; but the latter was strongly opposed to the attempt being made.

"In the first place, it would be impossible to get off those we might select," said Ben. "And then," he added, "this craft carries us very well in smooth water; but should it come on to blow, and a heavy sea get up, it's more than she would do if we had half-a-dozen more people on board. Then, you see, we have water and provisions for ourselves; but we should be on short commons if we had more people to consume it."

Ben's arguments prevailed; and though we felt sad at the thought of having to leave so many people to almost certain destruction, yet we could do no more.

The wind had now completely fallen, and as Ben and his companion, as well as ourselves, had been awake all the previous night, we felt too weary to continue working the oars. We were, also, both hungry and thirsty, though we had hitherto been too much excited to think about it. Halliday was, as usual, the first to cry out.

"Of course, we will get some food for you, sir. I forgot how sharp set you must have been," said Ben; "but as we have no galley aboard this craft of ours, you must be content to eat your supper raw."

"We shall be content to eat anything we can get our teeth into," cried Halliday. "Oh, do give me a cup of water, as we had only a few thimblefuls on board the big raft."

Ben quickly drew a small-sized cupful from one of several casks ranged round the raft.

"I should like to serve out more, gentlemen; but Mr Boxall will agree with me that it's necessary to be careful, as our stock is but small, and we shall not get more till we reach the shore—and perhaps not even then."

Ben had secured some flour, which he rolled up into small balls. We ate these thankfully, with some salt fish, from which they assisted to take off the saltness. We made a better meal than we had enjoyed since we left the ship; but I observed that neither Ben nor his companion ate anything.

Night now came on. The ocean was as calm as a mirror, and the stare came forth from the cloudless sky and shone down upon us, their soft light tending greatly to tranquillise our spirits. One of us kept watch at a time, while the rest lay down, with the sail as an awning, on the planks with which Ben had formed a raised deck to the raft. We could dimly distinguish the large raft in the distance; while voices, borne over the tranquil ocean with peculiar distinctness, reached our ears, though I could not make out what was said. Again there came shrieks and cries, then all was quiet. Once more loud voices—as if the people were holding a violent debate, or were fiercely disputing—reached us. After all was quiet, I lay down and slept as soundly as I had ever done in my life.

Chapter Five.

A frightful encounter with sharks—A chase, and an escape—
Land! land!—Breakers ahead.

I was aroused by a cry from one of my companions; and, sitting up, I
saw a small raft with four men on it approaching from the direction
of the large one. I at once knew that it must have been formed by
them during the night, for the purpose of trying to overtake us. The
men were urging it on with frantic efforts, evidently resolved to
board us; so we got out our oars, and began to row away to keep
ahead of them. Day was just breaking. They probably had wished to
surprise us during the darkness of night, but had been unable to
finish their raft in time. We were, it must be understood, to the
eastward of them, and a somewhat stiffish breeze had just got up,
blowing from off the shore, which, although the water remained
pretty calm, impeded our progress,—for our raft, though strongly
put together, and able to contend with a heavy sea, was deep in the
water, and could not be impelled by rowing at much speed. If
overtaken, we must expect, we knew, a fearful struggle; for though
we outnumbered those who were approaching, four desperate men,
all armed, might overpower us, as we possessed no missiles, not
even a boarding-pike or boat-hook with which to drive them off—
nor could we prevent them from getting alongside, or commencing
the fight till their feet were actually on our raft.

On they came, uttering fearful oaths. "They have probably attacked
the spirit-cask, and in their drunken fury are indifferent to
consequences," observed Boxall. "It will be madness to show them
the slightest mercy if they get up with us."

While we rowed away with all our might, I could not help frequently
turning my head to watch their progress. They had, I should have
said, stepped a mast on their raft, but had no sail; indeed, they could
not have used it had they possessed one. This was another sign of
the haste in which they must have embarked. Their raft was also, it
was evident, carelessly put together; and as it drew nearer we saw

that the men could with difficulty keep their feet on it—for the wind by this time having caused the sea to get up slightly, it rocked from side to side.

They were within half a cable's length of us, when the feet of one of the men slipped, and overboard he fell. His companions, not seeing him, continued to row on. He shrieked to them to stop; the man next to him was stooping down, holding out his hands to haul him in, when suddenly he too was drawn into the water. Piercing cries sounded in our ears. "See, see," exclaimed Ben; "the sharks have got them!" In an instant they had disappeared, while their companions looked on horror-struck. The next moment a huge shark rose to the surface. One of the men struck it with his oar, which was immediately torn from his grasp; and directly afterwards another shark darted at him. He seized his axe, and, holding on to the mast, attempted to defend himself, while the remaining man continued to row as desperately as before. We would gladly even then have saved the wretched men, but we were unable to do anything to help them. There must have been half-a-dozen sharks or more surrounding the raft, one after the other attacking the frail structure, and threatening every instant to capsize it. In vain the man on the fore-part of the raft attempted to turn it round; again and again the savage creatures assailed it; and at length one, more ferocious than its companions, threw itself upon the raft, and over it went—the two unhappy beings instantly becoming the prey of the monsters.

We turned our eyes away from the sight, not without a dread that we might ere long be attacked in the same way. We had, however, the advantage of a strong raft, considerably higher out of the water than the other; and thus we had less reason to fear that the sharks would succeed in upsetting it.

"It serves the fellows right," observed Ben; "though, villains as they were, I could have wished them a better fate."

Wearied with our exertions, and as there was no immediate necessity for rowing—seeing we could not hope to reach the shore until a breeze got up in our favour—we put in our oars to rest.

A FRIGHTFUL ENCOUNTER

"Of course, Mr Boxall, you will take command of the raft," said Ben, touching his hat; "and maybe you will think fit to pipe to breakfast, as, I dare say, Mr Blore and Mr Halliday are getting hungry again."

"That I will, very gladly," said Boxall; "and I will try, at all events, to do my best for all hands."

"Hungry! I should think I am," exclaimed Halliday.

We had some more fish, with some biscuit,—which, though soaked in salt water, afforded nourishment. The fish we could eat raw better than some salt pork which Ben told me he had on board. Although our food was not palatable, we had not much apprehension of starving. We were chiefly anxious about water, of which our supply was very small; and we could not help being struck by Ben's fidelity in coming to look for us, knowing, as he must, that we should consume so much of the precious liquid, which was little more than sufficient for himself and his companion.

The day wore on, and still no breeze got up. "I wish that we had had an oar apiece, as we might then have had better hopes of making progress with the raft towards the shore," I observed. Halliday, however, declared that he thought we were pretty well off as we were,—as it would be a pity to exert ourselves, and to find that after all it was of no use; for a strong breeze from the shore would send us back in an hour the distance we had made good during a day's labour.

"Still, if every day we make some progress, when the breeze does come from the westward we shall be so much nearer the shore," observed Boxall. "Therefore we ought, while we have strength, to do our best to urge on our raft."

Though we were all agreed as to the wisdom of this, yet the sun came down with such strength on our heads that we had little inclination to exert ourselves. We had also hopes that, when the breeze did get up, a sail might come near us. This, perhaps, made us exert ourselves less than we should otherwise have done.

The large raft, I should have said, was still in sight; and, looking through my telescope, I could see the people moving about on it,—though, as far as I could judge, there were fewer than there had been

63

when we left it. What had become of the others? Too probably many had been killed by the ruffianly mutineers; and some, having succumbed to hunger and thirst, had been thrown overboard.

As the day wore on, we could not help acknowledging that we felt weaker than we had been, while a strong inclination to sleep overpowered us. So, while we waited anxiously for a breeze, we spent some hours sleeping under the sail,—persuading ourselves that we should be better able to row during the cool hours of night, when we determined to set manfully to work.

I may venture to say, though I have not before taken notice of it, that a feeling of compassion made us unwilling to desert altogether the unfortunate people still on the raft until, for our own safety, we were compelled to do so. Before long, it was but too probable, their numbers would be greatly diminished. Already six of the mutineers had lost their lives, and their fate would, we hoped, be a warning to the others; perhaps, too, the better disposed people might gain the upper hand.

"Whether we can venture to take them off now, is a question," observed Boxall; "but we may possibly be able to reach the shore and gain assistance for them: and it would certainly tend to prevent them giving way to despair, could we, before we leave the neighbourhood, tell them of our intentions."

Halliday and I acquiesced in this; Ben was doubtful.

"After the spirit they have shown, I am afraid it would be of no use, sir," he observed. "They are not to be dealt with like Englishmen; and if we go near them, they will only try to get hold of our raft. I will ask José what he thinks."

The Spaniard shook his head. "They will not believe us, señor," he answered. "Our officers having deserted them, they will not believe that a party of foreigners can intend to treat them with better faith. As they have killed my poor brother, one of the best of men, so they will try to kill us."

I could not help thinking that there was much force in what José said; still, until a breeze should get up, we agreed to remain where we were.

Another day came to a close. Occasionally we could see the triangular fins of sharks gliding round the raft, their wicked eyes turned up towards us; but they made no attempt to attack us. After supper we again held a discussion as to what was best to be done. At last compassion gained the day, and we agreed to approach the large raft sufficiently near to hail the people, and to tell them that we would, if possible, send them assistance.

"You will do so at great risk," said José. "I warn you of that; but, at the same time, I will not be the one to oppose your kind intentions towards my countrymen."

We accordingly took our oars and began slowly to approach the large raft. As we drew near, we could hear the voices of the people on it; some shouting in hoarse tones, others shrieking and crying out, as if imploring mercy.

"It is useless to go on, señors," said José. "They will not listen to reason."

Still, impelled by a feeling superadded to that of the compassion which chiefly influenced us, and for which I can scarcely now account,—resembling that which is said to induce birds or other animals to hurry forward into the open mouth of the serpent,—we continued to row towards the fatal raft. Perhaps, too, Boxall, who was the person to order us to stop, still hoped that our presence, and the promise we were about to give, might induce the people to remain quiet till assistance could reach them.

At length we got near enough to hail; but it was some time before we could make our voices heard, or the uproar ceased. I desired José to tell them what we intended doing.

"Come nearer, come nearer," was the answer. "Give us a little water and a little food; and if you will take two of our number,—only two,—who are suffering greatly, it will show us that you are in earnest, and that you wish to save our lives."

"Don't trust them, don't trust them, señor," cried José, in an agony of fear. "They don't mean what they say. If once we get within their power, they will detain us."

I told Boxall what José said. He still hesitated, however. Just then I felt the wind fan my cheek.

"Here comes a breeze from the westward," shouted Ben.

"We have given our message," I observed to Boxall; "and I cannot help thinking that José is right. We must not forget the sample they have given us of their feelings."

"I am afraid it must be so," said Boxall with a sigh. "For our own safety, we must make for the shore without further delay. Hoist the sail, Ben. I will take the steering-oar; José can manage the bow oar; and you, Halliday, and Charlie can tend the halyards and sheet."

We assisted Ben to hoist the sail, which was somewhat large for the raft, except under a very light wind. Before the sail was set, however, the breeze had greatly increased, and scarcely had we brought the sheet aft when over went the mast, carried off at the heel. We of course set to work to get in the sail, while Ben, with an axe, endeavoured to cut out the broken heel from the step, in which he had fixed it. This took some time, as the raft was rocking about far more than it had hitherto done, and he could not work quickly in the darkness. Having at length succeeded, he had next to chop the heel of the mast to the proper size to fit the step. He was working away as rapidly as possible, and we were stooping down to assist him, when José shouted out, "They are coming, they are coming!" Looking round, we observed that the sail of the big raft was hoisted, and that she was coming towards us faster than we should have supposed it was possible for her to move. In little more than a minute she might be up with us; while the wild shouts and execrations of the miscreants who were on the raft rang in our ears, and showed us what he had to expect from them.

Ben worked away as composedly but as rapidly as he could, while we were engaged in taking a reef in the sail.

"It's done," cried Ben at last; and lifting the mast, we found, to our great satisfaction, that the heel fitted into the step. We immediately set up four stays.

"Be smart now," cried Boxall. "Hoist away with the sail."

He had good reason to give the order, for, as we looked round, we saw the head of the big raft with several people on it, some rowing to give it more impetus, while one stood with a boat-hook ready to catch hold of us. In another instant the fellow might have hooked on, or have run the point of it into the back of Boxall, who had again resumed the steering-oar; but, hoisting away with all our might, we got the sail up, and while Ben was making fast the halyards Halliday and I carried the sheet aft.

Over the now foaming sea we flew, while the big raft followed close astern,—those on it uttering the most fearful oaths and execrations as they found themselves disappointed in their project of seizing us. Our light raft went over the water far more rapidly than theirs, and we soon distanced them; but for long their shrieks and cries sounded in our ears.

"I thought, sir, that they intended treachery," observed José to me; "and we may be thankful that we escaped them." I agreed with him; at the same time, having escaped, we had the satisfactory reflection that we would have done our best to have rendered them assistance, and that we could not blame ourselves for deserting our fellow-creatures. What would now be their fate, it was not difficult to say. They might possibly reach the shore; but the large raft, hurriedly put together, was but ill calculated to resist the now fast rising sea, and we could not but fear that many of the unfortunate wretches would speedily be washed off it. Our little raft was tolerably strong, but the way the pieces of which it was constructed worked, gave us a notion what would be the fate of theirs.

We were tossed fearfully about, and had to run now to one side, now to the other, to balance it as it was lifted by the seas. Boxall kept his seat on a cask, endeavouring to steer it, but he had at length to call me to his assistance, while Ben helped José. On and on we flew. As the clouds gathered in the sky the night grew darker and darker, and we soon lost sight of the large raft, while the voices of those on it no longer reached our ears. I asked Boxall what he thought would happen to the miserable people.

"Too probably they have been washed off the raft, or it has been capsized, by this time," he answered. "I confess, I do not like to think of what must have been their fate."

Our thoughts were now turned towards what might happen to ourselves. We had no means of judging how far off we were from the coast, but I calculated that, as we had not seen it, we could not be within fifteen miles or so of it—an opinion which I expressed to Boxall.

"You forget that, low down as we are in the water, our horizon is very circumscribed; while for miles together, on this part of the African coast, the sandy shore rises but a few feet above the level of the sea," he answered. "It may therefore be much nearer, than we suppose. We must, at all events, keep a good look-out; although, with the wind blowing strong, and running as we are directly before it, we shall have no choice where to land, and shall have to make good our footing on the dry land as best we can."

We were silent for some time; indeed, we had enough to do to steer the raft.

"Keep a bright look-out, Ben," cried Boxall. "Do you see anything of the land?"

A NARROW ESCAPE

"No, sir," answered Ben, somewhat surprised; for he supposed, as I had done, that we were still a long way off. "I don't expect to see it for the next three or four hours."

"We may reach it sooner than you fancy," said Boxall.

"Very glad to hear that, sir," answered Ben; "for though I am very well satisfied with this craft of ours, I would sooner feel my feet on dry land than aboard of her, if it should come on to blow much harder than it does now."

I suspect we all felt as Ben did. The sea was fast rising, and as the foaming crests of the tumbling waves came hissing over the raft, we had to hold on tightly to avoid being carried away. But our chief anxiety was about our mast. Should that give way, the raft would be left tossing helplessly amid the seas, and in all probability be washed off. We had, however, stayed it up securely, and we could only hope that it would hold.

I now proposed taking another reef in the sail.

"No, we will let it stand," said Boxall; "we shall only run a greater risk than we do now of being pooped, should we shorten sail, and if the wind does not increase we shall easily carry it; indeed, by the look of the sky, I have hopes that the weather will not grow worse, — and perhaps by the morning we shall have it calm again."

"We may then congratulate ourselves on having had the strong breeze which is sending us along so famously," observed Halliday.

"We shall have reason to be thankful to Him who has caused the westerly wind to blow," answered Boxall. "It might have come from the eastward, and we should have been driven still further off the coast—when, if not swamped, we would in all probability die of starvation, did we fail to fall in with a passing vessel."

Fully two hours passed by, and still Ben's sharp eyes could not detect the land. We had been steering by the stars, and though they had for some time been obscured, we had reason to believe that the wind had not changed, and therefore, being directly before it, that we had kept the same course.

I asked Boxall how fast he thought we were going through the water.

"Considering the breeze we have got, I should say five or six knots an hour," he answered.

"Beg pardon, sir," said Ben, who overheard him; "you forget, I dare say, that this raft does not sail like a boat. I suspect that we don't get much more than three or four knots out of her."

"I believe you are right, Ben," answered Boxall. "In that case, it will take us an hour or so more than I calculated on to gain the shore. However, it may be to our advantage, for it will be far safer to land when it is calm than with so strong a breeze as is now blowing. At all events, unless the wind changes, we shall reach the shore at last."

Another hour went by. According to Boxall's predictions, the weather was improving. The dark clouds which had obscured the sky cleared away, and the stars shone forth brightly as before; still the wind did not decrease, and the seas kept tumbling, foaming, and hissing around us as before. More than once we looked astern, thinking it possible that the large raft might be again within sight; but no sign of her could be seen. By degrees we had got accustomed to the tossing and the occasional breaking of the seas over us, and even had we expected to perform a much longer voyage we should not have complained; indeed, it now seems surprising to me how little concerned we all appeared to be.

We were running much as we had been doing for the last three hours, when Ben exclaimed, "Land! land!"—and directly afterwards, "Breakers ahead!"

We all looked out under the sail at what appeared to be the dark outline of a hilly country,—it seemed strange that we had not seen it before,—while the intervening line of white foaming breakers stretched out parallel with the coast, and threatened our destruction before we could reach it.

"Do you see any opening through which we may pass, Ben?" asked Boxall.

"No, sir; none at all," answered Ben. "All we can do is to hold fast to the raft, and pray that we may be earned through the breakers."

"Had we not better lower the sail, then, and keep the raft off till daylight?" I asked.

"We may lower the sail; but all the strength we possess could not keep us out of the breakers," answered Boxall. "We had better do as Ben suggests—stand on, and hope to be carried safe through them. Hold fast, all of you!" cried Boxall; "here we are close upon them."

As he spoke, we saw the waters hissing and foaming and dancing up to a prodigious height, as it appeared, directly before us, while the land rose still more distinctly behind them. The next instant we were in their midst.

"Hold fast! hold fast!" again shouted Boxall, "and we shall be carried safely through."

The breakers did not appear so high as they had done a little way off, and we all had hopes that Boxall's predictions would prove correct. But we had not much time for thinking; my head whirled and I felt giddy as I looked at the tumbling, foaming waters surrounding us. The raft lifted on the top of a sea, and came down with a fearful crash on a rock; and I felt myself torn from the grasp I had of the raft, and carried far away from it. I looked for my companions, and distinguished Halliday struggling near me. Striking out, I caught hold of him and urged him to endeavour to reach the shore, which appeared at no great distance before us. I then shouted to the rest of my companions, and was thankful to hear Boxall's voice.

"Strike out ahead; we have not far to swim," he answered, and presently he was close up to us. Neither Ben nor José, however, replied to our shouts; but self-preservation compelled us to try and make the best of our way to the shore, without attempting to look for them.

We had not struck out far when I felt my feet touch something. For an instant the horrid thought occurred to me that it might be a shark; but I retained my presence of mind,—and directly afterwards, greatly to my astonishment, I felt my feet touching the ground. I told my companions; and soon we all found ourselves standing, with the water scarcely up to our armpits. Still, though we distinctly saw the shore, it appeared to be a long way off. We now stopped to look around us. Not far-off, on one side, rose a rock to a considerable height, as it seemed, above the water. Believing that we were on a sand-bank, and that we might possibly have to swim a considerable distance, we agreed to make for the rock and rest on it till daylight. Holding each other's hands, we accordingly waded on, when suddenly we found that we had reached the rock,—on which we without difficulty climbed. The upper part of it, which was much lower than we expected, was perfectly dry; showing that the sea, in moderate weather, did not break over it. Boxall was of opinion that we had struck on a reef which extended parallel with the coast, and broke the force of the waves, and that we were in an intervening lagoon,—so that should it be now low water, which he thought probable, we could have no difficulty in reaching the shore.

We again shouted to Ben and José, but no reply came; and fearing that they must have been lost, we gave up calling to them and sat down.

The wind fell soon afterwards, and wet through as we were, by sheltering ourselves in a crevice of the rock we did not suffer much from the cold. After waiting for some time, we found that the tide was ebbing.

"If we wait till the morning we shall have high-water again; and in my opinion we shall be wise to try and get on shore at once," said Boxall.

Halliday and I agreed with him; for, our strength being restored, we were anxious to find ourselves safe on dry ground. We could not, however, fail to grieve for the loss of Ben, who had been so faithful to us; and also for his companion, José, who seemed a truly honest fellow.

"Now," said Boxall, "let us start."

"We are ready," answered Halliday; and he and I following Boxall's example by slipping off the rock, found ourselves in water scarcely up to our middle and once more began to wade towards the shore.

Chapter Six.

A deceptive coast—What is it?—Our disappointment—A
strange apparition.

An attempt to cross an unknown expanse of water, such as seemed
the lagoon stretching out before us, was a hazardous experiment.
Still, the water was calm, and we concluded that it was shallow, so
that we hoped by perseverance to gain the dry land at last. There
was no time to be lost, however, as the tide might soon rise again,
and make the undertaking more difficult. I felt like a person in a
dream as we waded on, surrounded on all sides by water, over
which hung a peculiar silvery mist, curiously deceiving the senses,—
though perhaps I was not aware of it at the time. The appearance of
the shore even seemed changed. It looked altogether very different
from what we expected to find it. Instead of a low sandy beach, with
here and there hillocks of sand, it appeared to rise to a considerable
height, with hills and intervening valleys, and lofty rocks springing
directly out of the water. "We must have been further to the south
than we supposed," I observed to Boxall. "Surely we must be near
the French settlements. The shore before us cannot be on the border
of the great Desert of Sahara."

"I cannot make it out," he answered. "Still I am pretty certain as to
our latitude. The country, however, is but little known, and we may
have been thrown on a more fertile region than was supposed to
exist."

"I hope, then, that we shall be able to find some food," said Halliday;
"I am terribly hungry and thirsty. Don't you think that we may by
chance have got to the mouth of a river, and so may soon find fresh
water?"

"This, at all events, is salt enough," said Boxall, lifting a handful to
his lips. "No; it is merely a lagoon filled by the ocean."

We waded on and on, but the shore appeared no nearer.

"We may have a fearfully long way to swim, should the water grow deeper," observed Halliday.

"If it does, we can easily return to the rock and wait till the low tide during daylight, when we shall be better able to judge what course to take," I observed.

As I said this I turned round to look at the rock, and to see how far we were from it, when what was my astonishment to be unable to distinguish it! Behind us the lagoon appeared to stretch out to an illimitable distance, without a single object rising above the surface. To attempt to return would have been madness, as we should certainly have lost our way; we therefore could do nothing else than push boldly forward. The sand below our feet was smooth and even, but walking in water almost up to our middle was fatiguing work, and we made but slow progress. Still on and on we went, when suddenly we saw before us a high conical hill, and directly afterwards a bright light appeared beyond it. Presently the upper circle of the full moon rose behind the hill, though it seemed six times the size of any moon I ever saw; indeed, I could scarcely believe that it was the moon.

"I suppose that the African moons are much larger than those of any other part of the world. At all events, that is a whopper," exclaimed Halliday, without considering what he was saying.

"It will give us light to see our way," observed Boxall, "and we should be thankful for it. We had better keep to our right, however, where the shore seems somewhat lower."

He was turning aside, and I was about to follow him, when Halliday exclaimed—

"Look! look! what can that terrific creature be?"

We turned our eyes towards the summit of the hill, and to our horror saw an enormous animal with arched back and glaring eyes—so we pictured it—gazing down upon us, seemingly prepared to make a terrific leap right down on our heads. Such a creature I had never even read of; for it looked far larger than any ordinary elephant, and might have swallowed us all at a gulp.

A DREADFUL APPARITION

"What is to be done?" cried Halliday. "If we run, it will certainly be after us."

"We cannot run, at all events," said Boxall with less anxiety in his tone than I should have supposed possible, though I knew him to be a dauntless fellow. "We will keep to our right, as I proposed, and perhaps the monster won't follow us after all. It is not likely to come into the water to get at us."

We kept away to our right, and found the water growing shallower and shallower. It was now but a little above our knees. I confess that I turned my head very frequently, to see whether the monster was coming after us. There it stood, however, in the same attitude as before—which was some comfort, as it thus showed no inclination to act as we had dreaded.

"What can it be?" I asked of Boxall.

"A wild beast, certainly," he answered. "I might have supposed it a part of the rock, or some gigantic figure hewn out of it, but it is too much like a real creature for that; and I begin to think that the mist which hangs over the water must have given it its supernatural magnitude. I would have said, from its shape, that it was a hyena or jackal, but neither the one nor the other approaches to anything like it in size."

"Whatever it was or is, it has disappeared," I exclaimed; for on looking round once more, the monster was no longer to be seen on the top of the hill. The water was now but a very little way above our knees, while the ascent was much steeper than it had been.

"I only hope we shan't see the creature again on shore," said Halliday.

"We have not much further to go to reach it," observed Boxall. The last few yards we had taken we had rapidly shoaled the water. "Thank Heaven, we are ashore at last!" he added, as the light surf

ce around us, lighted up by the rays of the full moon, which

which rolled up slowly went hissing back and left our feet uncovered. A few paces more, and we were standing on dry sand.

"Halloa! what has become of the mountains?" exclaimed Halliday. "I thought we were going to land on a rocky country, but I see nothing but sand-hills around us."

Such indeed was the case. As far as our eyes could reach, we could discern, in the moonlight, only a succession of sand-hills, rising but a few feet above the rest of the country.

"I suspected that we should find that to be the case," observed Boxall. "If we were to measure the rock on the top of which we saw the monster standing, we should find that the creature's dimensions were not quite so gigantic as we supposed. However, here we are talking away, and neglecting to return thanks for our deliverance from the dangers we have gone through, and forgetting all about our unfortunate companions."

I felt rebuked by Boxall's remark, and so, I dare say, did Halliday. We all knelt down, and I know that I tried to return hearty thanks for our preservation; but my mind was still in a confused state, thinking of Ben, and our long wade, and the monster which we had seen, and of what might be our future fate. My strength, indeed, was fast failing me; and though I was generally stronger than Halliday, I was the first to sink down on the sand. He imitated me, and Boxall soon afterwards sat down beside us. We none of us felt much inclined to speak; yet we were afraid to go to sleep, when we recollected the creature we had seen,—which, though it might not be of extraordinary size, would, if it were a hyena, prove an ugly customer should it take us unawares. Otherwise, we had no reason to dread it. Such creatures, indeed, seldom attack human beings unless first assailed, as they five on carrion, and act a useful part as scavengers.

Wet through as we were, the night air chilled us to the bones; but we were too much exhausted to feel inclined to move about and try and warm ourselves. We sat for some time gazing on the wild, desolate scene around us, lighted up by the rays of the full moon, which seemed to increase its aspect of dreariness. On three sides appeared a succession of sand-hills, one beyond another; while before us was seen the lagoon across which we had waded, with the tumbling seas, on the crests of which the moonbeams played, breaking on the reef in the distance. Every instant the water in front of us became more and more agitated, as the rising tide flowed over the reef; and we could not but be thankful that we had crossed the lagoon when we did, as later the undertaking would have been far more difficult, if not impossible, and we should probably have been engulfed by the foaming waters, which now with greater and greater violence rolled up on the shore.

Our thoughts naturally turned to the future. How were we to support life in this dreary region? or, supposing it to be inhabited, what would be the character of, and disposition shown towards us by, the people we might encounter? I had read of the Arabs of the Desert, and of their generous hospitality to strangers, and I had hopes that such might be the people we should find. I mentioned this to my companions.

"Poets and romance—writers may have pictured them as you describe, but I am afraid that we shall find the reality differ greatly from their glowing accounts," observed Boxall. "My notion is that they are a set of utter barbarians, who will rob us of everything we possess, and only feed us for the sake of keeping us alive to work for them."

This was not encouraging, and I could not but hope that Boxall was wrong.

"We shall soon find out," said Halliday. "I only wish that in the meantime we had something to eat."

"Well, we are better off than poor Ben and José, who have lost their lives," I said.

"I don't think we ought altogether to give them up," said Boxall. "Now that we have rested, I propose that we go along the shore and look for them. They may possibly have been carried in a different direction from that which we took. I felt the current, though not very strong, setting to the southward as we crossed; and if they stuck to the raft, or any portion of it, not being aware that they could wade, they would be carried in that direction. I have been thinking the matter over, and believe that they may possibly have escaped."

As Boxall founded his opinion on sound grounds, I began to hope that Ben might still be in the land of the living; and as Halliday said he felt strong enough to walk, we set off along the shore. We every now and then shouted out, "Ben Blewett, ahoy! ahoy!" joining our voices to send them to a greater distance. But no answer came.

"I am afraid poor Ben must be lost," I said.

"He is not within hearing,—or, at all events, we are not within hearing of him; but let us still persevere. Had it not been for him, we should have lost our lives; and we are bound on every account to do our utmost to find him," observed Boxall.

We accordingly dragged on our weary feet through the yielding sand. Walking was now excessively fatiguing, as the sea had come up and covered that part of the shore which had been hardened by the constant washing of the water over it. Again we stopped and shouted, "Ben Blewett, ahoy! ahoy!" We waited, hoping against hope that a reply would come.

"I am so tired, I must sit down and rest for a few minutes," said Halliday. Boxall and I acknowledged that we felt much in the same condition, so we threw ourselves down on the sand. Scarcely had we lain down when the sound of a voice reached our ears. It seemed to come from a long way off, yet we all felt sure that it was a voice. We accordingly started up, forgetting our fatigue, and trudged on,—the sand seeming to our weary feet softer than ever.

We went on for some time, but still we saw no one. We began to fear that we had been mistaken; still we pushed on, and in another minute I saw a dark object in the water, which I took to be a rock, close to the white beach. Directly afterwards I made out a human figure, which appeared to be coming towards us. I had got a little ahead of my companions. I called to them, and we tried to hurry on through the soft sand, which seemed to mock our efforts to advance.

"Is that you, Ben?" I shouted.

"Ay, ay, sir," was the answer, in a tone which showed that the speaker had but little strength left. We soon reached him. It was indeed Ben himself.

"I am thankful to see you, gentlemen," he said. "It's what I little expected, when you disappeared from the raft. But how did you get on shore?"

We told him, and then asked how he had escaped.

"It's more than I can tell you," he answered. "All I know is, that I found myself floating alone on what remained of the raft, away from the reef, with the mast and sail gone and the oars lost. After some time I was carried again into the breakers, and, clinging on for dear life, though I couldn't tell where I was going, was sent right through them into smooth water. I looked about me, but could see nothing, nor hear any sounds. On I drifted, wondering what would next happen, when at last I was cast on shore,—the raft, which was turned over, being sent by a sea almost on the top of me. One of my feet, as it was, got caught; and if it had not been for the sand under it, my leg would have been broken: indeed, I had to dig it out before I could set myself free. Thinking that the tide might still be rising, and that I should be caught by it, I dragged myself on to the side of a hillock, where I lay down, and must at once have fallen fast asleep. I was at last awoke, I suppose, by your hails; though I first heard them several times in my dreams. I tried to hail in return, but felt my tongue clinging to the roof of my mouth; and it was not till after some time that I could open my eyes, and recollect where I was and what had happened. As soon as I did this, I got up as fast as I was able. And again I say, I am thankful to have found you, gentlemen; that I am."

"And we are very glad to have found you, Ben," I answered. "Do you think that poor José has escaped?"

"I am afraid not, sir," answered Ben. "He could not swim, and he must have been washed off the raft on the outside of the reef."

"Have you managed to save any of the provisions?" inquired Halliday.

"I am sorry to say, sir, that I am afraid they are all lost. The raft, however, was knocking about so much that I couldn't get hold of it by myself, to see if anything is still fast to it; but now you have come, we will try what we can do."

Weary as we were, hunger prompted us to exert ourselves; and approaching the raft, which was heaving up and down in the surf, we got hold of it, after some difficulty, and at the risk of being crushed, and succeeded in dragging it partly up the beach. On examining it, to our infinite satisfaction we found a pork-cask,— which Ben had fastened so securely that it had escaped being carried away. It was, however, almost crushed in two. We examined it eagerly, and found that, though part of the contents had been washed out, several pieces of pork still remained. The water-casks, which we should have been still more thankful to find, had, alas! been completely destroyed.

It required all the exertion we were capable of to secure the pork-cask, which we managed to drag out of reach of the water; and though very thirsty, our hunger induced us to eat a portion of the pork raw—which, however, we could with difficulty get down.

"Never fear! Chaw, sir, chaw!" cried Ben, as he saw me hesitating about putting a piece between my parched lips. "It will seem dry at first; but go on, and it will slip down easy enough at last, and do you good."

I followed his advice, and found that I could get down far more of the raw meat than I could have supposed possible.

The wind had in the meantime been increasing, and the surf broke with a loud, sullen roar on the beach. Having eaten as much as we could swallow, we now turned the undamaged side of the cask uppermost, so as to cover its contents; and then, at Boxall's suggestion, we made our way to a spot a short distance off, between some sand-hills, where, pretty well worn out, we threw ourselves down to rest.

Though thankful to get back honest Ben, we felt very melancholy at the dreary prospect before us. Strong as he was, he also appeared utterly worn out with his exertions; and, stretched at full length on the sand, he was soon fast asleep. I had rashly undertaken to keep the first watch.

"Awake me soon, and I will relieve you," said Boxall. "I am afraid you will not be able to keep your eyes open long."

"No fear," I answered. "I will do my best, depend on it; for I have no wish to be earned off by a hyena, or any other wild beast which may chance to visit us."

Boxall and Halliday sat with their heads between their knees, and very quickly dropped off. As long as I was able to remain on my legs and walk about, I proved a faithful sentinel; but feeling very weary, I at last sat down, and the natural consequences followed —I fell fast asleep. The howling of the wind among the sand-hills and the ceaseless roar of the surf rather tended to lull my senses than to arouse me from my slumber. I dreamed of the events which had occurred, and fancied that I knew exactly where I was and what was happening. Now I was looking towards the foaming sea, when I observed in the offing a vessel under all sail approaching the coast. Gradually she faded from my view. And now, turning my head, I saw to my dismay a pack of hyenas stealing silently along towards us. I started up, and was thankful to find that the hyenas had disappeared; but, near the spot where I had seen them, my waking sight fell on a strange-looking animal with a long neck, a pointed head, and huge hump on its back, which I at once recognised as a camel. It advanced at a slow pace, not regarding us, and making its way directly to the beach. Though unwilling to wake my companions, I could not help crying out, when Boxall and Halliday started up, though poor Ben remained as fast asleep as ever.

"What can that strange monster be?" exclaimed Halliday.

At which Boxall, though certainly not in a merry mood, could not help laughing loudly.

"Why, a camel, to be sure; coming down to the beach to get a lick of salt, of which most beasts are very fond," he answered.

"I wonder if it's a wild one, then," said Halliday; "if it is, we may hamstring it, or kill it in some other way, and it will give us an ample supply of food."

"There are no wild camels, that I ever heard of," answered Boxall; "and if we were to kill it, depend on it its owners would make us repent having done so. I suspect they are not far off."

The appearance of the camel, as may be supposed, completely aroused us, and we watched it as it stalked down to the sands.

"I propose that we catch it, and make it carry us somewhere or other," said Halliday. "Its back is long enough to let us all ride on it: you, Boxall, on the top of the hump, as the post of honour; Ben, astern; and Charlie and I in front."

I could not help laughing at Halliday's proposal; Boxall did likewise.

"We must catch the beast first, then get it to lie down while we are mounting. And then, should we ever get on its back, seeing that it has no halter, it would certainly carry us—not where we wished to go, but to the tents of its masters; who would probably knock us on the head, or, if mercifully disposed, make slaves of us," observed Boxall.

A MIDNIGHT INTRUDER.

"Then I vote we don't interfere with Mr Camel," said Halliday. "But perhaps, if we were to follow its footsteps, it might lead us to where we could get some fresh water; or, should it go back to its owners, we might have time to reconnoitre them at a distance, and judge whether it would be prudent to trust ourselves in their power."

"A very good idea," said Boxall. "If, however, we are to trace its steps, we must wait till daylight; for as it probably walks much faster than we can, we should very likely lose sight of it, and get bewildered among the sand-hills."

We were watching the camel as it came towards us, when, either seeing us or scenting us, it stopped short, poking out its head, as if wondering what curious creatures we could be. Then turning round, it stalked leisurely away, and was lost in the gloom.

"I hope it won't go and tell its masters—unless they happen to be well-disposed individuals," said Halliday. "I trust that they may prove friendly; and the camel, perhaps, has come to guide us to them."

"It seems to me that daylight is breaking," I remarked.

"We shall soon know all about the matter, then; only I do wish we could get something to eat," said Halliday.

"So do I; but there is no use talking about it," I observed.

"I am not much afraid of starving," said Boxall. "We may hope to find oysters, or some other shell-fish, in the lagoon. I am more anxious about water; but even that we may possibly find by digging in the sand."

Ben, overcome with fatigue, still slept on, undisturbed by our voices. I agreed with Boxall that he required rest even more than we did, and we therefore determined not to arouse him till daylight.

Chapter Seven.

Ben's dream—An unpleasant discovery—A search for
water—Friends or foes?—Boxall's ingenious mode of
obtaining a light—Our companion spirited away.

We lay on the ground, watching the stars gradually disappearing in
the sky overhead, and still unwilling to awake Ben, who slumbered
on, completely overcome by the fatigue he had endured for the last
few days. At length the sun, like a huge ball of fire, rose above the
region of sand-hills stretching out to the eastward. It was time
therefore for us to get up and obtain a supply of pork from the store
we had left on the beach, as also to commence a search for water. We
called to Ben; who, starting to his feet, rubbed his eyes and looked
wildly about him, as if not quite certain where he was.

"I mind all about it now," he said, slapping his leg. "But, bless me,
how I should like to have snoozed on: for I was dreaming that I was
away back in Old England, in my sister Susan's cottage, with the
youngsters playing about in front of the porch, and Betsy Dawson—
who has promised to marry me when I next get back—just coming in
at the door to have a cup of tea and a quiet chat; and I was putting
out my hand to take hers, when I found myself clutching a heap of
sand."

Poor Ben scarcely seemed to be aware that he was speaking aloud,
for when he heard our voices he cast a bewildered look at us. We did
not laugh at him, however,—that you may depend on.

"Well, well, Ben, we must be prepared for a good many trials and
disappointments; but I hope that we shall all meet them like men,"
said Boxall.

"Yes, sir, that we will; and I am ready for anything that turns up,"
said Ben, giving himself a shake. "We want water and we want food,
in the first place, I suspect."

"The water, I have a notion, we can get by digging, as we did on the sand-bank the other day; and as for food, it's hard if the sea does not give us something to eat, besides the pork," observed Boxall.

The hot sun having quickly dried our wet clothes, we felt, as we began to move, in somewhat better spirits. We soon reached the spot where we had left the cask,—being guided to it by the remains of the raft on the beach. Halliday was the most hungry, and ran on first.

"Hallo, the cask has been overturned; and what has become of the pork?" he exclaimed, as he began hunting about in the sand. "That monster of a hyena must have been here; and I am afraid the brute has not even left us enough for breakfast."

We hurried on, and speedily joined in the search.

"Here is a piece, fortunately, jammed between the staves," said Halliday, dragging forth the remnant of a joint of pork.

"We may be thankful to get even that," said Boxall.

We hunted round in every direction, but a couple of gnawed bones, with scarcely any flesh on them, were the miserable remains of the provision on which we had depended.

"There can be no doubt about the hyena being the thief," I observed.

"I am very sure of it," said Boxall. "Even had we buried the pork several feet deep, the creature would have dug it up; for the brutes are said sometimes to visit graveyards, and there to disinter human bodies unless carefully covered up with heavy stones."

I shuddered, and felt but little inclined to eat the meat which the animal had left us. However, Ben was not so particular, and offered to take the bones as his share—by which arrangement he got a larger amount than either of us. Hunger had compelled us to eat the pork raw; and this having the natural effect of increasing our thirst, we agreed to lose no time in looking for water.

The staves of the cask furnished us with tolerable implements for digging; and would serve us also for weapons of defence, in default of better. We fortunately had our knives, and as the wood was hard, we could shape them into wooden swords and sharpen the edges. So we at once began to search for a spot where a little verdure might tempt us to dig. For this purpose we scattered about, agreeing to keep in sight of each other, and the person who first found a likely spot was to wave his stave above his head.

The hot sun now getting high in the heavens, his rays beat down on our heads, and made us eager to discover the refreshing fluid. Boxall said he was sure it was to be found along the coast, although he acknowledged that such spots might be miles and miles apart. "However," he observed, "there is nothing like trying."

We agreed to go towards the south; one taking the beach, another on his left hand on the summit of the first line of sand-hills, the third further in, and the fourth in a like manner on his left. Ben took the beach, Boxall was next to him, but I was outside of all. It occurred to me that it would be wise not only to look for water, but occasionally to turn my spy-glass to the east in the chance of any natives appearing. I scarcely knew whether or not it would be desirable to fall in with our fellow-creatures, remembering what Boxall had said about the natives; but still I thought that we might trust to the generosity and hospitality of the Arabs, and therefore should have felt no apprehensions had any appeared. As far as my eye could reach, however, with the aid of my spy-glass, wide plains of arid sand, and sand-hills rising one beyond the other, were alone visible. It was a region in which it appeared impossible that human beings could exist. At last I shut up the glass, believing that we were not likely to be molested, and that we must depend on our own exertions for support. My mouth and throat were becoming dreadfully parched, and I would have given everything I possessed for a drop of pure water; but, from the appearance of the country, I now began to despair of finding any.

We had gone on for some miles, it seemed to me, when I heard Halliday give a shout, and turning my head I saw Boxall waving his stave. I hurried after Halliday, who was making towards him. There was a slight depression in the ground, with a little verdure. Boxall had already begun digging, and we all joined with an ardour inspired by the parched state of our tongues. We exchanged but few words; indeed, we could speak but with difficulty. The staves served very well the purpose of shovels; and remembering that by perseverance we had before reached water, we dug on and on, believing that our labour would not be in vain.

We had got down fully four feet, and yet no water appeared. "Dig away," cried Boxall; "even if we have to go two or three feet deeper, we need not despair."

At last our efforts were rewarded by the appearance of moisture, and after we had thrown out more of the sand a whitish fluid flowed into the hole. On tasting it we found that it was drinkable, though somewhat bitter and brackish.

"I have no doubt that it is wholesome, as the water which the Arabs dig for in their journeys is described in the books I have read as exactly like this," observed Boxall.

So thirsty were we that we did not allow it to settle, when it would probably have become more limpid. But we all felt greatly refreshed, and thankful that we had not been thrown on this desert region to perish with thirst.

Fatigued with our previous walk, we now sat down to rest. I turned my eyes in the direction of the reef,—which, however, was not visible,—and saw Ben looking in the same quarter.

"I wonder if we could repair the raft, and make our way to one of the settlements to the southward," I said. "We might land if we saw bad weather coming on; and we should not, at all events, be worse off than we now are."

"That's just what I have been thinking about, sir," observed Ben. "But then, do you see, we should not have fresh water, and we should have nothing to eat; and besides, I don't know whether there is enough of the raft remaining to make it fit for use—though, to be sure, we might pick up some more pieces along the beach."

"We need not give the matter much thought," said Boxall. "We are several hundred miles from the nearest settlement, and the want of fresh water alone would make the voyage impossible, even should we succeed in putting our raft to rights. All we can do is to push boldly on to the southward; and if we can obtain oysters or anything else for food, and retain our health, we may hope, with God's mercy, to succeed."

We were, it must be understood, seated on a sandy mound facing the sea, the light air coming from which enabled us to bear the heat of the sun. As we were about to get up and proceed on our journey, I caught sight of some objects moving among the sand-hills in the far distance. I told my companions, who threw themselves down on the ground; while, unslinging my telescope, I turned it towards the moving objects, which I at once made out to be two camels with riders on their backs.

The strangers drew nearer, and stopping, looked about them. "I am afraid their quick eyes have caught sight of the gold on our caps or the brass on my spy-glass," I observed. "What are we to do?"

"Remain perfectly quiet," answered Boxall. "We might possibly improve our condition by joining them, but it might become very much worse. We can now calculate pretty well what we shall have to go through; but if we place ourselves in their power, we may be ill-treated, or compelled to labour for them, if we are not murdered."

"Well, by all means let us keep out of their power. I for one have no wish to be reduced to slavery," said Halliday.

"And I am sure *I* don't want to work for these blackamoors," observed Ben.

WILL THEY DISCOVER US?

The general feeling, therefore, being against putting ourselves in the power of the Arabs, and thinking we could hold out, we remained perfectly still, completely concealed by the side of the bank. The strangers continued to approach, and it appeared very probable that we should be discovered. We lay quiet, however, and watched them; and at length, satisfied that they were mistaken, they continued their route to the southward, along the line of sand-hills which ran parallel with the coast. We watched them as long as they were in sight, and then descending to the sea-shore, the tide being out, continued our march over the hard sand. We had allowed the strangers to get so far ahead that we were not likely again to fall in with them.

"It strikes me, sir, that while the water is low we ought to be looking out for some oysters or mussels, or we shall have nothing to eat when dinner-time comes," observed Ben to Boxall. "I see some rocks on ahead where we are very likely to find them."

"You are right, Ben," answered Boxall. "I ought to have thought of that myself, but I was considering how we should meet the Arabs should we again fall in with them, or what bribe we could offer to induce them to conduct us either to Magador in Morocco, the nearest place where we shall find an English consul, or else to Saint Louis, a French settlement in the south, which is, I conceive, considerably nearer. It is a pretty long march either way,—half the width of the great Desert of Sahara, north and south."

"I can, at all events, make myself understood, and I will say whatever you advise," I observed.

"My opinion is, that on all occasions we should speak the truth," observed Boxall. "We must therefore say that we are British officers, wrecked on the coast, and that, if they will conduct us to any place from whence we can communicate with our friends, we will reward them handsomely." To all which, of course, Halliday and I agreed.

We had now reached the rocks where Ben had hoped to find some shell-fish. Taking off our shoes and socks, and tucking up our trousers, we commenced our search, armed with our knives and wooden swords. No oysters were to be found on the rocks, or in the shoal water in which we waded. However, we obtained as many mussels and some other shell-fish as we could carry in our pockets; and Ben captured a large crab, which was a prize, we agreed, worth having. And as by this time the tide was running in, we were now obliged to return to the shore.

"We must endeavour to light a fire and cook this food," observed Boxall. "If we attempt to live much longer on raw provisions, we shall be attacked by scurvy, and shall assuredly be unable to continue our journey."

"As there are no trees hereabouts, and as we have neither flint nor tinder, I don't see how we shall get a fire to cook our food," Ben observed.

"But there are roots on some of the sand-hills; and here is a stone I picked up, which I think is a flint," answered Boxall.

We could, however, find neither roots nor shrubs of any sort for fuel, and were obliged to content ourselves with chewing some of the mussels to stay our hunger as we walked along.

Having trudged on for some miles, some slight signs of verdure again greeted our eyes, although the bushes rose scarcely a foot above the ground. The branches, however, from their dry state, would, we imagined, ignite; though it would require a large number of them to make even a tolerable fire. We carried our fuel to a hole between two sand-hills, hoping that the smoke, by the time it had ascended above them, might become so attenuated as not to be observed by any passing Arabs. The difficulty was how to light our fire. We required first the means of striking a spark, and then the tinder to catch it, and finally to produce a flame. Boxall tried with his knife and the stone he had picked up, but was much disappointed when no spark proceeded from them, the knife and stone producing only a light with a phosphoric appearance. "We must not give it up, though," he said. "I have another idea—we must form a burning-glass."

"How is that to be done?" I asked.

"Let me look at your watch, that I may compare it with mine," he said. The glasses exactly corresponding in size, he took them both out. "Now," he continued, "by filling the interior with water we shall have a powerful burning-glass, which will in a few seconds set fire to any inflammable substance, or burn a hole in our clothes."

I bethought me at that moment of the inside cotton-wool lining of my cap, on which the rays of the sun had been beating all the morning, and I felt sure that it would quickly catch fire; so teasing out a small piece, I followed Boxall down to the beach, where he was employed in filling the two watch-glasses with water. I held the wool, while he lifted the glasses over it; and in a few seconds a hole was burned, and I observed some sparks travelling round it. I rushed back to the heap of fuel, blowing as I went; while Halliday stood ready with a leaf of paper, which he had torn from his pocket-book, and with a heap of withered twigs and leaves, which with infinite perseverance he had gathered together. By all of us blowing together a flame was produced, to our infinite joy. A milky sap, however, came from the shrubs, and only a small portion of them would ignite, while the smoke which ascended was so pungent and smelt so disagreeably that we could scarcely bear it. It had the effect, however, of keeping the mosquitoes, which had hitherto annoyed us terribly, at a distance. By degrees also a few burning embers appeared, and we placed our shell-fish upon them. Seeing Ben poking in his wooden sword, I asked, "Why are you burning that?"

"I am not burning it, sir, but hardening the point and edge; and I would advise you to do the same with yours."

And following his example, we found it greatly improved our weapons.

In a short time the shell-fish were cooked, and we enjoyed our repast, though we should have been glad to have had some substitute for bread to eat with the molluscs. Having cleaned out some of the larger shells, we cooked a further supply, which we packed within them, and then tied them up in our handkerchiefs, that we might be saved the necessity of lighting another fire. Indeed, we should, we knew, be unable to do so, except during the daytime, unless we could pick up a real flint—and that Boxall feared we were not likely to find.

Our hunger being satisfied, our thirst returned, and our next object, as we advanced, was to discover water. The tide being high, we were compelled to seek the harder ground on the summit of the sand-hills, as the mosquitoes and sand-flies rendered walking on the sand excessively disagreeable. We kept in a line, as we had before done in our search for water, at a short distance from each other,—Boxall having chosen a position on the left,—and had trudged on for a couple of miles or more, as we calculated, without discovering any signs which tempted us to dig; for we were unwilling to make the attempt without a prospect of success. I was next to Boxall; and after we had gone some way he came nearer to me, and shouted that he would diverge to the left, towards a slight elevation, desiring us to go on slowly, and to halt should we lose sight of him. "I will make a signal, should I find any sign of water," he added. By this time my mouth and tongue had become fearfully parched, and I earnestly hoped that he would succeed. Continuing to look out for the usual signs—a little verdure, with a slight depression in the sand—I went on slowly till I got near enough to Halliday to tell him what Boxall had said; and he repeated the order to Ben. We had not gone much further when I felt great hopes, from the appearance of a spot before me, that water might be found; so calling to Halliday and Ben, they joined me. I looked round to make the sign agreed on to Boxall, when, to our dismay, we saw an Arab on a camel rapidly approaching him! We had been partly concealed by a sand-hill, and so the Arab had not, apparently, observed us. It was evident, however, that Boxall had not a chance of escape. He must have thought so himself, as he stood calmly awaiting the arrival of the Arab, who pulled up his camel as he got close to him. We stood for a minute irresolute, not knowing what to do; but as the Arab did not raise his weapon, we believed he had no hostile intentions, and was not likely to injure our friend. Boxall had now thrown down his wooden sword, and was holding out his hand as if to greet the Arab in a friendly way. The latter also stretched out his hand, and we hoped that the interview would pass off peaceably, when, to our astonishment, we saw the Arab lean over from his saddle, and by a sudden jerk seize Boxall by the arm and place him by his side; then giving the animal a blow with his spear or goad, it set off at a gallop across the desert.

We now rushed forward, Halliday and I shouting to the Arab to stop, while Ben with loud cries advised Boxall to give the black rascal a thundering clout on the head, and that we would quickly come to his assistance; but I am inclined to think that neither the one nor the other heard us. Boxall did endeavour to release himself, but the Arab held him fast. Indeed, at the rate the camel was going, he could not otherwise have stuck on.

Fast as the wind, the fleet creature, regardless of the weight of the two men struggling on its back, moved across the desert, its broad feet scarcely making an impression on the sand. We ran and shouted in vain: the camel rapidly distanced us, and making towards the south-east, disappeared at length among the sand-hills; while we, almost exhausted, sank down on the ground.

All our previous misfortunes had not weighed so heavily on me as this. As far as we could tell, our friend might be carried into helpless captivity far away in the interior of Africa. Poor fellow! my heart bled for him. He had fully expected to obtain his promotion on returning home, and to be married to a very charming girl, of whom he had often spoken to me; for he had an independent property, though, having no interest, he had long remained a mate.

We felt ourselves still at liberty, and did not consider that his fate might probably be ours before long; for how could we hope, without the help of his judgment and thoughtfulness, to make our way over some hundred miles of desert? Had we known, indeed, one tenth part of the difficulties to be encountered, we should have said that it was impossible.

"We are not going to let Mr Boxall be carried off by that black chap without trying to get him back, I hope," exclaimed Ben at length.

A SINGULAR SIGHT

"Certainly not," I said.

"Of course not," exclaimed Halliday. "We must follow him till we get near the Arab camp, and then try and let him know that we are near at hand to help him to escape."

It struck me that this proposition was very good in theory, but unlikely to succeed in practice. I did not say so, however, as I was unwilling to damp the ardour of my companions, or to show any want of interest in our friend.

"If we are to overtake him, we must set forth at once," I observed. "It will be difficult enough to trace him in the daytime, and impossible in the darkness; and that fleet camel may have passed over many miles of ground before night sets in."

Halliday, I should have said, had a small compass attached to his watch-chain. It was a trifling little thing, and of scarcely any use at sea; but, placed on the ground, it would enable us to take the bearings of an object with tolerable accuracy. He at once put it down, and we marked the direction the Arab had taken; it was almost due south-east.

"Shall we make sail, sir?" asked Ben, who was eager to be off.

"Yes," I said. "You, Ben, lead, and keep straight ahead for the northern end of the most distant sand-hill in sight; while Mr Halliday and I will keep twelve paces apart, and twelve paces behind you. We shall thus form a triangle, and if we see you turning we will put you straight again. I think in that way we shall be able to keep a direct course."

"I understand, sir," said Ben.

Having measured our distances, we set off. We were already on the edge of the level desert, so that we had no impediments to interfere with our march. Had I been more sanguine of success, I should have gone on with better spirits; but with the slight hopes I entertained of overtaking Boxall, and suffering in common with my companions from excessive thirst, my spirits flagged, and I could with difficulty drag on my weary feet over the hot sand. But having reached the point for which we had been steering, we brought up; and again placing the compass on the ground, took a fresh departure. We had now no object by which to direct our course, and had it not been for the plan I had thought of, we should have had constantly to stop and ascertain by the compass whether we were steering right. The long shadows in front of us—or rather somewhat to the left—showed us that the sun was sinking low, and that unless we could reach the neighbourhood of the Arab camp before dark we should have to pass the night in the open desert. We pushed on bravely. Still, I confess I could hardly drag my feet after me; and I observed when I turned my eyes towards Halliday, that he was walking with yet greater difficulty, though unwilling to complain. Longer and longer grew our shadows—still the apparently illimitable desert stretched out before us—but nowhere was the camel to be seen. Influenced by Ben's zeal, I had been induced to undertake the pursuit; but I now began to repent having yielded to it.

At length Halliday cried out, "Charlie, I can do no more!" and sank on the ground. So I called to Ben to stop, and we threw ourselves down by our companion's side.

Chapter Eight.

The search for Boxall—The Arab encampment—We find water—Ben makes a "circumbendibus" of the Arab camp— Captured by black Arabs—Antonio's escape from the wreck—His reception by the Ouadlims.

Night found us in the midst of the vast desert, numberless low sand-hills scattered about around us, and the starry sky overhead. Here we must remain until daylight, or retrace our steps to the sea-shore. We might manage to get back, if we had strength sufficient to walk, as the stars would serve us as a guide, and a few points out of our direct course would not make much difference; whereas, should we attempt to keep to the south-east, we should very probably pass some distance either on the one side or the other of the line we wished to follow, and miss the Arab camp altogether. We could not hide from ourselves, too, the danger to which we were exposed from wild beasts; for besides hyenas—of the existence of which in the neighbourhood we had had ocular evidence—there was reason to believe that tigers, panthers, and even lions might be prowling about in search of prey; and our wooden swords, even though their points had been hardened in the fire, would be of little avail should we be attacked. I did not express my apprehensions to my companions, however, though I had no doubt they also entertained them. My duty, I felt, as the leader of the party in the place of Boxall, was to do my utmost to keep up my own and their spirits.

We sat silent for some time; Halliday was the first to speak. "I wish that I had a mouthful of water," he said, in a hoarse voice. "Should we push on and find none to-morrow, what are we to do?"

I could not answer his question.

"But we may find some, sir," said Ben. "The Arabs are sure not to encamp unless they can get it for themselves and their beasts."

"But suppose we miss the Arab encampment?" asked Halliday.

Ben could not answer *that* question. I thought it was time for me to speak.

"I am very unwilling to give up the search for Mr Boxall," I said; "but unless we are prepared to lose our own lives, with a very remote prospect of assisting him, I believe that our only course is to make our way back to the coast, where we have a better chance than here of obtaining both food and water. I propose, therefore, that we remain here till we are rested, and then make the best of our way to the sea-shore. We must manage, in the meantime, to do without water; and as we have a supply of cooked limpets in our pockets, we had better make our supper off them, and then lie down and rest. I am ready to take the first watch; you, Ben, shall take the second; and that will give time to Mr Halliday, who is more tired than either of us, to recover his strength."

My companions agreed to the proposal; and hunger being our sauce, we managed to get down a considerable portion of our store of limpets.

Knowing that should I go to sleep both myself and my companions might be pounced upon by some wild beast, I did not venture to lie down, but leaned forward as I sat on the ground, supporting my hands on my wooden sword; and the moment I began to get drowsy I rose to my feet, with the intention, as long as I could walk, of pacing up and down close to them. I had just risen, when, turning my eyes to the north-east, I observed a bright glare in the sky. My first idea was that it must be the moon rising; and then I recollected that it would not appear above the horizon for some hours, and was convinced that the light was produced by an extensive fire. Never having heard of prairie fires in that part of Africa, —there being little or no grass to burn, —I came to the conclusion that there must be a camp in that direction; possibly the one to which the Arab had carried off Boxall, though he appeared to us to have taken a much more southerly route. I watched the light carefully, till I was convinced that I was right, and that it came from an Arab camp; then I at once aroused my companions.

"Now is the time to get near them, then," exclaimed Ben. "We shall be able to see them though they cannot see us, and we shall thus have a better chance of finding out whether Mr Boxall is among them."

We at once got up; and, guided by the light, we made our way without difficulty. It evidently proceeded from a large encampment, as the fires covered a considerable extent of ground, — which showed us that there must be a number of bushes or trees in the neighbourhood, to supply fuel. On we went, the light still increasing, till we found ourselves on somewhat rougher ground, slanting upwards, behind which we had no doubt the camp would be found. After going on for some time longer, we could clearly distinguish the forms of a number of horses standing up, and of camels lying down, with their drivers among them — the light of the fires on the further side throwing them into bold relief. As we walked side by side, with our eyes turned up at them, we were all three nearly falling down together head foremost into a deep hole, to the edge of which we had suddenly come. Ben, who was the first to see it, caught hold of me, and I held back Halliday.

"What can it be?" he asked, kneeling down and peering into the hole.

"A well," I answered, "at which probably the animals from yonder encampment have been watered."

"I only hope, then, that they have left us enough to quench our thirst," said Halliday.

Ben offered to go down and explore the hole, for in the darkness we could not see how deep it was; and we knelt down, grasping him by the hand while he descended.

"It's all right," he said in a low voice. "I can touch the bottom — or a ledge, at all events; I will feel my way, and take care not to slip down into a bottomless pit."

It was too dark to see him as he moved about, but presently a slight splash of water sounded in our ears; after which we could hear it, as it seemed, gurgling down his throat.

In less than a minute he came close under us. "Put down your hands," he said; "here is something you will be thankful for."

We did as desired, and drew up a large wooden bowl attached to the end of a rope. I gave it to Halliday first, who I knew was suffering most; and between us we emptied the contents of the bowl, and then handed it down to Ben,—who went back with the same caution as before and procured an additional supply for himself and us. Having satisfied our thirst, we hauled him up; and then sitting down on the side of the well, we consulted what we should next do. I was of opinion that Boxall had not been carried to this camp; but that the Arab we had seen belonged to some other tribe, and probably had been reconnoitring in the neighbourhood, and, catching sight of Boxall, he had hoped to gain some advantage by making him prisoner. Ben, on the other hand, who was convinced that our companion had been carried to the camp, was anxious to be certain whether this was the case or not. I warned him of the risk we should run if discovered in the neighbourhood.

"Well, they can't do more than kill us," he answered. "If they make prisoners of us, we must do our best to escape; and if the blackamoors have got hold of Mr Boxall, and we find him, we shall be able to help him to get off too."

"But if we don't find him, we shall have had all our risk for nothing," said Halliday.

"Nothing venture, nothing win," answered Ben. "Just let me go, and I'll take good care that these Arab rascals don't get hold of me."

At length Halliday and I, won over by honest Ben's arguments, agreed to let him do as he proposed; it being settled that we should wait for him close to the well.

THE ARAB CAMP

"Thank you, gentlemen," he said. "I will make a 'circumbendibus' of
the camp; and if so be I can't get sight of Mr Boxall, I will be back
here in an hour at the furthest. If I am caught or knocked on the head

by the Arabs, it will all be in the way of duty; and you will say a good word for Ben Blewett if you ever get home."

Shaking hands with us warmly, as if he were going on a forlorn hope, he stole off round the well towards the Arab camp.

It did not occur to us at the time, but we had really chosen as dangerous a spot as any in the neighbourhood. In the first place, wild beasts prowling about at night were very likely to approach the spot to drink; and then, as a pathway led down to the well from the opposite side, the Arabs of the camp were sure, at early dawn, to come down to fill their water-skins,—so that should we, while waiting for Ben, fall asleep, we must inevitably be surprised. Fatigued by our long march, however, we could not resist the temptation of stretching our limbs on the sand, regardless of the risk we were running—but of which, as I have observed, neither of us thought at the time. We did our best to keep awake, however, and after, as we supposed, an hour had elapsed, began anxiously to look out for Ben.

The time passed by. "I say, Charlie, I am sure Ben has been gone more than an hour," said Halliday in a drowsy tone. I scarcely understood what he said; I tried to arouse myself—he repeated his remark.

"We must wait for him, at all events," I answered. "So, I say, keep awake, and rouse me up should you find me dropping off to sleep." But poor Halliday was even more sleepy than I was; and in another minute we must both have dropped off.

We had been sleeping, I suppose, for some time, when I was aroused by feeling a hand on my arm; and opening my eyes, I saw a black fellow scantily clothed standing over me. He put his hand on my mouth, as a sign that I must not cry out, showing the blade of a sharp dagger—which he drew from his side—to enforce his commands. I saw that another had hold of Halliday; while, to my sorrow, I found that they had also secured Ben. His hands, poor fellow, were tied behind him; notwithstanding which, he was making the most strenuous efforts to escape—though it would have availed him nothing had he succeeded, as he could not have rescued us, and must either have fallen into the hands of other Arabs or have died of starvation.

Compelling us to get up, our captors next secured our hands in the same fashion as they had done Ben's, and ordered us to move on. Instead of taking us to the camp, however, they began to drag us away in the opposite direction, towards the sea-shore, hurrying us along as fast as they could run,—making it evident that our captors did not belong to the camp we had seen, and were anxious to get a distance from it before daylight. In vain, therefore, did we try to get near Ben, to ask him if he had seen Boxall, and to learn what had happened.

I found, on looking up at the stars, that after going a short distance they turned off to the south-west, keeping on the harder and more elevated ground, but still verging towards the coast. This strengthened my conviction that they belonged to a different tribe from those in the camp, and that they had been on a marauding expedition when they fell in with us. Perhaps they believed that we belonged to their enemies, and hence their anxiety to hurry us away from the camp.

Day had just dawned when we saw before us a line of low dark tents, pitched on the side of a sand-hill just above the sea-shore, with camels and other animals standing near them, as if ready to receive their loads, in case an immediate start should be necessary. The light of day also revealed to us the hideous and savage countenances of our captors—their skins almost black, and in features, many of them, closely resembling negroes; though, from the dress of their chief, and their camels and tents, I should have supposed them to be Arabs. They had but scant clothing, in addition to the belts hanging over their shoulders, and to which their daggers were attached. Their other arms were short swords and spears.

Our arrival at the camp was announced by loud shouts from the people assembled in front of it; on which a number of other men, with women and children, came rushing out of the tents. Their chief, before whom we were brought, was a tall man, of rather lighter complexion than the rest, but with countenance not less hideous and sinister than those of his remarkably unprepossessing followers. He inquired, in a sort of mongrel Arabic,—which, however, I could partly understand,—who we were, whence we had come, and how we had been found. To the latter question alone, his people could give a reply. I heard him remark that there must have been a shipwreck on the coast not far off, and that we were some of the people who had escaped from it. The others agreeing that he was right, a consultation was then held as to the direction in which it had occurred. Thinking it was time to speak, I now stepped forward, and making a profound salaam—for I felt that it was wise to be polite to the savages—I said, in as good Arabic as I could command—

"Know, sheikh, that the ship on board which we were voyaging was consumed by fire; but the great Allah whom we worship allowed us to escape, and conducted us to your shores on a raft,—which, as a proof that I speak the truth, will be found a day's journey to the north."

The astonishment of the black Arabs, on hearing me speak in their own language, was very great.

"Who are you, and how is it that you can speak in our tongue?" asked the sheikh.

"It is the custom of my people to learn the tongues of the nations they are likely to visit, as they voyage to all the lands under the sun; and before long we hope that our countrymen will come here to take us off, and reward those who have treated us with hospitality," I answered, trying to look as important as I could.

"O Nazarene, you speak big words," exclaimed the sheikh. "But understand that your countrymen, however large their ships, will find it a hard matter to follow you into the Desert, should we think fit to carry you there."

"True, O sheikh; your wisdom approaches that of Solomon," I answered, trying to imitate the Arabic style of language. "But you will then lose the reward you would have obtained by restoring us safe to our friends. The few articles we carry about us, seeing that we could save nothing from the wreck, are not worthy of your acceptance. May I now inquire what powerful prince of the Desert I have the honour of addressing?"

The sheikh appeared somewhat pleased at this speech; but he did not relax the sternness of his features while he answered—

"Know, O Nazarene, that you are in the presence of the Sheikh Boo Bucker Saakhi, chief of the Ouadlims," was the answer.

Though the sheikh did not appear a man likely to be won over by soft speeches, I determined to persevere. Unslinging my telescope, I held it out to him.

"Here is an instrument which will enable a person who looks through it to see ten times as far as he can with his naked eye. I will present it to you, and show you how to use it, the day a ship appears in sight, and you enable us to get on board her."

I thought the sheikh was going to laugh; but he only grinned sarcastically as he replied—

"Know, O Nazarene, that I can at any moment take it from you, as well as everything else you carry, and strip you to the skin; so I value not your promise as you think I should."

"But, O Sheikh Boo Bucker Saakhi, we wish you to understand that our countrymen will reward you handsomely with numerous articles such as your soul desires, if you treat us with that hospitality for which you princes of the Desert are famed throughout the world."

"That may be true; but a bird in the hand is worth two in the bush," answered the sheikh. At least, he made use of an Arab proverb of a similar tenor. "However, I will consider the matter. In the meantime, I will receive you and the other Nazarene as guests in my tent, where you will be pleased to exhibit the various articles you possess."

Of course, I said that we should be delighted, though I suspected what would be the result of exhibiting our property.

"And who is yonder white man, who seems so greatly inclined to knock over my followers?" inquired the sheikh. "His dress, I observe, differs from yours. Is he one of your people?"

"That man, O sheikh, is a faithful follower of ours; a lion in war, and a lamb in peace when not interfered with," I answered, looking at Ben, who was at that minute engaged in a struggle with a dozen or more Ouadlims, from whom he had broken loose, and who were again trying to bind his hands.

"Let him be allowed to come here at liberty, and I will prove that what I state regarding him is true," I added.

The sheikh shouted to his followers, and I called Ben to come to us. As he did so, he pulled off his hat, which he flourished in the air, and made the sheikh a polite bow. Then putting out his hand, he exclaimed—

"Give us your flipper, old fellow, and we will be good friends!— only, tell your people to keep decent tongues in their heads, and their hands to themselves."

"What is he talking about?" asked the sheikh, who, of course, did not understand a word Ben had said, and was unable to comprehend his movements.

"He says that he is ready to fight for and serve you, O sheikh, as he has served his own chief," I answered. "You will find him faithful to yourself, and a terror to your enemies, while he remains with you."

I said this for the sake of getting Ben well treated, though it was an imprudent observation—and I was wrong in saying what was not the truth—as the sheikh might not be willing to part with Ben again. But for the present it answered its object; for the sheikh, bidding us all three follow him, led the way to the entrance of his tent, to the astonishment of his followers. Though it was considerably larger than a gipsy tent in England, it had much the appearance of one. The cover consisted of camel-hair cloth, supported by a couple of long poles in the centre, the skirts being stretched out and fastened to the ground by pegs. Heaps of sand were also piled up, as a further security to prevent it being blown away. The ground inside was covered with a dirty piece of carpet, while a few pots hanging to the tent-poles formed the whole of the furniture.

The women of the tribe were most of them even more ugly than the men; and though they were decently clothed as to quantity, their garments were dirty in the extreme. They appeared to go about the camp as freely as the men, who showed no anger or annoyance when we looked at them,—which, as Ben observed, was not surprising, considering how hideous they were. They gathered round, looking with curiosity at our white skins and strange dresses; but, out of respect to the chief, of whom they seemed to stand in awe, they did not further annoy us.

"Come into my tent, O Nazarenes, and we will talk this matter over more at our ease," said the sheikh, walking inside, and making a sign to Ben—who, from the character we had given of him, was looked upon as an important personage—to follow. The sheikh sank down on his carpet, and we imitated his example, endeavouring, like him, to tuck our legs under us—Halliday and Ben on one side, and I on the other. But our attempts were not very successful. Halliday tried two or three times in vain, and at last stretched them out comfortably before him; while Ben, after rolling from side to side, fairly toppled over on his nose, before he could get his legs stowed away—greatly to the amusement of the sheikh, in whose estimation he was thereby considerably lowered, I am afraid.

After we were settled, and the sheikh's cachinnations had ceased, he clapped his hands; on which one black damsel brought him in his hookah, while another appeared with a piece of charcoal to light it. He did not, however, hand us his pipe.

"You are hungry, strangers," he next observed.

"Yes, indeed we are, and very thirsty too," said Halliday, who had not attempted to speak till now.

"I forgot," said the sheikh; and calling to the black damsels, he ordered them to bring us food and water. In a short time one of them returned with a large bowl of couscoussu, a sort of porridge made of wheat beaten into powder. We had our fingers only to eat it with.

"Set to, strangers," said the sheikh, nodding; but he took none of the food himself.

"It is not bad stuff when a fellow is hungry," observed Halliday, stuffing the porridge into his mouth as fast as he could lift it with his fingers; "but it's very flavourless; I wish we had some salt to put into it."

"So do I, for more reasons than one," I answered. "I do not quite like the appearance of things."

"But he seems to be a pretty good-natured kind of fellow; perhaps he does not know we like our food salted," said Halliday.

"We must take people as we find them; and I hope he has not omitted the salt intentionally, though I suspect he has not made up his mind whether to trust us or not," I observed.

We all did justice to the sheikh's couscoussu, however; for, notwithstanding its want of salt, we had eaten no food so wholesome since we were on board the Spanish ship. Another girl next brought in an earthen jar of water, which we in a few minutes completely emptied.

"Thank you, Mr Sheikh," said Ben, after his meal; "long life to your honour."

"What does he say?" asked our host.

"He hopes that your shadow may never grow less, and that you may live to be a blessing to your people for as long as the patriarchs of old."

The sheikh seemed pleased, and answered, — "Your lion-hunter is a fine fellow."

I explained that I only said he was as brave as a lion; but the sheikh replied that his bravery must have been proved by his hunting lions — and that he, at all events, would give him an opportunity of exhibiting his prowess.

Ben, tired of sitting so long on his feet, now got up, and, pulling a lock of his hair, walked out of the tent. Not supposing he would be molested, we sat on, wishing to practise our Arabic by talking to the sheikh, who made numerous inquiries about our country and other parts of Europe, evidently being not altogether ignorant of what had been taking place of late in the world. We at last also got up, to take the fresh air outside, when he said —

"Stop, stop! young Nazarenes. You came here to show me the precious treasures you possess; I desire you to exhibit them."

"Of course we will," I said, unslinging my telescope.

He looked at it, putting the field-glass to his eye, when he saw his own ugly face reflected in it.

"Bismillah! it's wonderful," he cried out.

I explained that this was the wrong way to use it; and inviting him to come to the door of the tent, I put it to my own eye to show him how it was to be used. As I did so, turning it eastward, what was my surprise to observe a sail standing towards the shore.

"Thank Heaven! here comes a vessel which may rescue us," I exclaimed.

"Let me look at her," said Halliday, taking the glass from me.

"Look again, Charlie," he said, returning it to me. "I am afraid that it is only a small boat."

"You are right," I answered; "or rather, it is no boat at all, but a raft!" Indeed, by this time we could distinguish the raft with our naked eyes.

"What is all this about?" asked the sheikh, observing our agitation. I gave him the glass, but he could not fix it on the object. He saw the raft, however, without it.

"Allah be praised! yonder vessel will certainly be thrown on our shore, and we shall obtain a rich booty," he exclaimed.

I did not undeceive him.

"Can that be the large raft, I wonder?" asked Halliday. "If so, some of the poor wretches have escaped death after all."

I examined it attentively, and saw that it was very much smaller than the large raft, and could not support more than two or three people. I also now observed that a reef of rocks ran parallel with the coast for some distance, the sea breaking heavily upon it.

There was soon a general commotion in the camp, and all fully believing that a vessel was approaching which could not escape being wrecked, were highly delighted at the prospect of making themselves the possessors of her cargo. The sheikh was as eager as any one, and, accompanied by his family, hastened down to the beach, hoping to be among the first on board.

ANTONIO'S ARRIVAL AT THE CAMP

Nearer drew the raft, and at length I made out that only one person sat upon it, steering with an oar. The people—who were all by this time down on the beach—soon discovered their mistake, and began

116

to vent their disappointment by uttering curses on the head of the stranger,—we coming in for a share of their anger.

On came the raft, and presently, as we expected would be the case, was dashed on the reef, suffering even a worse fate than ours—being utterly broken to pieces. Its occupant, however, sprang forward, and we saw him striking out bravely in the calmer water, into which he had been thrown, towards the shore. He was followed by fragments of the raft, which I thought would strike him; but he escaped from them, and came on with rapid strokes towards us. The Arabs, some of whom rushed half-naked into the water, waved their hands and encouraged him by their shouts. As he drew near we saw that he was either an Arab or a black man; and before he landed we recognised him as Antonio, the black we had met on board the Spanish ship. The Arabs now stretched out their hands to help him, and he was soon in their midst, supported by their arms.

Whether he had recognised us or not we could not tell, for at first he appeared to be too much exhausted to speak; and from the eagerness with which the Arabs gathered round him, and his general appearance, we suspected that he either belonged to their tribe, or to some other tribe on friendly terms with them. Such we had soon too good reason to know was the case. Presently we saw him borne to the tent of the sheikh, where food and water were carried to him. Remembering his conduct to us on board the Spanish ship, we could not but fear that his coming boded us no good; still, of course, if he was an honest man he could not fail to corroborate our story, and so we waited with some anxiety to speak to him.

In the meantime the women and children gathered round us, the latter especially treating us with scant respect; the urchins, like so many imps, grinning from ear to ear at us, pulled at our clothes and pinched our arms and legs; while several of them, pious, I have no doubt, according to their notions, spit at us to show their hatred of the Nazarenes. We knew that it would be of no use to run after the little wretches and punish them, so we bore the indignities we received with as much stoical indifference as we could assume. A big fellow whom we heard called Sinné—one of the men who had captured us—encouraged them; and at last approaching Ben, he insulted him with abusive language and gestures, snatching at his hat, and even trying to pull off his jacket. On this, Ben, without considering the consequences, lifted his fist and knocked the fellow down. Sinné got up considerably cowed for the moment, and stalked away; but, from the malignant glances he cast at Ben and us, we could not doubt that he meditated vengeance.

"Come back, old fellow, and I will do it again," shouted Ben; but the Arab did not wish to put himself within reach of the seaman's sturdy fists.

"I wish that you had not knocked the fellow over, Ben," I said; "our only hope of escaping is to keep on good terms with the Arabs."

"And so I wish to do, sir," answered Ben. "It may be, if I knock a few more of them over, they will be all the better friends with us; and it may teach them that we will stand no nonsense!"

Certainly, Ben's mode of proceeding appeared at first likely to answer, for both women and children kept at a more respectful distance, while none of the men seemed inclined to molest us.

Being tired with our previous exertions, we now sat down under the shade of a tent, whence we could watch the wide expanse of sea stretched out before us; but our eyelids were heavy, and, in spite of the doubtful disposition of the natives, we all dropped off to sleep.

Chapter Nine.

An unpleasant change—Ben undergoes a severe trial—The Ouadlims receive an unwelcome visit—We are made peace-offerings—A curious spectacle—I make friends with the Sheikh's brother Abdalah—The shipwrecked party—Discover a valuable friend—Antonio's escape from the wreck.

We were aroused by the voice of the sheikh. "Get up, you lazy sons of dogs!" he was exclaiming in an angry tone. "You have been deceiving me, I find, by passing yourselves off as people of importance, when you are mere servants of servants. Get up, I say;" and he began to enforce his commands by kicks and blows. We sprang to our feet, and Ben, doubling his fists, would have knocked the sheikh down had I not held him back.

"What have we done to merit this treatment, O sheikh?" I asked.

"Told lies, vile Nazarene," he answered. "Henceforward know that you and your companions are to be slaves—should my people not prefer putting you to death."

The sheikh was heard by the rest of the community, who now gathered round us, delighted at being able to renew their insults,—some of them pulling off our caps, while others tugged away at our jackets and pinched us as before, even spitting at us in their fury. At length Antonio stalked out of the tent, casting malignant glances at us as he passed.

"I say, mate, you know what better manners are," exclaimed Ben. "Do try and teach these people to treat us decently."

Antonio made no reply, but, without even turning his head, walked on.

"You are a pretty fellow," shouted Ben; "I thought you would have wished to be civil, at least."

Remembering the black's behaviour on board the Spanish ship, however, I felt that it would be useless to appeal to him.

Presently we saw him returning, accompanied by Sinné and several other fellows, mostly as ill-favoured as himself. Approaching Ben, they threw themselves upon him, and, pinioning his arms, led him off, ordering us to follow.

"I am afraid they mean mischief," said Halliday in a melancholy voice. "Do you think, Charlie, that they intend to murder poor Ben?"

"I hope not," I answered, though I did not feel over confident about the matter. "I will do all I can to save him."

We followed Ben and his captors. He turned his head towards us, and, by his look, evidently thought that his last hour had come; so indeed did we, and very sad we felt. We walked on till we had got some hundred yards from the camp, when we saw a sort of bench formed by boards on the top of a sand-hill, to which Ben was conducted. Sinné and Antonio having led Ben up to the bench, made him kneel down before it; when, to our horror, the former drew a pistol from his belt and presented it at the honest seaman's head.

"Fire away, you rascals," cried Ben in a loud voice, fixing his eyes on his executioners. "I am not afraid of you!"

Every instant we expected to hear the fatal shot fired, but still Sinné refrained from pulling the trigger. Feeling sure that if we rushed forward to Ben's assistance it would be the signal for his death, we stood stock-still, not daring to move. In equally fixed attitudes stood the Arabs, evidently taking delight in our horror and anxiety. I dared not even pull out my watch to note how the time went by, but it seemed to me that a whole hour must have thus passed, — the Arab all the while standing motionless, till I thought his arm must have ached with holding the pistol. Halliday declared that he thought at least two hours must have elapsed, when Sinné, giving a self-satisfied grunt, restored the pistol to his belt, and stalked off towards the camp, followed by Antonio, and leaving Ben kneeling before the bench.

Ben, on finding that they were gone, got up and gave himself a violent shake. "I thought I was done for!" he exclaimed, with that cool air which an habitual indifference to danger can alone inspire. "I didn't care so much for myself; but I thought the villains would treat you in the same way as they were going to serve me, and I was terribly sorry for you, that I was."

We thanked Ben for his interest in us, assuring him how glad we were that he had escaped; and not having before had an opportunity of hearing the result of his expedition to the Arab camp, we inquired if he had seen Boxall.

"Not a glimpse of him," he answered. "I went round and round the camp, so if he was there he must have been inside a tent; but as a number of people, whom I took to be slaves, were busy either pounding corn or cleaning their beasts, I am pretty sure that if he had been carried there he would have been among them, and I should have seen him. I believe, Mr Blore, you were right after all; and that the Arab who got hold of him must have gone off to another camp. All we can hope is, that he is among better people than these black fellows here."

I hoped so likewise, though I began to fear that our chances of escape were very small, and that we should be doomed to perpetual slavery by our savage captors. Of course, from the first we had determined to escape if we could; but the question was, In what direction should we fly? The desert was terminable on the east by the Nile; on the north, by the barbarous empire of Morocco, or by Algiers, Tripoli, or Tunis; while to the south were hordes of savages of whom we knew nothing, with only one insignificant French settlement where we might expect a kind reception: and we should undoubtedly have many hundred miles of an almost barren region to traverse, either to the east or to the north or south, with but a bare possibility of escaping on board some vessel which might appear off the coast, provided we could keep along the shore and avoid recapture.

We were not allowed many minutes for conversation, for our savage tormentors quickly gathered round us again, and seemed to take delight in insulting and tormenting us in every way they could think of. We had been left for some time to the tender mercies of the women and children; the men having assembled together to hold, as we afterwards found, a consultation regarding our disposal—their savage yells and cries reaching our ears even above the shrill shrieks and shouts of the women. It was evident that our captors were engaged in a hot discussion, but not one of them, we had reason to suppose, was lifting up his voice in our favour.

At length Sinné appeared, and ordered us to accompany him. Advancing with rapid strides, he led us into the centre of a circle of Arabs; but as we glanced round at their scowling countenances, we observed no sign of kindly feeling or sympathy for our sufferings. The sheikh then calling to me, ordered me to interpret to the rest. He said that we were all three to be separated,—he himself intending to take me. Ben was to fall to the lot of Sinné; while Halliday was to become the slave of another chief man. This announcement affected us more than anything which had occurred. Together, we thought that we could have borne our misfortunes; but parted from each other, we felt they would be insupportable.

"You are all young and active, and can each do more work than any three women," he observed; "let me see that you are not idle, or you will repent it. And you shall begin at once."

On this some heavy mallets or pestles were put into our hands, and we were ordered to pound some corn in wooden mortars, which were brought out and placed before us, while our new masters looked on to see that we laboured with all our strength. Ben grumbled and growled, the only way in which he could express his feelings; but seeing Halliday and me working, he thought it prudent to obey.

I may say here that we had from the first observed that the people were in a somewhat uneasy state of mind, as if aware that an enemy was in the neighbourhood. No fires had been lighted. The tents had been pitched close to the shore, so that they and the camels were hidden, by the first line of sand-hills rising above them, from any one passing on the opposite side; while men on foot were sent out as scouts at night, to watch far and wide round the camp.

After we had finished our task we were told that we might go down to the beach and obtain shell-fish for our own supper. Our fare was not much better than we had before been able to obtain for ourselves; for, no fires being allowed, we were unable to cook our shell-fish—and only a small portion of porridge was given us, while we were compelled to drink the brackish water which we procured from a well dug in the sand some way off.

Darkness at length coming on, we were permitted to lie down, worn out with fatigue, outside the chiefs tent, thankful that we were not as yet separated from each other. The women and children, however, would not for some time allow us to go sleep; but again coming round us, joined this time by some of the younger men, amused themselves in jeering at and taunting us. But at length they retired, and we fell asleep.

Dawn had just broken, when we were aroused by the voices of the people in the camp; and on looking out, we saw a number of the scouts hurrying in, with alarm on their countenances. We were not kept long in doubt as to the cause of their agitation; for on glancing to the eastward we saw, coming over the hills of sand, several bands of Bedouins mounted on camels, their arms glittering brightly in the rays of the rising sun. On they advanced at full gallop, till they got within gun-shot of our camp, when they suddenly pulled up. The camels then slowly kneeling down, their masters dismounted, and secured fetters to their legs, to prevent them from going away. Two Arabs were mounted on each camel: the first seated on a small side-saddle, something in the style of a lady's; and the second as a man sits on horseback. We counted nearly twenty different bands, each composed of twelve men, who took up their stations one after the other. Whether they came as friends or foes, was at first difficult for us to determine; but, from the state of agitation and alarm into which the Ouadlims were thrown, it was soon clear that they regarded the strangers in no friendly light. To escape, however, was impossible, as they were greatly outnumbered by the new arrivals; who were also better armed, and under superior discipline, than the savage tribe into whose hands we had fallen. As we stood watching them, we saw in the far distance numerous other camels, as well as horses, and apparently sheep and goats, approaching.

The Bedouin sheikh and several other principal men now advanced, being well protected by the firelocks of their men, who stood in front of the camels. The black sheikh, Boo Bucker, being summoned, then advanced to meet them, with Sinné and other heads of families, cutting a very sorry appearance in the presence of the superior tribe. They had a long discussion, after which the whole party came to the top of the hill, where they could view the coast. No one hindering us, we drew near them; when, from the remarks made, I found they had supposed that a shipwreck had taken place, and their object was to participate in the plunder, or rather, to take it away from the Ouadlims should they have got possession of it—just as the frigate-bird seizes the prey which the smaller wild-fowl has obtained.

The new-comers appeared to be somewhat angry at being disappointed in their hope of obtaining a rich booty, and from the talking and wrangling which took place we thought they would have come to blows with our captors. The latter endeavoured to pacify them, however, and I gathered from what I heard that we were to be delivered up as a peace-offering. This to us mattered very little; indeed, we hoped that our condition would be improved by falling into the hands of a less barbarous tribe than those who had first taken possession of us. Still, it was not pleasant to find ourselves handed over, like so many sheep or oxen, by one party of savages to another.

Boo Bucker then coming up, seized me by the arm and dragged me forward to the strange sheikh; while another chief led Halliday. Sinné was about to seize hold of Ben; who, however, drew back, exclaiming,—"Come, come, old fellow, you are not going to touch me; I am going where my officers go, so don't you be afraid. And to show you that I don't harbour ill-will, here's my fist;" and he seized the Arab's hand and wrung it till the fellow cried out, and seemed glad to let him go. Ben soon came up to us, laughing and slapping his legs to exhibit his pleasure at the trick he had played the ill-favoured savage.

Still the Bedouins did not appear satisfied, and more wrangling took place. At length Boo Bucker and his companions retired to their camp, and in a short time reappeared, dragging forward Antonio, who seemed very unwilling to accompany them. Notwithstanding the resistance he made, however, he was brought up to the Bedouin chief, who placed his hand on his shoulder and claimed him as his slave. Antonio was at first furiously indignant at being so treated by his treacherous friends, but seeing that there was no help for it, he yielded to circumstances.

"I say, Charlie, it won't do to let these black fellows keep up our jackets and caps!" exclaimed Halliday. "Cannot you ask our new masters to get them back for us?"

"I will do my best, at all events," I answered; and turning to one of the Arabs who surrounded us, I inquired the name of their chief. The Arab seemed very much surprised at being addressed in his own language, and answered,—"Sheikh Hamed ben Kaid."

I thanked him in due form for the information he had given me; then stepping up to the sheikh, I made him a profound salaam, and addressing him by name, told him that we had been deprived of our garments, and begged that he would recover them. He at once turned to Boo Bucker, and upbraiding him for keeping back what ought to have been his, ordered him at once to bring the jackets and caps. The Ouadlim chief looked very much annoyed, as he had evidently expected to retain the articles; but a few menacing words made him hasten away, and return in a short time with the things, as well as my spy-glass,—all of which we expected would be restored to us. Such, however, we found to be very far from Sheikh Hamed's intention. He inquired if any other articles had been taken from us; and on my replying that everything had been given back, he ordered Boo Bucker to move with his people to the northward, as it was his intention to camp in the neighbourhood. On this the two parties separated; and we were not sorry to see the last, as we hoped, of our former masters.

Sheikh Hamed now mounted his camel, and ordering us to follow, moved on to the southward—to look out for a spot suitable for encamping, as we supposed. We marched on as directed; but Antonio, who showed an evident inclination to be refractory, was handed over to the keeping of some of Sheikh Hamed's followers. In a short time we reached a spot not far from the shore, which appeared to satisfy the requirements of the chief; and sticking his spear into the ground, he called a halt, when the various bands as they came up reined in their camels—the animals kneeling down as before, that their riders might dismount.

I looked out eagerly in the hope of seeing Boxall, but could nowhere discover him. I inquired of one of the people, who seemed inclined to be communicative, if a white man had been taken prisoner and brought to the camp. His answer fully satisfied me that the Arab who had carried off our friend must have belonged to some other tribe.

On the arrival of the baggage camels we were ordered to assist in unloading them and erecting the tents, and many a curse and blow we received for our want of skill in performing the operation. We took notice, however, of the mode in which everything was done, so that another time we should know how to proceed. The tents were quickly set up, much in the fashion of those of the Ouadlims,—though these were larger, and that of the sheikh had a somewhat better and cleaner carpet than the dirty cloth which covered the floor of Boo Bucker's tent. Having performed this duty, we were next ordered to assist in digging wells. Fortunately, we had retained our wooden swords. At first, the Arabs looked at them with contempt; but when they saw how we used them to dig up the sand, they treated them with more respect, and inquired if we could manufacture some for them. I replied that if we could find a cask on the sea-shore we could easily do so, but without the proper wood we could not gratify their wishes.

"Then look out and find a cask speedily," said the Arab who was superintending the operation.

The wells being dug, we had to bail out the water in wooden bowls, and carry it to the different animals. Fuel was then collected, and a line of fires kindled in order to drive away the mosquitoes and other insects, which appeared to torment the animals even as much as they did us. We were then ordered to assist the black slaves in cleaning the oxen and cows; which operation was managed in a curious way. The animals being seized by the horns, were thrown down on the sand, where they lay perfectly quiet, while the blacks with great dexterity cleansed their bodies from the insects. After this, they were washed with water from the sea. The cows were then milked.

These various processes employed the greater number in the camp till near midnight. We were then allowed to lie down inside one of the tents, already crowded with Arabs and blacks. Some sheep-skins were thrown to us for coverings; and though we did not require them for warmth—the heat was almost insupportable—they were a slight protection from the attacks of the mosquitoes which swarmed around us, and for long hours, it seemed, prevented us from falling asleep, weary as we were.

The next morning we were aroused at daybreak by several kicks from the foot of an Arab, who ordered us to go down to the shore and collect shell-fish—furnishing us with a basket for the purpose. Our taskmaster followed us, to see that we laboured diligently; and I observed that he and the other Arabs took great care not to wet their feet in the salt water. Believing that they would thus become defiled, when they were compelled to do so they invariably washed them afterwards in fresh water.

While we were thus employed in the grey dawn, the sheikh issued from his tent, and mounting the summit of the nearest sand-hill, shouted,—"Allah akbar!" (God is great!) At this summons the whole male population of the camp assembled in lines behind him, turning their faces eastward in the direction of Mecca; and as the sun rose above the horizon, they knelt down, and throwing sand over their bodies, bowed their heads to the ground, while they offered up their prayers, repeating,—"There is one God, and Mohammed is his prophet." The women at the same time came to the front of their tents, where they performed a similar ceremony.

We stood at a distance, struck by the solemnity of the scene.

"Well, after all, these appear to be decent fellows," observed Ben. "I only hope they will treat us in a proper manner."

But alas for Ben's good opinion of them! No sooner were their prayers over than the Arabs, with kicks and cuffs, set the slaves to work; while we had to return to the sea-shore to collect more shell-fish. We were thus employed for the greater part of the day, and could with difficulty obtain a little porridge, or get leave to cook our shell-fish at any of the fires.

Several days passed in a similar manner. We frequently met Antonio,—as I will still call him, though he had another name among the Arabs,—and he never failed to cast a look of anger at us, as if he supposed we had been the cause of his captivity. At length, every root and blade of grass in the neighbourhood being consumed, the sheikh gave the order to prepare for marching. The baggage camels were brought up, the tents struck, the animals loaded (we assisting), and every preparation quickly made. We had hoped to be allowed camels to ride on, but the sheikh ordering us to proceed on foot, we had no help for it but to obey.

On we trudged all day, under a burning sun, sinking up to our ankles in the soft sand. Ben did his best to keep up our spirits, talking away, and even singing; though neither Halliday nor I were able to join him. When we arrived at night, we had to assist in pitching the tents and grinding corn; while frequently we were sent to a distance in charge of flocks of goats. On such occasions, however, we were always separated from each other, and carefully watched, so that we could not attempt to make our escape.

THE BEGINNING OF OUR SERVITUDE.

The tribe, as it moved along through the desert, had the appearance of a large army. There were, to begin with, between eight and nine hundred camels, nearly two hundred of which belonged to the chief; and there were fully two thousand sheep, and nearly as many goats. There were also twenty or thirty horses, with a few jackasses; and numerous dogs, chiefly of the greyhound and bloodhound breed, which were used for the purpose of killing hares, foxes, and wolves. Each family possessed a tent, which, with their provisions, water, and effects, was carried by the male camels, while the young and the milch camels were not loaded. When we moved on, the sheep and goats of each family moved in separate droves—the animals keeping close together, and following their respective shepherds; but when we encamped or met with vegetation, they were allowed to spread over the country. They were again quickly collected by the shepherd's whistle, or, if at a distance, by the sound of his horn. However far-off they might be, the instant they heard the horn in they all flocked; having been taught to do so from their earliest days at the appearance of a wild beast, when their instinct showed them that it was the surest way of escaping from danger. On encamping at night, the camels and flocks belonging to each family took up their proper position in front of the respective tents, near the fires which were immediately kindled for cooking. On several occasions, when we were in what was considered a dangerous neighbourhood, either on account of hostile tribes or wild beasts, the tents were pitched in a large circle, the camels, flocks, and herds being placed in the centre. On such occasions the male camels and horses were kept saddled, while the men lay down by their sides, ready to start up at a moment's notice. The sheep and goats are much larger than any I have seen in England, with long legs and thin bodies; and when sufficiently fed they can keep up with the camels on a journey, and can run as fast as a greyhound. It is extraordinary, too, how long camels can go without food and water, and on what scanty herbage they manage to subsist.

From being able to talk to the people, Halliday and I had much softened their feelings towards us; and I determined to try what I could do to win the regard of the sheikh. He had a brother, Abdalah by name, a fine-looking young man, who thought a good deal of himself. Making him a profound salaam as he was passing one day, I said: "May your shadow never be less. O brother of the great sheikh, I have heard of your valour and prowess, and I doubt not that your generosity equals it! You see before you two young chiefs, who may some day become great water sheikhs, in command of many thousands of men; and knowing this, I trust you will not allow them longer to endure the pain and suffering they have gone through for many days."

"Bismillah! is what you speak the truth?" exclaimed Abdalah.

"Your servant would not condescend to speak a lie. Among our people it is looked upon as a disgraceful act," I answered.

Abdalah did not seem quite to understand this; but my bold address had some effect upon him, and he promised to make a request to the sheikh that we might be permitted to ride on camels when we had long journeys to take. Halliday and I thanked him; and I asked him if he had ever looked through my telescope, of which his brother had possession. He had not done so; and having described its wonders, I promised to show him how to use it the next day.

After we had performed our morning tasks, the sheikh pointed out two camels, with saddles on their backs, and told us that we might mount them. I then asked if Ben might have the same privilege.

"No, no," he answered. "You might take it into your heads to try and gallop off; and though you would not escape, it would give us the trouble of going after you."

As we rode along that day, I found that we were once more verging towards the sea-shore. While we were moving onwards, Abdalah came up with my spy-glass hung over his shoulder, and said that he wished me to show him its use. We soon afterwards — being a considerable distance ahead of the caravan — came to a halt, when, dismounting, I pulled the telescope out and put it to my eye. What was my surprise to see, in the far distance, a white spot on the beach, which on more minute examination I discovered to be a tent made of a ship's sails! Instead of letting Abdalah see it, I turned the glass towards some distant camels, which appeared mere specks rising out of the sandy desert. Abdalah's astonishment on seeing them, as it were, on a sudden brought within reach, was much greater than mine had been on catching sight of the tent.

After he had amused himself for some time, I informed him that I believed we should find some white men encamped at a distance of less than an hour's journey, and entreated him to be merciful to them. "That will be as the sheikh thinks fit," he answered evasively.

We were now anxious to hurry on, in order to ascertain who the people were; so, mounting our camels, we started off. I was considerably raised in the opinion of the sheikh and Abdalah when they found my prediction true. Dismounting from their camels, Halliday and I following them, they made their way towards the tent. As they drew aside a loose portion, a sad scene met the view. In the interior were a number of persons apparently in the last stage of starvation, whose haggard countenances, long hair and beards, and scanty clothing, showed the hardships they had endured. One of them coming forward, threw himself on his knees, imploring the chief in piteous accents to have compassion on him and his companions.

"Who are you?" asked the sheikh; but the man made no reply.

Halliday and I then stepped forward and looked on. I thought I recognised several of them, and at length was convinced that they were some of the people we had seen on board the Spanish ship. I then asked them if this was the case.

"Yes," answered the poor man on his knees. "We escaped in one of the boats, and after enduring many hardships were thrown on this inhospitable shore, — several of our people being drowned at the same time."

DISCOVERY OF THE SHIPWRECKED PARTY.

I told the sheikh of the sufferings they had endured, hoping to excite his compassion; but he seemed unmoved thereat, though he allowed Abdalah to show us a spot where, by digging, we could obtain some fresh water. The eagerness with which they took it when we carried it to them proved the amount of their thirst; indeed, I believe that all of them would have died in a few hours had we not arrived to their rescue, as they had long exhausted the small stock of water they had brought on shore, and had no idea that, by exerting themselves, they could have obtained a supply close at hand.

Among others I recognised the black boy, our young friend Selim, or Pedro as he was called on board. He at once came forward, expressing his pleasure at seeing us; for, believing that we had been left on board the burning ship, he supposed that we had perished. He had before shown so friendly a feeling towards us that we also were glad to meet him, especially as he did not appear to dread his future lot.

"I am at home everywhere, and I shall not find the Arabs worse masters than others with whiter skins," he said, shrugging his shoulders.

He and Ben—to whom he had been very attentive on board—at once became fast friends; indeed, he was the only person besides ourselves with whom poor Ben could converse. When the boy caught sight of Antonio, however, he looked anything but delighted. "What, he not drowned!" he exclaimed. "He too bad for that. Well, take care. He do some of us a mischief if he can."

Having myself formed a similar opinion of the big negro, I was not surprised to hear Selim say this of his countryman; and it was very clear that we must be on our guard against Antonio, who had already exhibited his ill-will towards us. At present our attention was taken up with the castaways, who were, we felt, still more unfortunate than ourselves.

Chapter Ten.

The fate of the shipwrecked party—The well in the desert—
We see Boxall—A panther visits the camp—Treachery—
Selim proves himself a true friend—Antonio made
prisoner—His escape—We rescue the sheikh from a
mountain of sand—The salt region.

The fate of the unfortunate people whose boat, after they had
escaped from the burning ship, had been wrecked, was cruel indeed;
their strength, reduced by famine, made them utterly unable to
work, while the hard-hearted Arabs not only refused to assist them,
but threatened them with perpetual slavery. The party consisted of
an officer of the ship, two seamen, Pedro the black boy, four
civilians, and an unhappy lady,—the wife of a Don Fernando, the
principal person among them, who had treated us with marked
contempt when we were on board the Spanish galleon. His manner
was now greatly changed; and we, of course, did not allude to his
former behaviour, which we endeavoured to forget. It seemed
wonderful that the poor lady should have survived the hardships
she had already endured. They were all reduced to the last stage of
starvation, with the exception of the black boy Pedro, or Selim,—as
will call him in future,—who, accustomed as he was to coarse food,
had flourished on the shell-fish, and the roots of some low bushes
which grew in the neighbourhood.

Notwithstanding the treatment we had received from some of the
unhappy people on board their ship, and though we had been
intentionally abandoned, we felt bound to do our utmost to assist
them. The camp having been pitched in the neighbourhood, the
sheikh ordered them to pack up their tent and move to it. This they
were utterly unable to do; but, after much entreaty, we obtained a
camel, on which we placed the canvas, arranging it so as to form a
seat for the poor lady—her husband mounting to assist in holding
her on. As we placed her on it, I doubted whether she would reach
the camp alive. The others were compelled to walk, and though
somewhat strengthened by the food we had obtained for them, they

could with difficulty drag their feet over the sand. On reaching the camp, we divided the canvas so as to form a small tent for the dying lady, and put up another for the rest of the party, who faintly expressed their gratitude to us.

We did not escape having to perform our allotted duties, for all that. The next morning, at daybreak, we were sent down with a couple of baskets to bring up shell-fish from the shore. On our return we found a party of strange Arabs in the camp, engaged in a discussion with the sheikh; and on drawing near I discovered that they were bargaining for the purchase of the unfortunate people who had just fallen into his power, and who, from their weakness, he did not wish to carry along with him.

They took the information I conveyed to them almost with indifference. "It matters little indeed into whose hands we fall," observed Don Fernando, the chief man among them; "but I beg you to say that if they will convey us to the neighbourhood of any place where a European consul resides, they will obtain a large sum for our ransom."

I told the strange sheikh this, and it made him ready to give a better price than he might otherwise have done, much to the satisfaction of Hamed.

On going to the tent of Don Fernando I found him stretched over the body of his wife, who had just breathed her last. Sad indeed was the poor man's fate, and we pitied him from our hearts, though we could do little to comfort him. His once haughty spirit was completely broken down. We at length aroused him; and calling Ben to our assistance, Halliday and I conveyed the body of his wife to a distance from the camp, where we dug a grave and buried her, he attending as the only mourner. He was then delivered over to his purchaser with the rest of the Spaniards, the young black alone remaining with us. We could not help pitying the poor people as we saw them carried away, though their fate might not be worse than ours; indeed, as they had some prospect of being redeemed, it might be better.

I must now give a more rapid account than heretofore of my adventures. Again we struck the tents and proceeded more inland, over hard ground producing wild bushes, but not a blade of grass or a drop of water. We then came to a region consisting of hills and valleys of sand, over which we had to trudge on foot, suffering fearfully from thirst. After proceeding about ten miles we saw before us a low circular wall of sunburned bricks, with a few stunted palm-trees. The Arabs pointed towards it eagerly, and even the camels and other animals lifted up their heads. It marked the position of a deep well, near which we encamped; and for the remainder of that day and the greater part of the next we were employed in drawing up water, not only to furnish ourselves and the animals, but to fill the water-skins carried by the camels, on which we were to depend for several days to come. This task accomplished, we continued our route over the sand. Here we saw a few deer, of a small size and of a somewhat yellow colour, with black streaks along their sides, and small straight horns; their legs were long and slender, and they flew over the sand at a speed which the fleetest greyhound could not equal. Here and there we met with small bushes of a palm-like form. When we halted at night we were employed in getting some roots which ran along the sand, and which were about the thickness of a man's finger. They were sweet as sugar, and the people as well as the cattle ate them. Barren as the region appeared, we saw three or four species of birds, the largest of which were bustards; and on searching in the sand we frequently came on their eggs, which afforded us the most satisfactory food we had yet enjoyed. About ten days we spent in passing through this sandy district. We then entered on a region of firm soil, sometimes presenting a hilly surface, and occasionally plains of hard clay sprinkled over with bushes, but without any other vegetation, and almost destitute of water. We were fully a month traversing this kind of country. We had left it a couple of days, when we saw before us a stream of running water. Oh, how eagerly we rushed forward, expecting to enjoy a draught; but when we knelt down and plunged in our faces, how bitter was our disappointment on finding that it was far too brackish to drink. However, Halliday, Ben, and I ran in and had the luxury of a bath; but the Arabs, being indifferent at all times about washing, would not give themselves the trouble of taking off their clothes for the purpose.

This was the first of several streams we met with of the same character. When encamping near them, however, the brackish water served to wash the cattle in the way I have before described. Again fresh water failed us, and in a short time the stock carried by the camels was exhausted, and not a drop remained in our skin-bottles. Nearly a whole day we had marched, under the fiery rays of the sun, our mouths so parched that Halliday and I thought we should sink to the ground; but knowing that we should meet with little or no sympathy from our task-masters, we did our utmost to keep up with Hamed and his brother. The ground was covered with bushes, and here and there a few stunted palm-trees reared their heads somewhat higher above the surface. At last I was obliged to cry out to Hamed that I could go no further.

"Courage, Nazarene! You will see water before long," he answered.

Scarcely had he spoken when we caught sight of a party of Arabs approaching from the opposite direction. Hamed and his followers urged on their camels; and it soon became doubtful who would first arrive at the water. If we did, by the law of the Desert it would be for our use and that of our beasts till all were satisfied; but the law of the Desert is often superseded by the law of the strongest. The other party still came hurrying on; when all at once we saw Sheikh Hamed, who had urged on his camel ahead of us, suddenly rein it in, and wave his spear. We therefore exerted ourselves, and were soon up to him. The strangers halted at a little distance off, under some palm-trees. There were five of them, besides three men on foot. We stood thus for some minutes eyeing each other. Would they yield to our inferior numbers? They stood still, as if in doubt—perhaps intending to wait till we and our beasts were satisfied, unaware of the numerous bands in our rear.

As I looked at them I could not help fancying that one of the persons on foot was a white man. I asked Halliday if he could make him out.

"A white man he certainly is, and it is my belief that it is Boxall," he answered.

I thought so too, but feared I might be mistaken. We waved our hands. He recognised us, I felt sure, though Halliday doubted it; at all events, we were about to hurry forward to meet him, regardless of our thirst, when the leading columns of the caravan appeared in the distance, and the strangers, seeing that they had no prospect of successfully disputing the water with us, hauled the men on foot up on their saddles, and went off at a round gallop. We were grievously disappointed at thus missing the opportunity of speaking to Boxall; and should he have failed to recognise us, the chances of our being able to hold any communication with each other would be greatly lessened. However, as he was in the neighbourhood, we might still hope to meet him, and concoct some plan for effecting our escape.

The pool over which the Arabs would have been ready to shed each others' blood was between thirty and forty feet in circumference, five or six feet deep, and contained little more than a foot or so of stagnant water; but, stagnant as it was, we drank eagerly of it. At the edge was sitting a huge frog, its sole living occupant, as far as we could see. We were about to drive the reptile away, when the sheikh exclaimed, in an agitated tone, "Stay, Nazarenes! disturb not the creature. It is the guardian of the pool, and should it be destroyed the water may dry up for ever." Obeying the sheikh's commands, we let his frogship watch on; but I suspect that he must have had an uneasy time of it, while the animals of the caravan were drinking up his water till every drop was exhausted.

As we travelled on, we frequently came in sight of other Arab tribes, but though moving in the same direction we never pitched our tents near each other. Occasionally, however, when the chiefs were on friendly terms, they would ride on together; though they always parted before the time of camping arrived. This was done because of the difficulty of finding water and food for their cattle. Sometimes we fell in with hostile tribes, when the cattle were driven close together, and the armed men drew up in battle array, ready to resist an attack. The Arabs do not, however, often engage in battle with each other, unless one party can surprise an enemy, or is much superior in numbers.

WHO IS THE WHITE MAN?

In vain did we look out for Boxall; and when I tried to ascertain from the sheikh's brother to what tribe the Arabs belonged whom we had seen at the pool, he would only tell me that they were enemies, and not good people.

At length, in the far distance, we caught sight of groups of tall palm-trees rearing their heads above the plain. At first, so accustomed were we to low bushes, I expected to see them only a little higher than usual, and was surprised at the length of time which elapsed before we reached them. We were delighted to find ourselves under their cool shade, and on the borders of a stream flowing in their midst. The Arabs, however, did not exhibit the same satisfaction; the animals were kept closer together than usual, while a vigilant watch was placed over them. I inquired the cause of these precautions, and was told that the forest was infested with wild beasts, and that we should be fortunate did we escape without being attacked. We had not gone far, indeed, when we caught sight of a lion stalking amid the trees; but after looking at us for some time, as if he would like to pounce upon some of the sheep or goats, he walked off, intimidated by the shouts and cries of the Arabs. We took warning, and did not stray from the camp.

Among many other trees in this forest, I remarked cocoa-nut, date, and wild orange trees; indeed, the region appeared so fertile, that at first it seemed surprising that the Arabs should not have taken up their abode there. There were many reasons, however, for their not doing so: the strongest was their unconquerable love of a wandering life through the desert wilds; another and very important reason was, that the vast number of wild beasts which inhabited the forest would have proved very destructive to their flocks and herds. There were also several tribes already in possession, who would have proved formidable enemies had they attempted to settle in the neighbourhood.

We had evidence the following day of the destructive power of the wild beasts. The caravan was already in motion, the chief men and the baggage camels being in front, a small guard only bringing up the rear. Halliday, Ben, and I, with our young negro companion

Selim, were tending the flocks placed under our charge—several of those belonging to other families of the tribe being on the outside of us. It was about noon, and the rays of the sun struck down between the lofty branches, rendering the heat almost insupportable. As we were moving on we observed the camels ahead hesitating to advance, notwithstanding the efforts of their drivers to urge them forward. A cry was then quickly passed from rank to rank that wild beasts were at hand; and the guards looked to their firearms. Suddenly a huge panther leapt from a thicket almost into the midst of the nearest flock. Muskets were discharged from all sides, at the no small risk of hitting either the shepherds or the sheep. Several men, bolder than the rest, rushed forward with their spears to attack the panther; but, with a blow of its paw, and regardless of the spears thrust at it, it knocked over two of its assailants; and springing at a third, who was endeavouring to make his escape, brought him to the ground. The panther was now in the midst of the flock; and while some of the guards were reloading their weapons, it seized a sheep, and, before they could fire, bounded off with it as easily as a dog would with a fowl. Though several shots were sent after it, the animal, unhurt, disappeared in the forest. And this was only one of several instances of a similar character which occurred during our journey.

We now ran to the assistance of the three men who had been struck down; but they were all dead. Loud wailings arose from their comrades, who, taking up their bodies, carried them to the spot where we halted for the night. Double guards were set, and fires lighted round the camp to frighten away the wild beasts. The night was spent by the Arabs in bewailing the loss of their companions; and at daybreak the next morning the dead were carried forth and graves were dug, when they were committed to the earth—some time being spent in piling up stones over their bodies, to prevent the hyenas or other wild beasts from digging them up.

The instance I have mentioned was too common an occurrence, however, to make much impression on the rest of the people.

Antonio had of late appeared to have forgotten his former animosity towards us, and whenever he could find opportunity he entered into conversation with Halliday and me. Still, notwithstanding the friendly manner he put on, I did not trust him; for there was something so singularly repulsive in his countenance, that I could not believe he was sincere.

He told us at last that we were approaching his country. "Now will be the time for you to make your escape," he said in a confidential tone. "You are weary of this life, I am sure; and if you will fly with me, you will be welcomed by my people, and be treated as great chiefs: besides which, as they have constant communication with the coast, you will without difficulty be able to return to your own country."

He was one day speaking in this way, when Selim, who was near, overheard him, but pretended to take no notice. The lad, however, watched for an opportunity when I was alone, and warned me not to trust the black, "He hates you and your friends, and has resolved on your destruction," he whispered to me. "I overheard him, when he did not know I was near, speaking to Abdalah, and it is clear that his intention is to betray you. Now, we will try to be even with him; the sheikh already mistrusts him, for he has been the cause of much trouble in the camp, about which I will tell you by-and-by. Do you therefore pretend to agree to his plans, and tell him that he must steal out first to a certain place beyond the camp, and that you will join him. I will then take care to let the sheikh know that he has gone, and that you have no intention of deserting, and will advise that men should be sent to seize him. If he is caught, it will prove that what I have said is true; and if he escapes, he will be afraid to return, and we shall be quit of him."

"But we should thus be acting a very treacherous part, to which I can on no account consent," I answered.

"You must leave that to me," replied Selim. "All you have to do is to listen to his plans: and depend upon it, if you do not, as I advise, pretend to agree with them, he will find some other means to betray you."

Notwithstanding what Selim had said, I, of course, could not consent to do as he proposed. However, I found he was not to be defeated. He managed to insinuate himself into the confidence of Antonio, and persuaded him that it would be imprudent to be seen conversing with me, but that he himself would act as go-between; and he was thus able to manage matters according to his own fancy. Had I known at the time how Selim was acting, I should have felt it my duty to put a stop to his proceedings, although they were intended for our benefit.

The very next night there was a commotion in the camp, and we heard that Antonio had been sent for by the sheikh. His name was shouted in all directions, but he was nowhere to be found. Soon afterwards a party, accompanied by Selim, set out from the camp; from which circumstance I had little doubt that the young black had carried out his treacherous plan. I could not help fearing, at the same time, that, notwithstanding his precautions, Ben, Halliday, and I might be implicated in it, and suffer accordingly.

We were still employed in our usual evening's occupation when the party returned, bringing back Antonio, with his hands securely bound together. As the light of the fire, opposite which he was led, fell on his countenance, it struck me that it had more of an angry and vindictive than of a downcast look. He threw his fierce glance on me especially, appearing even then to be meditating a bitter revenge, as he naturally considered that it was owing to my treachery that he had been captured. He was forthwith conducted into the presence of the sheikh, who, with his brother Abdalah and other elders of the tribe, was seated by a fire beneath a group of palm-trees. Here, squatting on the ground, with a guard standing over him, he was allowed to listen to the consultation they were holding as to the punishment he merited.

Selim, who managed to get near enough to hear what was going on, told us that some were for shooting him forthwith, or cutting off his head, while others considered that a sound beating would be sufficient to keep him in order. Though the Arabs are as well acquainted with the bastinado as the Moors and Turks, policy rather than mercy decided them on not inflicting it, as he would thus be unable to march, and it would be necessary to burden a camel with him for many days to come. It was at length decided that he should receive a severe beating; and that, should he still be refractory, he should be sold to the first slave-caravan for any sum he would fetch. That might seem a light punishment; but, as strong slaves are often compelled to carry burdens as well as work hard, should he be sold he would have to march for many months over the burning desert, — and as slave-merchants keep a watchful eye on their property, he would have but little chance of escape: so the fate in store for him was calculated, it was considered, to keep him on his good behaviour.

"The camp will not be long troubled with him, however," said Selim, when he had finished his account. "He is sure before long to create a disturbance, and the sheikh will sell him to the first caravan we meet with."

The Arabs, however, little knew the man they had to deal with. A guard was set over him; but though watchful enough when an enemy is expected to attack them, the Children of the Desert are, when in charge of a prisoner, as liable to yield to drowsiness as other people, under the belief that he too will fall asleep. Such, probably, was the case in the present instance. When morning dawned, Antonio was not to be found. His guards declared that they had seen a thick smoke ascend from where he lay, and that when they went to the spot he had disappeared, — thus proving without doubt that the Jins (or evil spirits) had carried him off. A diligent search was made round the camp, but no traces of him could be found, and no one could guess the direction he had taken.

We now again moved forward, and were once more in the open country. By Selim's advice, Halliday and I did our best to ingratiate ourselves with the sheikh. "He thinks well of you already," he observed, "because you can speak his language; and if you can gain his confidence you will certainly be better treated, and perhaps be able to obtain your liberty." We were well-disposed to take this advice. The sheikh, I considered, was only following the instincts of his nature in making us slaves; and I hoped, by working on his good feelings (supposing he possessed any), ultimately to obtain our liberty: and, at all events, we should be better off while we remained with him.

I must briefly describe the chief incidents of our journey. We had now again obtained the use of camels, and were riding on ahead with the sheikh, who usually liked to converse with us, as we could tell him of strange countries, and of events of which he had no previous conception. The noonday sun was beating down on our heads, without a breath of wind to cool the air, when we saw before us a vast, almost perpendicular wall of sand, which seemed completely to bar our way, extending as it did so far to the east and west that it might require not only one, but several days' journeys to get round it. The sheikh, though at first somewhat daunted at the appearance of the barrier, declared that there must be a passage through it, and that through it we must go if such passage could be found.

Turning to the left, he led the way under the sand cliff, narrowly eyeing the ground in the hope of finding the footmarks of any camels which might have preceded us. On we went, the remainder of the caravan waiting for a sign from their chief to advance. At length there appeared a gap in the cliff, if I may so call it, —just as if a violent current of wind had forced its way through the barrier. The sheikh examined it, evidently doubting whether it would afford a safe passage for himself and his numerous followers, with their flocks and herds.

At last he moved forward ahead of us, to examine the passage more narrowly; now looking to the right, now to the left, as if disliking the appearance of the towering masses of sand above his head. At length he exclaimed, "If it is the will of Allah that we should perish, why longer hesitate?" and waving his spear, he urged on his camel into the centre of the gorge.

THE ARABS DISCUSSING ANTONIO'S PUNISHMENT

I was on the point of shouting to him to stop, for I observed the summit of the cliff begin to tremble ominously, as if it felt the effect of the camel's feet at its base; but in another instant down came the avalanche of sand, entirely surrounding the sheikh, who in vain endeavoured to force his way out. Higher and higher it rose, his camel struggling violently—while he clung to its back, knowing that should he lose his hold he himself would be speedily overwhelmed. His brother and the rest of the leading party stood aghast, afraid of sharing his fate should they attempt to go to his rescue; while, regardless of what might be the consequences to myself, I dashed forward, calling to Halliday and Ben. Fortunately, I carried secured to my saddle a long coil of rope, which I had found useful in surrounding my flock at night; and telling my companions to hold fast to one end, I took the other, and, throwing myself from my camel, dashed into the midst of the sand. I knew, however, that at any moment, should I be completely overwhelmed, they could draw me out.

I made my way with great difficulty, almost at times covered up by the sand, till I succeeded in crawling rather than walking up to the spot where the sheikh was struggling.

"I have been sent to your rescue, O sheikh," I cried out, throwing him the end of the rope. "Secure this to your camel's body." He quickly did as I advised him.

"Is it secure?" I asked. The reply was in the affirmative.

"Hold on then, O sheikh, and we will draw you forth!" I exclaimed; when, hurrying back to my companions, we fastened the other end of the rope to our three camels, which with might and main we urged away from the bank.

Faster and faster came down the sand from above; but we pulled and pulled, while the sheikh's camel struggled, trampling the sand down with its fore feet; and in a few seconds we had hauled him out from the midst of the sand, and once more safe among his followers—who rode up to congratulate him, and to compliment us on the service we had rendered.

"You have done well, O young Nazarene," he exclaimed, turning to me; "and from henceforth know me as your friend. Though I cannot grant you your liberty—which in this place would be of no use, as you would certainly be murdered were you to attempt to cross the desert alone—yet, on my return to the north, I will venture as near the settled districts as I can, that you may have an opportunity of reaching your countrymen."

I thanked the sheikh in proper terms, assuring him of the satisfaction my companions and I felt at having rescued him from the dangerous position in which he had been placed.

Quickly recovering himself, and being quite indifferent to the quantity of sand clinging to his garments, he rode along in search of a more practicable opening. This at length was found; and as the valley was much broader, and the sand slanted more gradually on either side, there appeared a fair prospect of our being able to pass through. The whole caravan then entered the defile between the sand-hills; but we were fully three hours travelling between those prodigious masses of sand. Sand was below our feet, sand in front and behind, sand on each side. A sudden blast would inevitably cover us with it for many feet. It was nervous work. Fatalism alone could have induced men, fully alive to the danger they were incurring, to venture into such a position. To add to our danger, the loaded camels frequently fell down, and we were compelled to take off their burdens to enable them to rise.

At length, overcome with fatigue, the whole caravan emerged from the defile on firm ground, where we encamped,—but without a drop of water to quench our burning thirst. The only liquid that we could procure, and that in very small quantities, was milk from the camels and goats.

We at length reached a pool of brackish water, which somewhat restored us. Further on we passed over a region of salt. Here the ground, as we advanced over it, gave way under our feet, producing a crackling noise, just as snow does when trod on after being slightly melted and again hardened by the frost. I observed numerous heaps of beautiful crystallised salt, perfectly white, arranged in peculiar order and symmetry. This salt region was of considerable extent. In certain places we found that the ground had been dug up; and I heard that caravans came there for the express purpose of loading their animals with salt, to convey it to far-distant parts of the continent.

Though the sheikh may have thought it beneath his dignity to express many signs of gratitude to us for the service we had rendered him, yet our condition was considerably improved, and we had less hard work than usual to perform; still, we were by no means allowed to eat the bread of idleness.

As we were travelling on, when I happened to be in the rear I observed in the far distance a small black object, which, from its constantly appearing in the same direction, I could not help believing was some person following the caravan. The Arabs did not seem to have noticed any one; but my mind instantly fixed on Antonio, and I felt sure that he had some treacherous object in view. However, until I had ascertained that I was right in my conjectures, I thought it would be more prudent not to tell the Arabs, as, should he be pursued, he would in all probability make his escape or hide himself, and I should be accused of creating a false alarm, and might be ill-treated in consequence. I contented myself, therefore, with merely telling Halliday and Ben, who were of opinion that I was right; and we agreed to be on the watch, lest he should steal into the camp at night with the intention of murdering us, or watch for us should we venture outside. At all events, we were certain he was capable of any treachery, and that he would run any risk for the sake of gratifying his revenge.

Chapter Eleven.

Conversation on religious matters with the Sheikh and Marabouts—The slave track—At the shrine of the saint—I start on a journey—The sheikh grants me a favour—An unpleasant duty—attacked by a wild beast—Antonio haunts our camp—Arrival at our destination.

Day after day we continued to travel southward—further and further from home, as it seemed to us. Whenever we could meet, Halliday, Ben, and I—not trusting to the sheikh's promises, of whose fickleness we had many proofs—eagerly discussed the possibility of escaping. Ben's idea was, that if we should arrive at length at a river running into the sea, we might either steal a canoe or build a raft, and float down the stream. We might thus escape from our present masters, who, unaccustomed to the water, would be unable to follow us; but we should run the risk of falling into the hands of still greater savages, who might very likely murder us. Still, our present slavery was well-nigh unbearable, and we were ready to run every risk to escape from it. We were doubtful whether we might venture to take Selim into our counsels. He seemed attached to us, and especially to me; but then, as he had shown a readiness to act treacherously in the case of Antonio, he might, should it be to his interest, play us a similar trick, Halliday thought. I was more inclined to trust him; I liked the expression of the lad's countenance, and he had hitherto, as far as we could judge, been faithful to us. During the time he had been on board an English ship-of-war, he had learned the truths of Christianity from the boatswain and three or four of the men, who, having become truly converted themselves, had endeavoured to win over their shipmates, and had taken great pains with him. He had been the only survivor of a boat's crew wrecked on the northern coast of Africa—he, being an excellent swimmer, having gained the shore. He had been kept in slavery a year or more by the Moors; but he at length managed to swim off to a Spanish vessel, and afterwards entered on board the galleon where we first met with him. Accustomed, therefore, to the habits of the Moors, he was able to conduct himself discreetly towards them; and passing for a good

Mohammedan, he had in a considerable degree gained their confidence. He had, however, expressed to me more than once his regret at having to play the hypocrite.

"What can I do?" he would observe. "I know that Mohammed was a false prophet; but if I were to say so I should have my head cut off— and to that I cannot make up my mind. Every time I cry out 'Allah is great, and Mohammed is his prophet,' I know that I am telling a lie, and pray to be forgiven. Do you think that the true God will forgive me?"

I replied that it was not for me to decide, but that I thought he was bound to try and escape from such thraldom on the first opportunity.

"That is what I shall do," he answered; "but I will not escape without you; and as I know the ways of the country, and can speak the language of the black people further south, I may, I hope, be of use to you."

After this conversation, he came to me one day and told me that the sheikh and two marabouts, or priests, who were in the camp, had resolved to make me and my companions turn Mohammedans. "I warn you, that you may know how to behave. Let me advise you not to show any indignation, but rather to pretend that you are ready to listen to what they call the truth."

The very next day the sheikh summoned me into his presence. I found him seated with the two marabouts; and they at once explained the doctrines of the Mohammedan faith, and to which, according to Selim's advice, I listened with all the respect I could assume.

"Are you acquainted, O sheikh, with my religion, from which you wish to turn me?" I asked quietly.

"Yes; you worship Jins, and have dealings with the Evil One," he answered in a confident tone, as if he knew all about the matter.

I have since met others, in more enlightened lands, equally confident as to their knowledge of the religious opinions of those who differ from them, and equally wrong.

"You have been misinformed, O sheikh; pardon me for saying so," I replied calmly. "I worship the one true God. Listen to the prayer I offer up every morning." I then repeated slowly, and with all due emphasis, the Lord's Prayer. The sheikh and marabouts listened with astonishment depicted on their countenances.

"Can this be so?" asked the sheikh. "Such a prayer as that any true believer might be ready to offer up."

"Forgive us our offences, as we forgive them that offend against us," I said slowly, looking at the sheikh. "Can you pray thus and expect to be forgiven?" I asked.

"Truly the young Nazarene has put a puzzling question," observed the sheikh, turning to the marabouts. They shook their heads, unable to reply, but still unwilling to confess themselves defeated.

"Now, O sheikh, understand that we Christians desire to follow that precept, not from cowardice or a mean spirit, but from obedience to our Lord and Master; and would you therefore wish to induce me and my companions to abandon a faith inculcating so pure and holy a precept? Understand that where it is practised, blood feuds, and the many other causes which produce the quarrels and bloody wars so constantly prevailing in this region, are impossible. Peace and prosperity reign in exact proportion as the true Christian faith gains the ascendency among a people."

"You argue well, young Nazarene," said the sheikh. "I may not see with your eyes, but I respect your opinions."

We said much more on the subject, and I had reason to hope that, without sacrificing my principles, I had gained the respect of the sheikh; but one of the marabouts, at least, was far from contented with the result of our conversation. He constantly afterwards attacked both Halliday and me, endeavouring to convert us, and threatening us with severe penalties if we refused.

We had now got a considerable way to the east, and were passing along the track of caravans moving northward with slaves, collected in the Black States, to the southward of the Desert. The whole road was marked by the skeletons of human beings, who had expired from thirst and hunger. As I was riding along on my camel, dozing in consequence of the heat of the sun, I was awoke by hearing a crashing sound, and on looking down I saw that my beast's feet had stepped upon the perfect skeletons of three or four human beings, which gave way beneath them. The head of one of the skeletons, detached by a kick from the animal's foot, rolled on like a ball some way before me. The Arabs took no notice of the occurrence, however, remarking that they were only those of black slaves, and of no account.

It was about this time that several of our camels knocked up; and seeing that they would not live, the sheikh gave the order for them to be killed. I was struck with the savage expression of the Arabs, who stood ready with their knives in their hands, waiting for the signal to plunge them into the bodies of the poor animals—which, before they were cool, were cut up to supply food for the caravan. The head of the camel to be slaughtered being turned towards the east, an Arab stuck his dagger into its heart, when it almost instantly dropped dead.

A good many camels having been thus lost, Halliday, Ben, and I were compelled, as at first, to trudge on on foot.

All this time I had not forgotten Antonio, and I was sure that I occasionally caught glimpses of him. How he managed to subsist, might seem surprising; but he had armed himself, and was thus able to kill any animals he might meet with: he might also pick up subsistence from the remains of the camels, sheep, and cattle which dropped on the road. Possibly, too, he had some confederates in the camp, who might have hidden food as well as ammunition,—which, when we moved on, he would know by certain marks where to find.

We at length reached a somewhat more fertile region, where date, cocoa-nut, and other palm-trees were once more seen; while beyond it was a large lake, on the borders of which we heard was the shrine of a Mohammedan saint, at which the people of the caravan were about to worship. Out of the lake, we learned, ran a broad river to the westward; a fact which created in us the most lively interest, for it might afford us the long-looked-for means of making our escape.

As we neared the sacred precincts, the marabouts again endeavoured to make us change our religion. On our refusing, as formerly, to do so, they became very angry, even the sheikh himself appearing to be much disappointed. While we lay encamped, a day's journey, I understood, from the shrine, —which was to the eastward of us, —he sent for me, and expressing his confidence in my fidelity, informed me that he intended to trust to my care the widow and children of a friendly chief, who had died while visiting the tomb of the saint. "Her relatives, to whom she desires to return, dwell about twelve days' journey off; and you will return before we again set forth on our journey northward. I will send two guides with you who know the country; but as our camels require rest, you will be compelled to proceed on foot. The widow and her children will, however, be provided with a camel; and the guides will conduct another laden with provisions and water. Here," he said, giving me an old-fashioned, large-mouthed pistol, "is a weapon with which you can defend yourself and your charges; and here, also, is a pouch with ammunition. You will set out to-morrow morning; and may no harm befall you on the way!"

I hardly knew whether to be pleased or not at the confidence placed in me. Halliday and I had been hoping that while at this spot we might find an opportunity of escaping down the river, as we had proposed, —and should I be separated from him and Ben, our plan might be defeated. So as soon as I had left the sheikh I went in search of them, and told them of the expedition I had been ordered to make.

"I am afraid you will have to await my return before we can venture to carry out our plan."

"I don't quite see that, sir," said Ben. "You are going to the west; and that is, I suppose, the direction the river takes. Now my idea is, that if we can make off while the Arabs are praying to their saint, we can meet you half-way on your return; and then we can all steer for the river together, and either borrow a canoe or build a raft, as you proposed."

"But the risk of missing each other is very great," I answered. "I am therefore still inclined to hold to my opinion, that it will be better to wait till I can get back; and if I can give a favourable account of my mission, the sheikh will place more confidence in us, and we shall be less strictly watched than heretofore."

"I propose that we consult Selim," said Halliday. "He has been making inquiries about the country, and has picked up a good deal of information which might be useful to us."

"I am sure, from what he has said to me lately, that he can be trusted, and that he is as anxious to escape as we are,—so I agree with you, Halliday," I said. "Perhaps the sheikh will allow him to accompany me; if so, he will be of great assistance in enabling me to find you out. I might ask to have him, on the plea that he understands the language of the people."

My companions agreed to this proposal, and I undertook at once to petition the sheikh that he would allow me to take Selim. It was also settled that my friends should endeavour to escape from the camp exactly twelve days after I had left it, when they were to make their way along the banks of the river for six days, and then look out for me. I undertook, on my part, to return eastward for the same length of time, also keeping as closely as possible to the river. By this plan we had good hopes of meeting, though we could not conceal from ourselves that there were many dangers to be encountered; but yet no more feasible plan presented itself.

So confident did I feel in Selim's honesty, that, without speaking to him, I at once went back to the sheikh and boldly requested that he might be allowed to accompany me. To my great satisfaction, he at once consented.

"He is a sharp lad, and you will find him of great use on your journey," he added.

Selim, whom I soon afterwards found, was greatly pleased at what I told him.

"We may hope, then, to shake the dust of the camp off our feet for the last time," he said quietly.

I had fixed my eyes on Selim's countenance as he spoke. He turned his on me with so honest a look, that I was more than ever convinced he was sincere. I took his hand, and said,—"We understand each other, then; if we escape to my country, notwithstanding the difference in the colour of our skins you shall be my friend for life."

"I hope so," he answered. "Though we may be wide apart, our hearts may be joined; and we may meet above, in that happy land to which all Christians are bound."

I had no longer a shade of doubt as to Selim proving faithful.

Next morning Selim and I, according to the sheikh's directions, waited outside the camp, when he, his brother Abdalah, and two other chiefs appeared, conducting a couple of camels. On the first was placed a palanquin of wicker-work, ornamented with silk hangings, and a tuft of feathers on the top. Within it was seated a veiled lady and three small children, whose black curly heads made them look more like negroes than Arabs. There was apparently some mystery in the matter, into which it was not my business to inquire. Leading the other camel, which was laden with provisions and a small tent, were two guides, both of whom were negroes, though dressed in the Arab fashion. The sheikh then uttered a benediction on the occupant of the palanquin and her young family, and ordered us to advance. The guides, with Selim, went first, by the side of the baggage camel; and I, with the veiled lady, followed. Whether I was to see her face or not, I could not tell, nor was I very curious about piercing the mystery connected with her.

AN UNPLEASANT DUTY

The sun was still rising at our backs, as, moving forward at a tolerably quick pace, we soon lost sight of the camp.

We had gone several miles, Selim always keeping ahead with the guides, with whom he was apparently engaged in an interesting conversation. I was already beginning to feel somewhat tired, when a voice from the palanquin desired me to take out one of the children, as the little urchin had a fancy to be carried instead of being cooped up within it. Unwilling to disoblige the lady, I obeyed; so, placing the child on my shoulder, we again moved on—though, as I dragged my weary limbs along, I felt very much inclined to let the young urchin drop. Feeling, at last, that I could no longer carry him, I begged the veiled lady to take him in again; but she, looking on me as a slave bound to obey her commands, replied that he preferred riding on my back, and that I must carry him as long as he wished. Accordingly, to avoid a dispute, I again took up the urchin and staggered on, strengthened by the hope that my days of slavery would soon come to an end.

I had not forgotten my suspicions about Antonio, and wondered whether he was still in the neighbourhood, or if he had observed us quitting the camp. If so, I had little doubt that he would follow in our footsteps, and attack us should he find an opportunity. He might, indeed, at the present moment be stealing upon us to shoot me, and carry off the lady, before the guards could be aware of his approach. As may be supposed, therefore, I very frequently turned my head anxiously round, almost expecting to see him. I also began to think that the sheikh had acted very imprudently in sending the lady with so small an escort, and I regretted that I had not begged to have a greater number of guards; at the same time, it occurred to me that I should have had more difficulty in escaping from them than from the two men who accompanied us.

The thought of the possibility of being suddenly attacked by Antonio added not a little to the annoyance I felt at having to carry the little blackamoor. Still, unwilling to offend his mother, I went on without complaining as long as I could walk. I felt very much inclined, I confess, to pinch his legs and make him cry out, especially when he amused himself by pulling at my hair, evidently thinking it very good fun.

We had gone some distance when, turning my head, I saw—not Antonio, but a large panther, stealing out from a thicket at some distance on our left, and approaching us with stealthy steps. "Now, lady, unless you wish your child to be gobbled up by yonder monster, you must take him," I cried, throwing the urchin, without waiting for a reply, into the palanquin, and shouting out to Selim and the guides to come to my assistance, as I had only my pistol slung to my back—a very unsatisfactory weapon with which to encounter a wild beast. The guides had carbines and spears, indeed; but it was a question whether they would use them or run away.

Selim at once gave proof of his courage and fidelity, however, by snatching a carbine from one of his companions, and rushing back at full speed towards me. "Don't fire your pistol," he cried out; "keep that, lest my carbine fail to kill the beast."

The panther came on, in spite of the shouts which the guides set up, while they waved their cloaks and spears, and did their utmost to frighten it away. When within about a hundred yards of us, however, the savage creature stopped. This encouraged the guides, who now moved hesitatingly towards us. But again the panther crept on, though with less boldness than at first, as if it had expected to pick off the rearmost of the party, and was disappointed in its object. Seeing that should we move on the panther would follow with rapid bounds, I ordered the guides to stand still; and snatching the carbine from Selim's hand, I knelt down that I might take a surer aim. Knowing, however, that the Arabs' powder is often very bad, and that, consequently, their weapons frequently miss fire, I felt very doubtful whether such might not be the case on the present occasion.

"Silence!" I cried out to my companions, who were still shouting and hurling fearful epithets at the head of the panther. "Only cry out should it attempt to spring."

The savage brute came on, and was now within twenty paces. Two or three bounds might bring it upon us. So, praying that my weapon might prove faithful, I drew the trigger, aiming at the panther's breast. The piece going off, I was knocked over by the rebound; for the owner, in loading it, had put in a double charge: indeed, it was a wonder that it did not burst. When the smoke cleared away, I caught sight of the panther struggling on the ground, a few paces only in advance of the spot where I had last seen it; and the Arabs, shouting "E'sheetan! E'sheetan!" now rushing forward, plunged their spears into the creature's body, uttering a curse with every thrust they gave it.

"Allah akbar!" exclaimed one. "It was a regular Jin."

"No doubt about it. You Nazarene have done well; for if you had not killed him, he might have carried one or all of us off," cried the other.

I felt very thankful at having succeeded, because I had not only killed the panther, but had risen considerably in the estimation of my companions. I should have liked to have had the animal's skin; but I was unwilling to delay our journey, and we therefore pushed on. I beckoned to Selim to walk alongside me; and I still carried the carbine, which I had reloaded from the guide's pouch.

"I think we shall do well," said Selim; "I have been talking to those men, and they are well-disposed towards us. We shall, therefore, have no difficulty in escaping from them; indeed, one of them was once a slave himself, and would like to leave the tribe altogether. I have been telling him of the countries I have visited and the wonderful things I have seen, and he is eager to go and see them."

"They may be well-disposed; but we must take care, Selim, that we are not betrayed by them," I observed. "We must first accomplish the object of our mission; and we have a good many dangers yet to encounter." I then told him of my apprehensions regarding Antonio, and charged him to keep a good look-out himself, and warn the guides also to be on their guard.

Selim listened with attention to what I said.

"I am afraid that you are right," he answered. "Last night, while we were encamped, I fancied that I caught sight of an object moving in the distance. I took it for a wild beast, and accordingly threw more wood on the fire and made it blaze up, and thus, as I supposed, frightened the beast away. I remarked, however, its extraordinary shape, and for some moments believed it to be a man; but as I gazed towards it, it disappeared in the darkness, and so I thought that my fancy had deceived me."

From what Selim said I now felt perfectly sure that Antonio was following us, and so determined the next night to remain myself on the watch, with the carbine by my side. Accordingly, after we had pitched the tent and had taken our supper, I lay down close to the camel,—the palanquin, which had been taken off its back, assisting to form a screen. The other camel lay on the opposite side,—the fire being in the centre,—while boughs of prickly pear, which we cut down, formed the remainder of the circle. This was our usual style of encampment, and it afforded a tolerable protection against wild animals.

I had not been long on the watch, when, as I was looking eastward, I saw a shadowy form slowly emerge from the darkness; as it approached it resolved itself into the figure of a man of gigantic size, as it appeared to me, but having certainly the air of Antonio. He stopped, and appeared to be surveying the camp. I saw that he grasped a large scimitar in his hand; but he had evidently no firearms. This accounted for his hesitation about attacking us unless he could take us by surprise. I could have shot him where he stood, but, though convinced that he meditated mischief, I could not bring myself to do so unless he actually attacked us.

I lay quiet, attentively watching him; and at length he began to move forward, grasping his sword. On seeing this I started up, and the light of the fire behind me brought my figure into view. He immediately turned and fled, and in a few seconds I lost sight of him. He would now be aware, however, that we suspected his design, and were on the watch; which would make him approach more cautiously another time.

THE WIDOW'S RECEPTION.

Calling up Selim, I told him to take my place while I got some sleep, which I much required; but the night passed away, and nothing more was seen of Antonio.

I cannot describe each day's journey. We kept along the skirts of a woody country, occasionally crossing shallow streams which furnished us with an ample supply of water. On two other occasions we caught sight of that mysterious figure, —once in the daytime, and once at night; but we were at both times on our guard, and he did not venture to approach. Still, the knowledge that he was following us, evidently with sinister intentions, caused us great anxiety, for we could not tell at what moment he might make a dash at us, at all hazards, and wreak his vengeance on our heads. Selim and I would certainly be his first victims, and probably he would put the rest of the party to death.

At length the guides told me that we were approaching the end of our journey, and that the tents of the black sheikh were not far off. It had been arranged that we should encamp at a short distance from them, when I was to go forward with the camel, and deliver the widow and her children to her father.

I had expected to see an encampment somewhat similar to the one I had left; but, as we drew near, a few low, cotton-covered tents alone met my view. The lady desired me to make her camel kneel down, saying that she, with her eldest child, would go forward, and begged me to take charge of the younger ones. I did as she wished; and, taking a basket which contained her valuables, she advanced with trembling steps towards one of the tents. Two figures stood at the entrance: one was a gigantic negro, with about as ugly and sinister an expression of countenance as I ever saw; the other was a veiled woman, whom I concluded to be the sheikh's wife. They received the poor lady without the slightest expression of pleasure or affection, and seemed to be demanding why she had come back; but, on account of the distance I was from them, I could not hear what was said. The widow had, I concluded, a long story to tell, and the black stood eyeing her with a look of contempt, which showed me that her reception was anything but a pleasant one. The old dame—for such,

I was convinced, she was, though I could not see her features — stood quite still. At last I saw the widow go forward and kneel at the sheikh's feet; when, lifting her up, he seemed, as far as I could judge, to be assuring her of his protection, and forgiveness for any fault she might have committed. She then turned round and beckoned to me, when I brought forward the other two youngsters. As her father did not invite me to remain, however, I made my salaam to the lady and returned to our camp.

I told Selim what had occurred.

"The sooner we are away, the better, then," he said; "that sheikh is one of the fiercest and most barbarous in this part of the country, and it is impossible to tell how he may act towards us."

I agreed with Selim, that if such was his character his countenance certainly did not belie him. It was then too late to move, however, so we arranged with the two guides to stop till the following morning, when we proposed setting out at daybreak.

Having lighted our fire, and formed our camp as usual, while the guides lay down by the side of their camels, Selim and I sat and talked over our plans for the future. The question to be decided was, How could we best separate from our companions without being followed? There were difficulties, but we hoped to overcome these. Selim was of opinion that the safest plan would be for me to run off a couple of hours before dawn, — when he, taking the carbine of one of the guides, would set out as if in pursuit of me. The guides, finding that we did not return, and the one afraid of losing the other, would proceed on their journey, and report at the camp that we had been lost. Should Halliday and Ben, in the meantime, have been unable to make their escape, this would prevent suspicion being cast on them.

To this plan I agreed, provided no better should present itself.

Chapter Twelve.

I escape from the camp—A terrible encounter—Selim
arrived—We cross the stream—A joyful meeting.

Having but a small stock of provisions and little water to carry,
Selim and I rode on one of the camels, while the guides mounted the
other, and we made the first part of our return journey more
pleasantly and rather more rapidly than we had come. We at the
same time kept a good look-out for Antonio, but not a glimpse of
him could be seen, and I began to hope that he had abandoned his
design of murdering us,—if he had entertained it,—and had gone off
to try and reach his own country.

We at length arrived at the spot where Selim and I had agreed to quit
the camp and strike off for the river, which we believed to be not
more than a day's journey to the south of us. The country was wild
and barren in the extreme, here and there a few cacti and stunted
shrubs alone being visible. It would be imprudent to attempt
escaping by day, with the possibility of being followed by the
guides; even should they not follow us, they would naturally, on
their arrival at the camp, inform the Arabs of the direction we had
taken. Of course, we might have shot them, or have hamstrung the
camels; but though Selim suggested that such might be necessary, I
would not for a moment entertain the idea. If we were to escape, we
must escape with clean hands and clear consciences. I would only
consent to Selim carrying off one of the carbines, and as much
ammunition as he could obtain; while I provided myself with as
many dates and as much other food as I could stow away.

We determined to commence our enterprise that very night, as soon
as the moon had risen. I believed that I should have no difficulty, by
the aid of her light, in making my way due south; and I agreed to
stop at daybreak to look out for Selim. He would follow as soon as
he thought that I had got to a sufficient distance to render it unlikely
that the guides, should they propose to accompany him, would

overtake me; and even in that case he hoped to be able to slip away from them.

We encamped as usual, when Selim and I undertook to keep the first watch; and the guides, unsuspicious of our intentions, went to sleep. We had intentionally kept only a small fire burning, and as soon as the guides' eyes were closed we let it get still lower. Selim might have made his escape with me, but then he would have been unable to obtain one of the carbines and the ammunition, which it was essential for our future safety we should possess,—and which, according to the Arab fashion, the men slept with close to their hands, ready for instant use.

Having fully agreed as to our future proceedings, so that there might be as little risk as possible of missing each other, I looked once more to the priming of my pistol, took a draught of water (that I might require none for some time to come), and then stole noiselessly out of the camp. I waited for a minute to ascertain that the Arabs were really asleep, and not watching me; then I took another survey in every direction, lest Antonio might possibly be in the neighbourhood; but no one appearing, I started off, running towards the south.

I had before dark carefully surveyed the ground, and ascertained that it was perfectly level, without any impediment to stop my course. As soon as I had got out of sight, however, I went on more leisurely. The moon did not rise so soon as I had expected, while clouds gathering in the sky obscured the stars, and made it more difficult to keep a direct course. Still I hoped that I was steering to the south, and so continued on. Now and then I stopped to listen, but no sound reached my ears, and I was satisfied that I was not followed. On and on I went, anxious to reach some wood or thicket in which I could conceal myself should the guides, contrary to our expectations, accompany Selim.

Often had I found trudging over the desert with bare feet in the daytime very painful, but at night, unable to discern the inequalities of the ground, and the prickly plants which grew on it, I suffered far more than I had ever done before, hardened as my feet had become by going so long without shoes. I had hitherto reached no trees, and although I tried to pierce the gloom I could discern no trace of the forest I expected to meet with in the distance. The moon now rising, enabled me better to see my way; but, though my feet pained me greatly, finding that I was making slower progress than I had calculated on, I pushed forward, still hoping before daybreak to reach some spot where I could conceal myself. At length I could bear the pain no longer, and, overcome with fatigue, a faintness seized me, and I sank down on the ground.

How long I had continued in this state I could not tell. When I came to myself the moon was high in the sky, occasionally obscured, however, by the clouds which a strong wind drove across it; now her rays cast a bright light over the desert, now all again was in comparative darkness. I could only hope that no wild beast, prowling in search of prey, might find me, as I could, I felt, offer but a slight resistance. With the thought that such a thing might possibly occur, I took my pistol, which I had carried slung to my back, and grasped it in my hand.

Again the faintness seized me, and I lay stretched out on the hard ground. As my senses returned, my ear being close to the ground, I fancied that I heard a footfall. Opening my eyes,—a cloud at that moment having passed the moon, which now shone brightly forth,—I saw approaching, a few paces off, the figure of a tall black man, with a scimitar raised in his hand—the light of the moon revealing to me the vindictive features of Antonio. In another moment his weapon, raised to strike, would have descended on my neck. His attitude convinced me of his intentions, so there was not a moment for deliberation. I was unwilling to have his blood on my head, but had I even ventured to speak my life would have been sacrificed. Suddenly lifting my pistol, I fired. The shot took effect. Raising his hand to his head, and dropping his sword, the black fell backward to the ground.

DEATH OF ANTONIO

For a moment it seemed as if I had been in a fearful dream, but the still smoking pistol in my hand convinced me of the reality of what had occurred; so, rising, at length I staggered towards where

Antonio lay. Not a limb, not a muscle, moved, however. He had been shot through the heart. Feeling a horror of remaining near the dead body, and knowing also that it would certainly attract beasts of prey, I was anxious, in spite of the pain my feet suffered, to get to a distance. Reloading my pistol, therefore, and taking the scimitar, — which might enable me to defend myself against savage beasts as well as human foes, — I hurried forward as fast as my maimed feet would allow me.

At length I made out a dark mass rising above the ground, which I hoped was the commencement of the forest bordering the river; and in a short time I reached the trunk of a large tree, which stood out at some distance from the others, when, unable longer to endure the pain of walking, I sank down at its base. It was just the sort of place in which I knew Selim would search for me. Suddenly the dreadful thought occurred, Had Antonio first encountered him, and taken his life? Such, I feared, was but too possible, as the savage black must have discovered our camp after I had left it, and pursued me to the spot where, intending to take my life, he had met his own doom. This idea caused me much anxiety, and greatly damped the satisfaction I felt at finding myself free. How many difficulties and dangers also yet lay before me! Should I meet Halliday and Ben? I asked myself. If not, what would become of us all? Could they find their way to the sea alone? Could I, indeed, expect to do so? How deeply I regretted having been separated from Boxall, who, with his good sense and courage, was far better calculated than any of us to conduct to a successful issue the hazardous undertaking proposed.

Afraid of going to sleep, lest Selim should approach or any wild beast find me, I watched the moon sinking lower and lower, till she gradually disappeared altogether at the break of day. As the light increased I found myself on the borders of a forest, denser than any I had yet seen in Africa; while to the north the wide plain over which I had passed lay stretched out before me. I looked out anxiously for any figure which might prove to be that of Selim. Strange birds flew overhead, and a herd of deer went bounding by at no great distance. Had I possessed a more efficient weapon than my clumsy pistol, I should have tried to shoot one of the latter, in the hope of being able to manufacture shoes or sandals out of the hide to protect my lacerated feet, which were so swollen that I felt it would be almost torture to proceed further without some protection for them. As soon as there was sufficient light, however, I employed myself in picking out the thorns, with which they were full; after which operation I felt some slight relief. I then looked around for water in which I might cool them, but no stream or pool was in sight—though I knew, from the appearance of the vegetation, that water could not be far-off; and I felt sure that if I could but drag myself to it, I should soon be able to proceed.

As the sun rose, his rays threw a bright glare across the plain, almost roasting me where I lay. To avoid the heat, I moved round to the western side of the tree, in the cool shade of which I stretched myself out at my length to rest my weary limbs, and turned my anxious eyes northward—from which direction I expected Selim would come. At length some one appeared on the top of a small hillock in the far distance, and stopped and looked about him. It must be Selim, I thought; and yet, until I was certain, I did not like to show myself. I anxiously watched the person. "Yes, it must be Selim," I exclaimed aloud. My fear was that, not seeing me, he might go off to the east or west. I knew that my voice could not reach him at that distance. I tried to drag myself up by means of the trunk, so as to lean against it when I was on my feet; but I could stand with difficulty even then. The only means I had of drawing Selim's attention was to fire off my pistol, but I was unwilling to throw away any of the ammunition. The person was by this time about to descend the hillock. With great pain and difficulty I got round the tree into the sunlight, and fired. Immediately the person began to run towards me; when, unable longer to stand, I sank down on the sand, fearing that after all he might be an enemy. I reloaded my weapon, therefore, and leaned back against the tree, with the scimitar I had taken from Antonio in my hand, determined to defend myself to the last.

The person approached rapidly, stopping every now and then to look about him—surprised, apparently, at not seeing any one. As he came nearer, to my great joy I saw that it was no other than the faithful Selim. He bounded forward as he caught sight of me, uttering exclamations of joy; but his joy was turned to sorrow at finding me in the painful condition to which I had been reduced.

"But still I have reason to be thankful that you are alive," he said. "Soon after you had gone, what was my dismay to catch sight of Antonio's shadowy form in the distance. He had apparently been watching the camp, and must have seen you leave it; but I suspect he was waiting to ascertain whether any person would follow you. Had I had the carbine in my hand, I might have been tempted to fire at him; but I should thus have awakened the guides, and your flight would have been discovered. I went up, as it was, to the sleeping men, to try and get one of their carbines, but found that I could not do so without arousing them; and when I looked again, the mysterious figure had disappeared. I trembled for your safety, but notwithstanding my anxiety I had to wait till the time agreed on. Then, arousing the guides, I told them that I thought you had escaped; and while they were rubbing their eyes, and trying to understand what I had said, I got hold of one of their weapons, with a bag of ammunition, and shouting out that I would quickly overtake you, rushed forth from the camp. 'Take care of the camels, or they will escape,' I exclaimed as I dashed forward. They, believing that I should soon be back, did not follow, and I was soon out of their sight.

"I was hurrying on, when I fell over the dead body of Antonio. My mind was greatly relieved, for I was satisfied that, instead of his killing you, you had killed him; and with revived spirits I pushed on till I reached the sand-hill and heard the report of your pistol. We have, however, no time to lose, for when the guides find that I do not return, they are very likely to come in pursuit of us."

I told Selim how unable I was to walk.

"I see that," he said; "but I must carry you till we get to water."

"But you have not strength enough," I said.

"Try me," he answered, and insisted on taking me on his back; and, though I was fully as heavy as he was, he managed to carry me with far greater ease than I should have supposed possible.

We were soon making our way through the forest, which was more open than it had appeared at a distance. It contained a great variety of trees, few of which I had ever seen before. Many bore fruit and nuts, which Selim told me would furnish us with an ample supply of food. Among them were several shea-trees, from which vegetable butter is prepared; the fruit greatly resembling a large olive.

At length we caught sight of water glittering amid the green foliage. Selim staggered on towards it, though his strength was well-nigh giving way. It was a comparatively narrow stream, running, we supposed, into the main river which we wished to reach. We had great difficulty in making our way amid the tangled foliage which grew on its banks; but at last we succeeded in finding a tree which had fallen into the water, and by scrambling along it we were able to reach the edge of the stream.

"We must take care not to be picked off by any passing crocodile," observed Selim. "Stay, I will get a long stick, and, by splashing it in the water, we shall soon drive the creatures away, should any be near."

He did as he proposed, and then we stooped down without fear and took an ample draught to satisfy our burning thirst.

I quickly felt a beneficial effect from sitting with my feet in the stream and cooling them, Selim carefully beating the surface all the time; and being much refreshed, we soon returned to a more open part of the forest, where we sat down to rest, and to satisfy our hunger with the dates I had in my shirt, and some fruit which Selim collected. He also got some large leaves, possessing, he said, healing qualities; these he bound round my feet, and they produced even a more soothing effect than the water had done. Soon, relieved of pain, I felt excessively drowsy; and Selim promising to keep watch, in a few seconds I was fast asleep.

When I awoke I found that the day was far advanced. Selim had been busy, in the meantime, in making me a hat with palm leaves—which, he said, I greatly required to shield my head from the sun. He had also, from the same material, manufactured a pair of slippers, which assisted to protect my feet, though they could not defend them altogether from the thorns which lay on the ground.

Knowing that he must be in need of sleep, I told him that I would watch while he got some rest. He acknowledged that he should be very glad of it; and in a few seconds he was fast asleep. I sat with his carbine in my hand, ready to fire at any wild beast which might approach us; but happily none came near. And in a couple of hours or less Selim awoke, and declared that he was quite able to proceed.

Our first object was to gain the bank of the river, to look out for Halliday and Ben, whom we hoped might have found their way to it. Though I still walked with difficulty, I managed to get along. We had not gone far when Selim observed a tree from which, he said, the people in his country were accustomed to manufacture bows.

"I must make one at once," he observed; "it will save our ammunition—which will serve to defend us from human foes or wild beasts, while we can shoot small birds or animals with arrows."

He quickly cut off a branch which he fixed on for the purpose, and as we walked along he began to shape it with his knife.

We had followed the course of the stream, which, as we caught glimpses of it through the trees, widened considerably. We had now arrived near the point where the stream joined the larger river, but both of us felt that we could go no further. We had still a good supply of dates, and Selim quickly collected some fruit, which enabled us to satisfy our hunger. We then cut down a number of saplings and a quantity of branches, with which we constructed a hut between the buttressed roots of a gigantic baobab-tree, with a strong barricade in front. Here we hoped to rest more securely than we had done for a long time, as we could not be attacked in the rear, and we believed that no wild beast would attempt to break through it; then, as we had met with no traces of inhabitants, we consequently did not expect to be attacked by human beings. We had our hut completed before dark; and in the meantime Selim managed to collect a number of reeds for arrows, and the strong fibre of a plant to twist into a bow-string. We had thus plenty of occupation—till night coming on compelled us to retire within our hut, and build up the barricade in front of it.

When I awoke in the morning, I found that Selim had completed his bow and arrows; so as soon as we had breakfasted on our remaining stock of provisions we set out towards the bank of the main river. It should be understood that we were on the eastern side of the stream. We had not gone far down it when, coming to an opening amid the numerous trees which lined its banks, I caught sight of a human figure moving, at some distance off, on the opposite shore. Telling Selim, in a whisper, what I had seen, I dragged him behind a tree, from whence we could look out and observe the stranger. We eagerly watched him; and presently we saw him joined by two other persons.

"Why," exclaimed Selim, "they are our friends!"

"If so, Boxall must be with them," I said joyfully.

The uncertain light of the forest had before prevented me from distinguishing them; but as we made our way to the bank I was convinced that Selim was right. They had their backs turned towards us, and were proceeding westward, or down the river. We shouted to them; but our voices were lost amid the forest, or they did not recognise them, for they hurried on, and were soon lost to sight.

Fearing that we should miss them altogether, we now determined to swim the stream—without reflecting on the dangers we might run. Selim fastened his bundle of arrows and my pistol on his head, and lifting his carbine and bow in one hand, he boldly struck out. I followed his example; but, laden though he was, he swam better than I did. Happily the stream was not very rapid, and a draught of water which I took as I swam across contributed to restore my strength; so in a few minutes we were on the opposite bank.

HOW WE CROSSED THE STREAM.

Losing no time in shaking the water from our clothes, we hurried on, shouting to our friends. Again we caught sight of them. They looked round, and seeing us coming, hurried towards us.

The meeting, as we all grasped each other's hands, was indeed a happy one. But how Boxall had fallen in with them I could not conceive.

A few words, however, sufficed to explain how it had happened. It was he, as we had supposed, whom we had seen at the water-hole; and the tribe among whom he was a captive had, like many others, travelled south to worship at the shrine of the saint. A far greater intimacy than usual had taken place between the people of the different camps which at that period had assembled in the neighbourhood, and he thus came to hear that three Englishmen were held in slavery by Sheikh Hamed. He of course guessed that we were the persons spoken of, and resolved to communicate with us, though he knew that he ran a great risk of being severely punished should he be discovered. He took the opportunity, while all the men in his camp were worshipping at the shrine of the saint, to wander as far away as he could venture without creating suspicion in the minds of those who might be watching him, in the hope of meeting with one of us, or with some of our people who might give him information and take a message from him. He had proceeded further than was prudent, when, as it happened, a party of our Arabs returning to the camp caught sight of him, and supposing, from his white skin and dress, that he was one of us, seized and bound him, and carried him off as a prisoner. His capture, as he afterwards learned, was observed by a shepherd and some boys of his own camp, who carried back intelligence of what had occurred.

Fortunately, Ben, who was outside our camp, met the party, and recognising Boxall, claimed him as a friend; telling him, without loss of time, of our intention of escaping. This made Boxall—who had been well treated by his captors, and expected to be liberated on his return to the north—abandon his resolution of going back to them, if he could escape from our camp. He pretended, therefore, to be well satisfied with his change of masters, and—as was really the case—to be delighted at finding an old friend. The Arabs, being thus deceived, believed that there was no necessity for watching him, and gave him over without hesitation into Ben's charge.

Now, as I had left the camp secretly, it was not known by the people generally, and especially by the women, that I was absent, and Ben calculated rightly that Boxall would be mistaken for me. He accordingly conducted him boldly into the camp, where they soon found Halliday; and it was agreed that as soon as night came on they should all three make their escape together. This they had done; and having supplied themselves with food and some leathern bottles filled with water, they had pushed on during the night and the whole of the next day, till they reached the shelter of the wood. Arriving at the very stream we had discovered, and supposing that they would find us on the western side, they had crossed it, and had been waiting the whole day in expectation of our arrival.

Boxall had gone through numerous adventures; but having been fortunate enough to cure some of the sheikh's family and several other persons by practising the slight knowledge of medicine he possessed, he had been held in high estimation, and had gained the confidence of the sheikh and all the chief people,—so that he had had few of the irksome duties to perform which had fallen to our lot.

I now fondly hoped that, with Boxall as our leader, though we might have many difficulties to encounter, we should be able to overcome them, and finally reach the sea. We all agreed, however, that, from the direction the caravans had taken, we must still be at a considerable distance from it, and that we should certainly have a long voyage to perform on the river.

"No matter how long it is," exclaimed Ben in a confident tone; "if we can get a few planks under our feet, and a bit of canvas for a sail, with Mr Boxall as captain, we'll do it!"

Chapter Thirteen.

The raft upset—We discover a canoe—A fight for liberty—
Recaptured—The black woman's kindness—The black
sheikh better than he looks—Sheikh Hamed's anger—A
frightful doom—Rescued.

We did not spend much time in relating our adventures—knowing
that we should have opportunities enough by-and-by of spinning as
many yarns about them as we might.

Boxall approved of our plan of trying to find a canoe; or if not, of
building a raft on which we might float down the stream until we
could fall in with one; so we accordingly made our way at once to
the bank of the river. It was not so broad as we expected to find it,
yet the volume of water was sufficient to make us suppose that it
flowed on in an uninterrupted course to the ocean. Of the character
of the natives we knew nothing; indeed, we believed that no
European had ever explored that part of the country. Selim alone
could give us any information. His idea was that the people were
among the most barbarous of any to be found on the borders of the
Sahara. This was not satisfactory, but we could only hope that we
might escape them.

"At all events," observed Ben, "I have a notion that four Englishmen
with a carbine, a large pistol, and a Turkish cutlass, backed by an
honest black fellow with his bow and arrows, are a match for any
number of savages; so if they come we must give them a thrashing—
and that's what I've got to say about the matter."

Though not quite so confident as Ben, we hoped that we should be
able to keep at bay any enemies who might attack us.

The bank of the river was thickly wooded, and we made but slow
progress. Despairing at last of finding a canoe, we determined to
build a raft. Reaching a part of the bank where a few feet of open
ground gave us space to work, we commenced operations. My

cutlass was invaluable, as it enabled us to cut down a number of young palms, the wood of which was soft and light. There were also plenty of creepers, which served instead of ropes for binding the logs together. We first placed a row of young trees side by side, and then secured another row at right angles upon them. By evening our raft was complete. We also provided ourselves with long poles, which would enable us to guide it in shallow water or keep it off overhanging trees; and, in addition, we formed five rough paddles — one being larger than the rest, for steering. We intended also to form a triangle, between which we could spread our shirts to serve as a sail should the wind be fair. Well satisfied with our day's performance, we launched our raft, which had been built close to the water, and secured it to the bank. It floated us all well; and as it was likely to afford a more secure resting-place than the shore, we lay down on it to sleep — two of us at a time keeping watch, lest any wild beast might, attack us. But although lions were heard roaring all night long, and other strange sounds came out of the forest, we slept securely on our floating bed.

At daybreak, and in good spirits, we commenced our adventurous voyage. At first we floated tranquilly down the stream, having only occasionally to use our paddles to keep the raft off from the trunks of sunken trees — called snags, in America — which appeared above the water. In a short time, however, the current became more rapid, and we found, by the way the water leaped about, that we were being carried over a shallow part of the river. Our poles, too, showed that the depth was not above three or four feet. Presently the water became more shallow and more agitated, and we thought it wise to make for the bank. We were steering towards it, when the raft, striking an unseen rock, was whirled rapidly round and round: the water rushed over it, and we ourselves were swept off; while the raft, freed from our weight, was carried downwards, and quickly dashed to pieces among a number of rocks, over which the water furiously rushed, not a hundred yards below us. Happily we were all good swimmers, and we managed to reach shallow water and climb up the bank.

"What has become of our weapons?" was the first question we asked. They, with my Moorish sword, had been placed in the centre of the raft, and so had been lost. We had cause to be thankful however, for having escaped with our lives.

Undaunted by the accident, we determined to persevere, and to try and find a canoe in which to prosecute our voyage. Ben had saved one of the long poles, which, after sharpening at the end, would serve as a weapon—the only one we now possessed. Selim offered to supply us with bows and arrows, which might serve to kill birds for our meals. He showed himself one of the most active of the party, too, and as he went on ahead he looked into every little bay or hollow in which a canoe was likely to be concealed.

At length we caught sight of some low, conical-shaped, thatched huts in the distance, and Selim said he was sure he could find a canoe not far off from thence. The only doubt was whether he should take it without asking the owner's leave, or try to obtain the loan of it: but then we had absolutely nothing to offer in return; and the natives might not only refuse to give it us, but might make us prisoners—and perhaps carry us back to the Arabs from whom we were escaping, or sell us to some other tribe.

"Beggars must not be choosers," said Ben. "To my mind, if we can find a canoe, we have a right to her, considering that we have been kept in slavery, and worked pretty hard too, by the friends of these people."

Certainly, I would rather have bought the canoe; but as that was out of the question, I could not help agreeing with Ben.

We had not gone far, when we came to a path evidently made by human feet. "This probably leads to some plantation, or to another village, through the forest," observed Boxall. "We must proceed cautiously, so as not to come suddenly upon the natives."

Selim offered to go on first and explore the way.

In a short time he came running back. "I have discovered a canoe afloat and secured to the bank," he said. "She has paddles in her, so the owners cannot be far-off. We are indeed, fortunate, and must not lose the opportunity of escaping, as we are not likely again to meet so good a one."

We hurried on. There lay the canoe, as Selim had described; she was large enough to hold us all—indeed, large enough to navigate the river to its mouth. Without further consideration we stepped into her, and seizing the paddles, cast off the painter, and shoved out into the stream. We did not feel quite as happy as we might have done had we been able to obtain her by lawful purchase from the owners. They would naturally be enraged on discovering that we had run off with their property, and if they could obtain the means, would, of course, follow us; we hoped, however, by paddling on, to get well ahead before being discovered. We should be in most danger when passing the village we had seen on the bank some way down the stream.

Boxall told Selim to take the helm—as his black face might make the natives suppose that we were a party of white slaves sent down the river by our owner—while we four paddled with might and main. As we neared the village we plied our paddles harder than ever. Just as we got abreast of it, we saw a native in the front of one of the huts. Discovering us, he shouted to some others, who rushed out of their huts and followed him down to the river. We did not stop to ascertain what they were about to do, but paddled on. We had not got far, however, before we saw a canoe being launched from the bank. We might easily have distanced her, and were expecting to do so, when there appeared two more canoes some way ahead of us, putting off from the shore, evidently with the intention of intercepting us. Our only hope now was that we could fight our way past them. Had we possessed our firearms, or even Antonio's scimitar, this we might have done without much danger; but with only our paddles and Ben's long pole for weapons of defence, we should run, we knew, a great risk of losing our lives: still the attempt must be made.

We paddled on boldly, shouting at the top of our voices, in the hope of intimidating our enemies. Those in one of the canoes seemed doubtful about attacking us, but the others came boldly on, sending, as they got near, a flight of arrows towards us. Selim shouted to them, telling them to keep off, and saying that we only wished to be allowed to pass in peace. To this they paid no attention, however, but, uttering loud cries in reply to our shouts, came dashing towards us. Ben, who had got his long pole ready, sprang up, and plunged it with such force that it ran through the body of one of the savages, who was dragged overboard. The others, alarmed by the death of their companion, paddled to a distance, and assailed us with fresh flights of arrows. Happily, they were not well aimed, and none of us were struck.

We now began to hope that we should escape, though, as we paddled on, we were hotly pursued by two canoes. We were, however, distancing them, when we found that the river made a sharp bend, and ran back close to the village we had at first seen. At the same time we caught sight of four or five large canoes putting off from the shore, evidently for the purpose of intercepting us. In vain we attempted to escape; the canoes completely surrounded us, and unless we had resolved, rather than yield, to sacrifice our lives, resistance would have been useless. We merely, therefore, warded off with our paddles the blows aimed at our heads, while we cried out to the people that we were ready to give in if they would desist from striking. Before they understood us, however, we had received several cuts and bruises, and in a pitiable condition were conducted on shore.

On landing we were placed in an open space on the ground, with guards over us; while the more influential persons seated themselves under a widespreading baobab-tree, and discussed what was to be done with us. Though we could not hear clearly what was said, from their gestures we fully believed they contemplated putting us to death.

"We might as well have made a stouter fight for our liberty," observed Ben, who seemed to be sorry that we had yielded so easily.

"If they believe that they can make anything by us, they will not kill us," said Boxall. "We may still, I hope, escape death."

Anxiously we watched the gestures of the assembly. They were savage-looking fellows enough, but yet it soon became evident that some were for mild measures; and Selim, who understood better than we did what they were saying, caught a few words, and told us that they were waiting the arrival of some one, who had been sent for, and who was to decide our fate.

Some hours passed, during which we were kept without food, and exposed to the burning rays of the sun. At length there was a movement among our captors, and we caught sight of several horsemen coming through the forest, with a person, who was evidently a chief of importance, at their head. As he approached, we recognised the black, ill-looking sheikh to whose camp we had conducted the veiled lady. My heart, I confess, sunk within me, for I expected very little mercy at his hands. Without dismounting, he listened to the account the chiefs of the village gave of our capture. When they had finished, I thought it was time for me to speak, and I knew that by so doing I could not make our case worse; I therefore addressed him in Arabic, which, at our former interview, I found that he understood. I reminded him that I had conducted his daughter and her family, placed under my charge, in safety to him; and that, having faithfully performed my duty, I felt that I had a right to escape from slavery, and to try and get back to my own country; that on my way I had fallen in with my present companions, and that when we were captured we were only doing what he and any of his people would, under similar circumstances, have attempted.

He seemed more moved by my address than I had expected. "What you say is true, O Nazarene," he answered; "but those from whom you have escaped are my friends, and they will demand you at my hands. You know the penalty you have incurred by attempting to escape, and you must be prepared to pay it."

ATTACKED BY SAVAGES.

I felt it would be of no use pleading for mercy with the savage, or I would have entreated him to set us at liberty, and to allow us to continue our voyage down the river. I had frequently heard, too, of the fearful cruelties which were practised on slaves who attempted to escape from their Arab masters, so I could not help thinking of those we should be doomed to suffer were we to be delivered up to Sheikh Hamed.

The black sheikh now held a short consultation with the chiefs of the place and with those who accompanied him, and finally decided that we were to be carried next day to his camp. We were, in the meantime, thrust into a small hut, there to remain till the following morning, when we were to set out. Of course, we could not help being greatly cast down by the turn affairs had taken; Boxall, however, did his best to keep up our spirits, and urged us to look above for that strength and courage which we required in our time of need. "Our lives have been preserved when we expected to have lost them. Let us hope that even now some means of escape may be found," he observed.

"I wonder whether the savages think we can live without eating," said Halliday. "I wish they would bring us some food."

Not many minutes after this the door opened, and a black woman appeared, carrying a couple of baskets containing a bowl of couscoussu, a calabash of water, and some fruit. Though her countenance was shrivelled, it beamed with kindness.

"I heard that there were white men starving, and in captivity, and I hastened from my home down the river to bring food to them," she said. "Here it is. Eat, strangers, and may your strength be restored."

We thanked her for her charity.

"I myself have reason to be thankful to white men," she answered. "When I was young, and just married, our village was attacked by a party of Moors, when my husband and I were carried down to the coast, to be conveyed across the wide ocean to slavery in a distant land. While waiting to embark, the kind governor of the place purchased us, kept us in his house, and fed and clothed us; and at last, when the country was at peace, he sent us back to our own home. There we continued to live, and my husband is now a rich man. Our great pleasure since then has been to help those white men who have been made slaves by the Arabs, or who are otherwise in distress."

As she said this, the hope arose in me that she might possibly help us to escape. I asked her without hesitation if she could do so. She shook her head. At last she answered: —

"My husband is now old, and has no influence with the people of this place. They respect me, so they allow me to bring this food to you, but my power extends no further; still, I will do what I can. I must not now delay, or I may be accused of endeavouring to assist you to escape."

Of course, after hearing this we could not detain the kind negress; and wishing us good-bye, she took her departure, while we set to at the welcome food she had brought us.

"We have indeed reason to be thankful for this unexpected assistance," observed Boxall. "He who put it into the heart of this kind negress to bring us this food, will find us the means of escape."

With our spirits somewhat raised by this event, we stretched our weary limbs on the hard ground, and were all soon asleep.

We were awakened at daybreak by one of our guides, who told us that we must immediately set out on our journey. We had barely time allowed us to eat the remainder of the provisions the good negress had brought us, and were compelled to abandon any hope we had entertained of escaping by her assistance.

We had now to march with guards on either side, and our hands tied, two and two: Boxall and I, Halliday and Ben, with Selim bringing up the rear. The journey was a fatiguing one, for after we had left the belt of forest which bordered the river we had a wide expanse of open country, where we were exposed to the rays of the hot sun. It was not desert, however; for numerous plantations covered it.

At length we reached another woody district on the very borders of the Sahara, where the chief had pitched his camp. He had preceded us, we found; for on our arrival he appeared at the door of his tent, and called me up to him.

"I have saved your life and that of your companions," he said; "but as you were attempting to escape from bondage, I am bound to deliver you up to Sheikh Hamed Aben Kaid, who will treat you as he thinks fit. All I can do is to report favourably of the way in which you conducted yourself towards my daughter and her children, and this may tell in your favour; but I warn you that a severe punishment awaits those who attempt to fly from their masters. You will set out to-morrow morning. And take my advice: as soon as you arrive you must express your desire to become faithful followers of the Prophet, and all will be well; if not, you may expect no mercy."

I thanked the black sheikh for the kindly feeling which prompted his advice, but did not say whether I intended to take it. I felt very sure that my companions would suffer anything rather than turn Mohammedans, and I hoped that even the fear of death would not make me do so.

For the remainder of the day we were placed in a tent by ourselves, and were amply supplied with food. As soon as we were alone, I told my friends what the black sheikh had said. Their answers were as I expected; and we all agreed to support each other in the resolution we had formed to be firm to our faith.

Next morning we set out at daybreak on our dreary journey, escorted by a party of black troops on foot, with a few camels to carry provisions. We kept the road I had come, turning neither to the right nor to the left. Nothing occurred to us during the march worth narrating; we were not ill-treated, and were sufficiently supplied with food, our guards wishing to bring us back in good condition. We had got within about a day's journey of the camp, when we saw a party of Arabs approaching, mounted on camels, and as our guards did not appear alarmed we knew that they must be friends. As they drew nearer I recognised Sheikh Hamed at their head; and as he saw us a frown gathered on his brow, and he inquired of the leader of our guards how we had been taken. On being told what had happened, his anger increased, his own people gathering round him and crying out that we deserved nothing but death. While he and they were discussing the matter, one of the marabouts, who had taken part in the discussion I once had with the sheikh on religious subjects, proposed that we should be forgiven, provided we would acknowledge Mohammed as the Prophet of God, and conform in all other respects to the true religion, as he called it. As the question was not formally put to us, we had no reason to reply, and therefore stood silent while the discussion was going forward. As soon as it was over, the marabout came to us and inquired whether we were willing to conform to the faith of the Prophet, promising that if we did so our lives would be spared. We answered boldly, and at once, that we would not be hypocrites, and that we had resolved to abide by the religion in which we had been brought up.

Our determined answer greatly enraged the marabout, who had expected to make easy converts of us. "Then you must be prepared for the fate you have brought upon yourselves," he answered.

As evening was approaching, both parties encamped; and we were left during the night in doubt as to what our punishment would be.

Ben was as firm as any of us. "A pretty sort of prophet Mohammed must have been, if he could not teach his followers to behave themselves better than they do," he exclaimed. "I cannot say but what they bow and pray enough, and go through all sorts of curious forms, but to my mind it's all outside show; and if their religion don't teach people to be kind and merciful, and to do to others as they would others should do to them, it's not worth a bit of rotten rope yarn."

Selim, who had hitherto professed to be a follower of Mohammed, declared, after hearing our conversation, that he was ready to acknowledge himself a Christian, and to die with us if we were to be put to death. Boxall thereupon spoke very earnestly to him, as he had done to us, and urged him to adhere to his resolution. "It is far better to die than to live a hypocrite, or to acknowledge that Mohammed was a true prophet of God, when we know that he was an emissary of Satan sent to deceive the world," he observed.

Next morning, after the Arabs and blacks had gone through their usual ceremonies, we were brought out, with our arms bound to our sides.

The marabout had, in the meantime, been among the people, endeavouring to excite them against us, and they now gathered round from every side with savage gestures, hurling bitter curses at our heads, calling us vile Christians, despisers of the true Prophet, Nazarene dogs, accursed infidels, children of Satan, and similar names, till they had exhausted their vocabulary of abuse.

The two sheikhs and the other chiefs now appeared on the field, and were received with loud acclamations. "Allah, Allah! God is great, and Mohammed is his Prophet!" shouted the crowd surrounding us, while their countenances exhibited their hostile feelings.

Terrible was the doom preparing for us; whatever might have been the wishes of Sheikh Hamed and the black chief, the voices of the marabouts and the people prevailed. We were doomed to a fate scarcely less terrible than that of Tantalus. We were condemned to be buried alive, with our heads above the sand, — water and food being placed just beyond our reach, so that we might see the means of saving life and yet be unable to profit thereby. Certainly, I think, the vivid imaginations of the old heathens could not have invented a more horrible punishment.

Again the marabouts came to us, and asked whether we would become faithful followers of the Prophet; promising to receive us as brothers, and to raise us to rank and honour in their tribe, if we would do so, and pointing out the dreadful fate which would be ours if we refused. But we all remained firm, declaring that we could not embrace a religion in which we did not believe.

Selim, influenced by our example, shouted out, — "I once professed to be a follower of your false prophet, and I am sorry for it. I don't believe in him, or the Koran, or in the wrong and foolish things it teaches. You may kill me, along with these white men; I would rather die with them than live with such wretches as you are." The marabouts, as he spoke, rushed forward and struck him, and tried to drown his words by their shouts and execrations. Boxall, Halliday, and I, seeing no advantage in irritating the fanatical feelings of our captors, had said nothing, except that we would not turn Mohammedans; but Ben shouted out, in the best Arabic he could command, — "I believe in one God; but I know very well that Mohammed was not one of His prophets; and only blind, ignorant fools such as you are would believe in him or the stupid book he wrote. You may bury me, or do what you like; but as long as I have got a tongue above ground to wag, I will not knock off speaking the truth. — I say, Mr Blore, I don't think they quite make out what I mean. You just tell them, please; and give them a bit of your own mind too."

Fortunately for Ben, only the first words of his speech were comprehended, and many of the people fancied that he was ready to turn Mohammedan; so that, instead of attacking him, many of them demanded that he should be set free and allowed to do as he wished. Indeed, by his good-humour, and readiness to help any one who wanted assistance, he had become a general favourite in the camp. The marabouts, however, suspecting, from his tone of voice, that he was not very complimentary to them or their religion, answered that he must be left to share our fate. They were also greatly enraged against Selim, and decided that he (in consequence of his perversion from the true faith) and Boxall (as the eldest of the party) should be the first to suffer.

In the meantime, preparations were being made for our punishment; spades had been brought, and two holes dug in the sand about six feet apart.

AN OPPORTUNE RESCUE

While we lay bound on the ground, the marabouts again came forward, and asked Boxall if he would turn Mohammedan; reminding him that he would be the cause of our death, and that of the young black, if he refused, as we should all undoubtedly follow. It was very clear that they would rather make converts of us than put us to death.

"No, my friends," answered Boxall calmly. "In our country each man is allowed to believe as he thinks best; and I tell you that I cannot believe as you do."

"Then take the consequences of your obstinate unbelief," answered the marabout, making a sign to the people surrounding us.

They instantly seized Boxall and Selim, and dragged them to the holes, into which they thrust them, — one facing the other, and with their arms bound tightly down by their sides, — till their heads alone were visible above ground. The sand was then shovelled in till their bodies were entirely buried; after which a bowl of water and two pieces of well-cooked meat, emitting a pleasant odour, were placed between them, at such a distance that they could not possibly be reached.

The Arabs had begun to dig two more holes, when we observed some disturbance among them. Presently the sheikh hurried to the top of a neighbouring mound, while all eyes were turned northward across the Desert. Leaving Boxall and Selim in their fearful position, and entirely disregarding us, those possessing firearms began to look to the priming, and all appeared to be getting their weapons ready for use, when, even as we lay on the ground, the heads of men in a long line came into view above our limited horizon. Then we could distinguish camels—of which there seemed to be a hundred or more—advancing rapidly in close order. On they came, — the ground shaking beneath their tread, — surrounded by clouds of dust stirred up by their feet.

The two sheikhs now marshalled their men, and calling on them to fight bravely and merit paradise, led them forward to meet the foe. We watched them with painful interest, for our lives depended on the result. Whether the strangers had come for the purpose of rescuing us, we could not tell; but should they be defeated, there could be little doubt that our present masters would carry out their intention of putting us to death. If, on the contrary, the strangers gained the day, we had good hopes that we should be rescued, though we might still be kept in slavery.

Sheikh Hamed and the black chief fought bravely; but they and their followers were but ill-armed, and greatly outnumbered. Back and back they were driven, and many soon lay stretched on the ground. Still others, who had remained as a reserve, advanced, rushing with their muskets and swords right up to the camels; but they too were driven back, while many of them took to flight. I prayed that the tide of battle would not sweep our way, lest we might be trampled to death. Several of the blacks, however, passed us, but these were in too great a hurry to escape to knock us on the head.

Ben, meantime, had been working away desperately to get his hands free. "Hurrah! I have done it," he shouted, and instantly came and released Halliday and me. We then hurried to the assistance of Boxall and Selim, and with one of the spades which had been left behind we quickly dug them out. It was fortunate that we were not delayed, for they were already beginning to feel the weight of the sand pressing round them, though they might possibly have lived for many hours in that position.

We had been so eager in extricating them, that we had not observed how the battle went, till, looking round, we saw the new-comers in full pursuit of our late owners, many of whom had been cut down. No prisoners had been taken, however; for it being known that the blacks were followers of the Prophet, it was not considered worth while to capture them, as they could not be held in slavery.

Boxall, on catching sight of the victorious party, at once recognised them as his friends; and as they now halted and drew together, he led us towards them. Their leader at once knew him, and gave him a cordial welcome, expressing his satisfaction at having rescued him. Boxall then introduced us, and said that we wished to place ourselves under the protection of him and his tribe. The sheikh then ordering five of his followers each to take one of us up behind him on his camel, the victorious party rode off with us across the Desert, in the direction from which they had come, carrying away with them some of the arms and a few camels which they had captured.

The band of warriors who had so opportunely come to our rescue belonged, I learned from the man behind whom I rode, to the powerful tribe of the Sheikh Salem Alsgoon, between whom and Sheikh Hamed Ben Kaid a feud had long existed. Although they could not come to blows at the tomb of the saint, a constant watch had been kept on the movements of Sheikh Hamed; and when it was found that he had set out from his camp to meet us, an expedition had been despatched with all haste to surprise him. To this circumstance we owed our preservation. Sheikh Salem, however, would have had sufficient excuse, according to the law of the Desert, for attacking Sheikh Hamed, on account of his having, as was supposed, carried off one of his slaves; indeed, the desire to recover Boxall was one of the motives which had induced him to undertake it. Had we not been found, he had ordered his people to make a few prisoners, in order that they might be exchanged for Boxall. Thus the very circumstance which at first appeared the most disastrous to us, as is often the case in life, resulted ultimately in our favour.

Chapter Fourteen.

The old recluse—Description of the camp—Night intruders—Bu Saef—The mirage—Overtaken by a sand-storm—Fearful sufferings—Arrive at an oasis—Falling fortunes—Another conversation with Marabouts—Visitors at the camp—Sold—Arrive at a town.

We rode on without stopping till the sun had sunk low in the western horizon, the object of the Arabs being to join the main body by daylight,—for our leader well knew that Sheikh Hamed, having escaped, would hasten back to his camp and summon his followers to pursue us; and as we had to pass at no great distance from the camp, there was every probability of our party being overtaken.

Sheikh Salem's people, however, were full of fight, and boasted that, even should the whole of the hostile tribe come up with us, they would quickly put them to flight. They nevertheless dashed on with unabated speed, and never had I before ridden so fast through the Desert.

Although rescued from a cruel and lingering death, we could not expect that our lot in other respects would be greatly improved. We were going back to slavery, and our new masters were likely to treat us as the others had intended doing, should we attempt to escape or refuse to embrace their religion.

Just at sunset we reached a hollow with a few bushes growing at the bottom, from the midst of which sprang up a strange figure. It was that of an old man of most repulsive appearance, with a long white beard, a dark ragged garment thrown over his withered body, and a long stick in his hand. He was, I was told, a holy recluse, who lived upon the alms of passing pilgrims. He saluted our leader as an old acquaintance, and mounting on a camel, offered to guide us on our way during the night. It is no easy matter at any time, even for the Arabs, to find the way in a direct line across the boundless Desert; and when clouds obscure the stars, it is almost impossible without a compass. The old recluse, on seeing white strangers, cast a look of disgust and disdain at us, expressing his surprise that any true believers should allow infidel Nazarenes to remain in their company. But our leader only laughed, and answered that, as we had not eaten pork for a year, we had become almost as clean as Arabs. Considering that we had had a bath only a few days before, we considered ourselves a good deal cleaner. However, we did not say so, but let the dirty old saint abuse us to his heart's content without replying.

Even camels cannot go on for ever; and at length we reached a rocky ridge with a hollow beyond it. Crossing over the ridge, we descended into the hollow, where we at length halted to spend the night. On this ridge several sentries were placed, to give early notice of the approach of the foe. No fires were lighted; and each man, having taken his frugal meal of dates and flour-cakes, lay down among the weary camels to rest.

The night passed off without any alarm, and before daybreak we were again mounted and proceeding on our journey. Just as the sun was about to appear a halt was called, when all the men dismounted, and prostrating themselves towards the east, threw sand on their heads, while they uttered aloud their prayers as the sun rose above the horizon. Though anxious to push forward, as our pursuers would be employed in the same way, yet they did not hesitate to expend the time required in offering up their prayers. They mounted again as soon as possible, however, and once more we went ahead.

A sharp look-out was kept for the camp, of the position of which the old Arab did not appear certain; for the tribe had been moving on for the last two days, in order to put as wide a space as possible between themselves and their foes. At length we saw a horseman spurring across the plain, when, catching sight of our camels, he turned and galloped towards us. He was one of several scouts who had been sent out to look for our party. Guided by him, we now went forward with confidence, and soon came in sight of numerous troops of camels, spreading, it seemed, right across the horizon; while Arabs were arriving from all directions,—some mounted on camels, others on foot. Passing through the line of camels, we saw before us a number of low tents, pitched at a short distance from a pool of water bordered by tall reeds, stunted palms, and other trees. As our party approached, we were welcomed with loud shouts. No sooner had we dismounted than the wife of the sheikh—a tall woman of commanding aspect—advanced from her tent to meet Boxall, who went forward with confidence, we following. I cannot say that she looked benignantly at us, for her countenance was stern, though unusually handsome for an Arab woman of her age. She gave orders that a tent should be prepared for our use, however; and as soon as we had taken possession of it she sent us a bowl of couscoussu, with some dates and camel's milk, so that we fared sumptuously after our fatiguing ride.

"I feel almost as if I had got home again," said Boxall, as we lay at our ease with our legs stretched out on the carpet covering the floor of our tent. "I am really thankful to have you with me. Besides, we enjoy an advantage in being under the protection of a powerful sheikh, though I am afraid that our chance of escape is as remote as ever; while I suspect, notwithstanding the sheikh's promises, he will be very unwilling, when the time comes, to give me my liberty."

AN ARAB ENCAMPMENT

"Where there's a will there's a way; and we must look out for that way," observed Ben. "I only hope that we shall some day get back to the sea, or be in the neighbourhood of some town where Christian people live. We must look out, at all events, for a chance of giving our friends the slip. I, for one, have no fancy to spend my days among these fellows, who never think of serving out an honest piece of roast beef, and turn up their ugly noses at a man because he may chance to have a liking for boiled pork and pease-pudding."

We were not allowed to remain long in quiet. After we had enjoyed a couple of hours' rest, our tent was besieged by a number of people who came to have a look at the strangers. Among them were the two daughters of the chief. They were not much darker than Spanish women, and had graceful figures and really beautiful features. Their teeth were brilliantly white; and their eyes full of expression and vivacity, heightened by the colour they had given to their eyelashes and eyebrows by means of a blue stone. Their dress consisted of a woollen robe, which covered them from the shoulders, where it was secured by a silver buckle, and hung in folds down to their feet. They asked us all manner of questions, some of them very difficult to answer. Unfortunately, we had no presents to offer them in order to gain their goodwill. They looked upon us as their father's chattels, and with a mixture of contempt and curiosity, as if we were strange animals. Nor can I say that they appeared to feel any of that pity for our condition which we might suppose would animate the hearts of such lovely damsels. In truth, I fear that Ben was right when he observed, — "The good looks of them gals is only skin-deep; we may depend on that. They are more likely to do us an ill turn than a good one. I can tell it by the eyes they cast at us; so we mustn't be taken in by them." Alas! the Arab maidens had none of that true beauty which adorns the mind, for which our own fair countrywomen are so justly celebrated, and without which all outward beauty is a mockery and deception, as Ben justly remarked in his own way.

I must here describe the encampment, which was similar to many others we met with during our wanderings. It was about ten or twelve hundred yards in circumference. The tents were made of camel-hair cloth, manufactured by the inhabitants. They were supported in the middle by poles, round the top of which was some basketwork, to give them ventilation; the lower edges being fixed to the ground by pegs, and further weighted by stones or sand. The sheikh's tent differed but little from those of his people, being only more spacious, and rather higher. It was pitched in the middle of the enclosure; the others being on either side, according to the rank of the occupants. A large part of the ground within was covered over with carpets, on which the family slept; the tents of the less wealthy people being furnished with mats only. On a few short poles stuck in the ground were hung the goat-skin bottles containing milk or water; as also arms, and a few garments, which, together with some wooden bowls, jugs, small millstones for grinding corn, cooking utensils, looms for weaving camel-hair cloth, and sundry small articles, constituted the whole furniture of the habitations of these wanderers of the Desert.

The people continued to press around us in a most annoying manner. Boxall said he would complain to the sheikh's wife, in order that we might be allowed to rest in peace. He accordingly made his way through the crowd—who treated him with more respect than they did the rest of us—and that lady soon made her appearance, and in a threatening way ordered them to disperse. Though they obeyed her, they cast no very friendly glances at us; and in a short time many returned—with others who, though they did not enter the tent, crowded round the opening to have a look at us. Indeed, not till some time after night closed in were we allowed to rest in quiet.

We had been asleep some hours when I was aroused by a shout; and starting up, I heard Ben cry out, "Hallo! what do you want with us, old fellow?" Selim gave a shriek, and Boxall and Halliday sprang to their feet, when by the dim light of the stars I caught sight of a number of heads, adorned with horns and long beards, at the entrance of the tent. The creatures, undaunted by our shouts, rushed in, butting against us, and evidently determined to take possession of the tent. We soon discovered them to be goats, which had been turned out for our accommodation, and now seemed inclined to dispute possession and reclaim their former abode.

"Since you have come here you shall pay for your footing, and give us some milk for breakfast," exclaimed Ben, trying to seize one of them. The creature, however, was not to be easily caught; and eluding his grasp, it bolted out, followed by the rest, which we in vain tried to secure. They did not return, and we were allowed to pass the rest of the night in quiet.

The next morning, after the usual form of prayer had been gone through, the scouts reported that Sheikh Hamed's people were nowhere in the neighbourhood, and the order was given to strike camp. The women immediately began to lower the tents, and to roll up the coverings in packages suitable for stowage on the camels' backs. Even the sheikh's wife and daughters performed their part, with our assistance. The men were in the meantime bringing in the baggage camels—which, kneeling down, were rapidly loaded.

We marched much as we had been accustomed to do with Sheikh Hamed's tribe: a strong guard of armed men brought up the rear, scouts were sent out on our flanks, and another body, with which the sheikh generally rode, went ahead,—the whole covering the plain for an immense distance. There must have been three thousand camels, at the least, with several thousand sheep and goats, and a considerable number of horses and asses. Thus we moved forward day after day towards the north-east; not in a direct line, however, for we had frequently to make détours to reach wells or water-holes, or spots where water could be obtained by digging. Sometimes, too, we had to push across sandy regions in which not a drop of water could be found. On such occasions the poor animals, with the exception of the camels, suffered greatly; and even they became sensibly weakened, while we ourselves suffered greatly, from the want of water.

We were allowed to ride on camels, but were otherwise—with the exception of Boxall—treated as slaves. I was allotted to the sheikh's wife, who proved a very imperious mistress. Ben had been claimed by a relation of the sheikh, the owner of a camel of the celebrated Bu Saef breed, noted for its speed, which it was his especial duty to tend; while Halliday and Selim became the property of other principal men related to the sheikh. Boxall, in his character of a doctor, belonged to the sheikh, though he was allowed to practise among all in the camp who claimed his services. My condition, from being able to act as interpreter, was better than it might otherwise have been; and I often blessed my old friend Andrew Spurling for having incited me to study Arabic. Boxall, however, confessed to me that he was on dangerous ground. Had he possessed a stock of simple medicines with the properties of which he was well acquainted, he believed he might have been the means of alleviating the sufferings of many; but he was well aware that if any patient should die to whom he had given a draught, he would be accused of murdering him, and in all probability be put to death. He had therefore to confine his skill to bruises, wounds, or broken limbs, which he invariably treated with the cold-water system whenever water was to be procured; and as his patients recovered, his reputation was thus maintained.

I cannot recount one tenth part of the adventures we met with during that long march northward across the Sahara. Occasionally the monotony of our life was diversified by hunting ostriches and several kinds of deer. The former were run down by horsemen, who formed a large circle, compelling the birds to turn round and round till their strength was exhausted.

Water became scarcer as we advanced into the Desert. The camels and other animals had drunk their fill at some pools in a valley, the water-skins had been filled, and we had now an immense extent of arid sand to traverse before we could reach another well. There was no means of avoiding this region, which even the bravest looked on with dread. We commenced our march before the sun was up, stopping only for a hasty prayer, and then pushing on again. Instead of spreading over the plain, as usual, the camels and other animals were kept close together, forming a broad, dense line. A few hours of rest were to be allowed at night; we were then again to advance; and so we were to proceed till the oasis could be reached, as the destruction of the whole caravan might be the result of delay. Almost in silence we moved over the glittering plain. The fiery sun struck down on our heads, and the heat was such that the air seemed to dance around us. Hour after hour we moved on, a few words being now and then exchanged, or songs sung by the light-hearted, or tales told by the most loquacious of story-tellers. I observed skeletons of camels and men sticking out of the sand, as the caravan deviated slightly to avoid them; for they extended across the plain half a mile or more. On making inquiries, I found that the skeletons were those of a caravan which, while crossing the Desert on their way south, had been overtaken by a simoom, and had perished, when only half a day's journey from the pools we had left. The sight certainly did not tend to raise our spirits; we had nearly three days' journey before us, and in the course of that time we might be exposed to the same danger.

We encamped for a little at night, but having no fuel, were compelled to eat our provisions cold.

During the next day the heat was more intense than ever, and our thirst increased in proportion. Soon after mid-day, a bright lake of shining water, as it seemed, appeared before us, with animals feeding on its banks; the walls of a city, with its domes, and spires, and tall palm-trees, behind. How delightful was the spectacle! Eager to reach it, I could not help urging on my camel; many others did the same, but our leaders proceeded as deliberately as before, regarding the spectacle with no concern; when, as we advanced, it suddenly vanished, and I found that we had been deceived by a mirage, so common in the Desert.

The atmosphere had hitherto been calm, not a cloud dimmed the bright blue sky; but before long the wind, hot as from a furnace, swept by us, the sun struck down on our heads with irresistible force, while the azure of the sky changed to a lurid tint. I saw the Arabs looking anxiously at each other. Stronger and stronger came the wind, blowing the sand like spray from off the ground. Turning my head, I observed a dark cloud advancing towards us, sweeping over the ground. On it came, rising upwards, and completely obscuring the heavens. In vain would we have attempted to escape from it; almost immediately we were enveloped in a vast mass of sand, through which even the sun's rays, with all their power, could not penetrate. Darker and darker it grew, till we could scarcely distinguish those who rode on either side of us; while sand filled eyes, ears, and mouth, and covered our hair, even penetrating through our clothes. The Arabs shouted to each other to keep together, and dashed forward; but thicker and thicker came the storm. My tongue felt as if turned to leather, a burning thirst attacked me, and it was with difficulty I could speak; while others were suffering even more severely than I was.

The sheikh had called a halt; and those in the rear came crowding up, almost riding over the front ranks before they were aware that they had reached them. Men and animals stood huddled together in a vast mass. To lie down would have been death; had any attempted to do so, they would either have been trampled under foot or have been buried beneath the sand. The fierce wind rendered it useless to pitch the tents, seeing they would have been blown down as soon as erected, or carried away before the blast. Occasionally those nearest each other would ask whether the storm was at the worst; but no one dared reply.

The clouds of sand became thicker and thicker; we seemed to have death alone to expect. Complete silence prevailed; the horses hung their tongues out of their mouths, the camels drooped their heads, while the sheep and goats struggled to free themselves from the sand collecting around them.

Thus hour after hour went by, and many of the Arabs, though accustomed to such storms, gave themselves up for lost. But suddenly the wind changed, and seemed to drive back the clouds which surrounded us; objects hitherto obscured came into view; and once more the voices of the leaders could be heard. The order to advance was given, and again we dashed forward, though so exhausted with thirst that we could scarcely keep our seats, while those on foot with difficulty dragged on their weary limbs.

At nightfall we encamped, and small measures of water, or of such milk as the camels and goats could yield, were served out to the people; but the portion we obtained was scarcely sufficient to cool our parched tongues. Our very skin felt like leather, and was cracked and scorched all over. A short time only could be given for rest, however; another blast might sweep up clouds of sand and overwhelm us; another fatiguing march during a day and night over the Desert had to be passed. Besides, every drop of water was expended; and though the camels might go on with comparative ease, we must all of us expect to suffer dreadfully,—but more especially the women and children.

Again we advanced; but another day might witness the destruction of many who had hitherto held out bravely. We went on as fast as the camels could move their limbs. The expectation that water would be found ahead incited us to exertion, I suppose, otherwise many would have sunk down and resigned themselves to their fate. At length the faint outline of palm-trees was seen in the far distance. Shouts of joy were uttered by those in advance, and taken up by the multitude in the rear. Soon the palm-trees became more and more distinct; and even the animals seemed to know that relief would soon be obtained.

In a short time the whole caravan was collected round a large well, from which eager hands were employed in drawing water. Some time passed, however, before we could obtain a draught, as even the animals were considered more worthy to enjoy the water than we Nazarenes were.

We here encamped, that both human beings and animals might recruit their strength. It was curious to remark the contrast between the flocks which came up to receive water at the well and those which had already slaked their thirst; the latter bounded and leaped about, showing how quickly the refreshing liquid had restored their strength.

I have elsewhere described the appearance of our camp, and the mode of proceeding never varied. Before we started in the morning, the male part of the population were called out to prayer; the herdsmen then departed in all directions to tend the camels, horses, sheep, and goats while grazing. As the day advanced, the extreme heat, and the absence of most of the men, deprived the camp of all its bustle: a few women were alone to be seen, occupied in grinding between two stones the barley which was to serve for the evening repast; others were employed at their looms, weaving camel-hair cloth, within the shade of the tents.

In the evening the whole scene became one of the greatest animation. Various travellers were arriving, and seeking the hospitality of the sheikh and his people: some came in troops, lightly mounted; others with camels loaded with articles to dispose of in the Desert. The sheikh sat on his carpet in front of his tent, calmly smoking his long hookah, and habited in a white haique of extreme fineness, which hung over another garment of sky-blue, ornamented on each side of the breast with silk embroidery of various colours. On his feet were red morocco boots, tastefully figured; while, instead of a turban, he wore round his head—which was entirely shaved—a band of blue silk, a sign of his rank. Each Arab as he arrived made his camel kneel before the tent, and then, holding his musket in one hand, he touched the sheikh's head with the other in token of respect. The sheikh congratulated each one on his arrival, and returned the numerous salutations, without even inquiring from whence the traveller came, or whither he was going.

Before dark, all were assembled for evening prayer; after which the travellers formed themselves into groups, partaking out of one common bowl the couscoussu prepared for them by their hosts. As night approached the camels and flocks came trotting in; and by a peculiar instinct each herd arranged itself before the tent to which it belonged, the women hurrying out to milk the she-camels and goats. The hubbub which ensued, caused by the numerous animals assembled, may be imagined. A perfect calm then succeeded the bustle: the inhabitants retired to their tents—the travellers, enveloped in their cloaks, lying down with their camels by the side of the waning fires; the cattle, closely packed together, remained immovable till morning,—and, notwithstanding the number collected, not a sound was heard during the night.

The routine of every ordinary day, when we were not travelling, was similar to that I have described.

Our position in the camp had not improved of late. By some means or other I had offended my hasty mistress and her young daughters, and this prejudicing the mind of the sheikh against me, I was ordered to perform the same sort of service as that to which Halliday and Ben had been condemned; while we were told that from henceforth we must march, like the other slaves, on foot. This encouraged a marabout, who hitherto had not interfered with us, to insist that we should turn Mohammedans; and every day we were summoned to hear him abuse the Christians, and to listen to his arguments in favour of the faith of the Prophet. Boxall, too, had not been so successful in his cures as at first. One of his patients, suffering from some internal disease, and who had broken his arm by a fall from a camel, died, and Boxall was accused of killing him — though he protested his innocence, and even the sheikh said that the man might have died from other causes. But from that day the people lost faith in him; and he was finally reduced from his post as surgeon-general of the tribe to serve with us as a camel-driver.

Though the life he had now to bear, however, was one of daily toil, he accepted his position without complaining. "I confess, my dear Charlie," he said to me soon afterwards, "that I often felt ashamed of myself, while I was enjoying the favour of the sheikh and the abundant food he provided for me, — simply because I happened to know a little about medicine and surgery, — to see you and Halliday ill-treated and badly fed, and to be unable to help you. However, now that we are together, perhaps we may be better able to manage some means of escape. I have been endeavouring to calculate our present position, and I believe that we are not more than four hundred miles south of the borders of Morocco or Algiers. Should we reach Morocco, we might not be much better off in some respects than we are at present, as the Moors are even more fanatical than these wandering Arabs; but we might find the means of communicating with one of the English consuls on the coast, and probably obtain our release: whereas, if we could get into the neighbourhood of the frontier of Algiers, we might, on escaping, place ourselves under the protection of the French. To reach one of their outposts would, of course, be a difficulty; for, even supposing that we could escape from the camp, a journey by ourselves of three or four hundred miles across the Desert would be dangerous in the extreme, with the probability of being pursued by the Arabs. Notwithstanding this, I am inclined to the latter plan, provided my calculations of our position should prove correct."

"So am I," I answered. "As for the dangers we may have to encounter, I am perfectly ready to face them; so I am sure will Halliday, Ben, and Selim—for we must not on any account leave the black lad behind."

The plans for escape formed the subject of our conversation whenever we met. We were all of one mind about it, and we resolved not to desert each other, but to remain or escape together.

Seeing I could converse with the Arabs with greater ease than the others, Boxall charged me to try and ascertain exactly whereabout we were, adding—"But be cautious about exhibiting any special interest in the matter."

Whenever strangers came into the camp, therefore, I got into conversation with them, and tried to learn whence they had come, and how long they had been on their journey, hoping to find some one who had visited either the Atlantic or Mediterranean shores of the continent; but no one I had met with had performed less than a journey of thirty days in coming from the city of Morocco, or forty or more from Fez—which of course placed us still a long way to the south of Algiers. We had therefore to wait patiently till the sheikh should move his camp further northward. We heard, however, of several large cities in different parts of the Desert: Timbuctoo, a long way to the south; Tintellust and Agadly, to the east; Tafleet and the beautiful oasis of Draha, to the north-west of us,—to all of which places travellers were proceeding.

Ben was at this time in a better position than we were. Being a handy fellow, and understanding something of smith-work, he had mended the locks of some of the Arabs' firearms; and the whole of his time, when not occupied in tending his camel, was employed in repairing the damaged weapons of our masters. He held his position, however, among those capricious people, by a very uncertain tenure. The marabouts fancied, from his easy, good-natured manner, that they could without difficulty induce him to turn Mohammedan, and set to work with him, as they had done with us, to show the excellence of their religion.

"Look you here, my friends," answered Ben, after listening with perfect gravity for some time, when one evening he and I, with the rest of our party, were seated on the ground at our supper, and two of these so-called holy men came up to us. "If it's a good thing for a man to have a dozen—or even fifty—wives, to cut throats, to steal, and commit all sorts of rogueries, then your religion may be a good one; but if not, why, do ye see—begging your pardons, no offence being intended—to my mind it was invented by the devil, and your Prophet, as you call him, was as big a rogue as ever lived.—Just tell them, Mr Blore, what I say; for I never can make these marabout chaps understand my lingo."

Knowing that Ben's remarks would not be favourably received, I confess that I did not translate them literally, but replied: "My brother listens with all respect to the wisdom which has proceeded from your mouths. We all acknowledge Allah, and look to him for everything we possess; but we have been taught to put faith in another Prophet, whom we believe to be greater than any human being, and therefore we cannot deny Him by acknowledging any other."

"Mohammed was superior to all other prophets!" exclaimed the marabouts. "Those who do not believe this are worthy of death and eternal damnation."

"It is just on that point we differ, my friends," I answered with perfect calmness. "You believe one thing, we believe another. In the end we shall know which is right. In the meantime, why should we wrangle and dispute? or why should you grow angry with us because we do not agree with you?"

"The more we love you, the more anxious we are for your conversion," answered the marabouts.

"You take a curious way of showing it," I could not help observing, causing thereby something like a smile on the grave countenances of the priests—who did not, however, again attempt a theological discussion with us. Ben managed to make his opinions known, though, and received very severe treatment in consequence. The sheikh no longer continued to protect him any more than he did us; and when the tribe moved forward, he was compelled to trudge on foot, separated from his camel—which on such occasions was bestrode by his master.

Many a weary day's march we had to make. Sometimes, however, we remained for several weeks together at an oasis, where wells would be found, and herbage for the beasts, with groves of date-trees. Here we had time to regain our strength; and our masters being generally in better humour, we were in consequence less harshly dealt with.

Still, our existence was daily becoming more and more unendurable, and only the hope of ultimately escaping kept up our spirits, and prevented us sinking altogether into despair. Had we consented to abandon our religion, our homes, and civilisation, we might have been raised to a high position among these barbarians; and I believe that Boxall and I might have become sheikhs ourselves. The beautiful Coria, the youngest of the sheikh's daughters, showed me at first many marks of her esteem; but my refusal to embrace their religion, even for her sake, changed her love into hatred, and she became my most bitter persecutor.

At length we heard that we were approaching a town, which we hoped might prove to be at no great distance from the borders of Algiers. Our knowledge of the interior of Africa, however, was very imperfect; or, I may say, we knew nothing at all about it—our only recollection of the Desert being a vast blank space, with a few spots upon it marked "oases," with Lake Tchad and Timbuctoo on its southern border, and a very indefinite line marked Algiers and

Morocco. The place we were approaching was, we heard, the permanent abode of the sheikh; and the country, though arid according to European notions, was more fertile than any we had yet seen—palms and other trees being scattered about, with ranges of hills in the distance.

The Arabs manifested their joy by singing and uttering shouts of delight, praising the country to us as if it were a perfect paradise. Here and there were fields of barley, with some low tents in their midst; and a grove of date-trees circling a well, near which was an open space. The sheikh advanced into the centre, and the camels immediately halting, they were unloaded, and all hands set to work to erect the tents. The tribe had reached their home, after their long pilgrimage.

There seemed, however, no prospect of our lot being improved. We had not been long settled when a cavalcade arrived, the persons composing which differed greatly in appearance from those among whom we had so long lived. Their leader was a handsomely dressed, fine-looking Arab. He wore a haique, over which was a cloak of blue cloth, with a well-arranged turban on his head. The costume of his followers was nearly as becoming; their horses were large and well-caparisoned, their saddles being covered with scarlet cloth, to which hung enormous silver stirrups; while they were profusely covered with ornaments of the same material. Each horseman was armed with a poignard and sabre, and pistols in his sash; while he carried before him—the but resting on the saddle—a fine silver-mounted Moorish gun.

The same ceremonies as I have before described were gone through; an entertainment also being prepared for the new-comers.

After some time we were summoned to attend the sheikh, when we found that he was offering to sell us to his visitors. The price to be paid we could not ascertain, nor the object of our proposed purchasers; our only consolation was that we were to be sold together, and should not thus be separated.

A NIGHT MARCH

What other object the visitors had in coming to the camp we could
not learn. I had my suspicions, however, when I heard the young

sheikh—whose name was Siddy Ischem—invite our master to accompany him.

"No! Allah be praised, I have never been accustomed to towns and their ways; and within stone and brick walls I hope not to enter, unless I go at the head of my people, sword in hand, to plunder and destroy the cursed infidels,—when, with the blessing of Mohammed, I will get out again as soon as the work is accomplished."

"Each man to his taste," answered Siddy Ischem. "A city affords its pleasures as well as the Desert."

The greater part of the next morning was spent at the camp. We were then ordered to be ready to march. Siddy Boo Cassem, owner of the famous Bu Saef camel, with several of his tribe, accompanied our party. No camels or horses were allowed us, however, and having to march on foot, a dreary, fatiguing journey we found it. Some of our masters rode on either side of us, to prevent the possibility of our running away; though where we could have run to it was hard to say. We travelled on all day, the night overtaking us while we were still on the road. In about an hour, however, the moon rose, and enabled us better to see the path.

Not long afterwards, we caught sight of a lofty tower rising out of the plain, and the dark frowning walls of a fortified town; and from the remarks of the Arabs we learned that this was our destination. We soon came under the walls, when the leaders of our band began to defile through a narrow archway. My heart sank within me, for I felt that the difficulties of escape would be increased. I expressed my feelings to Boxall; but he rejoined,—"Such walls as these can be easily scaled; and if we once get on the outside, we are not so likely to be observed and followed as from an open camp. Cheer up, Charlie; 'it's a long lane that has no turning.'"

Even he, however, felt somewhat dispirited when we were conducted to a long, low building, into which we were thrust, and the door closed upon us. All we could discover in the gloom was that the walls were of bare stone, with rings and chains secured to them, and that the floor was excessively dirty. We were so tired from our journey that we longed to lie down; but we were unable to do so until we could scrape from the floor the offal which thickly covered it.

"I hope they are not going to send us supperless to bed," exclaimed Ben. "Can't you sing out that we are in want of food, Mr Blore, and that we shall be much obliged to them if they will send us something to drink at the same time?"

There was a single, strongly-barred window in the room, looking into the street. I went to it, and cried at the top of my voice, "Oh, pity! oh, pity! oh, pity! Will any one have compassion on us, and bring us some food to supply our wants?"

My appeal was not in vain, for before long the door opened and a veiled female appeared, bringing a basket with the universal couscoussu, some dates, and a bottle of water. Without uttering a word she placed the basket on the ground, and retired as silently as she had entered; not even allowing us time to thank her for her kindness. All we could do was to bless her after she had gone, and wonder who she could be; and then we set to with hearty appetites to devour the viands she had brought us. Finding some pieces of wood, we next scraped a spot in the corner of our prison clear of dirt; and then throwing ourselves on the ground, forgot our cares in sleep.

Chapter Fifteen.

Ben displays his ability as a gunsmith—I act the part of eavesdropper—How Siddy Boo Cassem obtained Bu Saef—Selim goes on a dangerous expedition—Its result—Boxall doctors Siddy Boo Cassem—We take French leave of our masters.

Scarcely had daylight appeared when the door opened, and a number of inquisitive faces—belonging to people of all descriptions who had come to see us—appeared at the entrance. Some gazed in silence, but many amused themselves by abusing us, and bestowing on us all sorts of uncomplimentary names. We endured the abuse for some time without replying; but at last I got up and said—

"What is it that excites your curiosity, O followers of the prophet Mohammed? Are we not formed like yourselves? In what do we differ, except that your skins are dark and ours light; that you are at home, and we come from a far-distant land; that you speak one language, and we speak another—although Allah has given us the power of acquiring yours? We have no wish to insult you, and why should you take a pleasure in insulting us?"

The people were greatly astonished at hearing me address them in their own language. What I had said had also considerable effect, for they instantly ceased abusing us; and several of them began to ask questions about our country, and the business which had brought us to Africa.

Affairs were taking a more favourable turn, when one of those abominable marabouts came in and reminded the people that we were Nazarenes, and haters of the Prophet, and endeavoured thus to incite their fanatical zeal against us. What would have been the result I do not know, had not Siddy Ischem made his appearance. As we had become his property, he had no wish to see us injured; so he quickly drove the people away, and ordered us to accompany him to the house where he was staying.

We soon reached a one-storied building, having a gateway, through which we passed into a courtyard, round which ran a colonnade. Part of the courtyard was covered with an awning, under which, on a carpet, sat a richly dressed Arab, by whose side Siddy Ischem took his seat, and then calling us up, desired us to narrate our adventures. I did so, explaining that three of us were officers who had been wrecked on the coast; that I felt sure a handsome price would be paid for our ransom; whereas, if we were kept in slavery, though we might labour ever so hard we could be of little profit to our masters.

I do not know whether the sheikh was moved by what I said, but he told a slave standing by to bring us some food, and desired us to sit down in the shade and eat it. He then ordered us to go to the stables and groom the horses, saying at the same time that we must be prepared to continue our journey the next day.

We found that the town in which we were, was one of those built by the Romans when their colonies spread over the northern shores of Africa. The town had long fallen into decay, the sands of the Desert having gradually encroached on it till the greater portion of the land fit for cultivation had been overwhelmed. The only habitable houses were one story in height, composed of sunburned bricks, and with flat roofs, on which the occupants seemed to spend most of their time.

I forgot to say that we discovered our abode, which we at first took for a prison, to be merely a stable, and that the rings and chains were simply intended to secure refractory horses.

We performed the duties assigned us as well as we could; and Ben's talent as a gunsmith being noised abroad, he was called on to repair all the damaged firearms in the place—we assisting him as well as we could—at a smith's shop to which we were conducted.

"What wonderful people are these Nazarenes!" observed some of the bystanders. "They know everything."

"Yes," remarked others; "the Jins teach them. It is their turn now; but they will burn throughout eternity. Curses rest on them! Allah is great; we have paradise for our portion."

Similar remarks were made during the time we were at work; while some of the spectators, to show their contempt, spat at us; and several came up threatening us with their fists, to prove their zeal for their religion. But we had been too long accustomed to this sort of treatment to take any notice of it; and even Ben went on with his work, filing, hammering, and screwing away,—only remarking, when he understood what was said, "That's all you know about it."

Those who had their weapons mended went away contented; but as we could not repair half the number brought to us, the owners of the rest were very indignant, and we were glad to get back to our dirty stable out of their way.

During the evening, Siddy Boo Cassem, Ben's master, made his appearance, and informed him that he was to remain in his service, to attend to his Bu Saef camel when he himself was not riding the animal.

"Not a few clever rogues have attempted to run off with the creature, which is to me as the apple of my eye; but I know that you Nazarenes would not know where to run to, so I can trust you," he observed.

I told Ben what Siddy Boo Cassem had said.

"Let him give me the chance, and I will see what I can do," he answered.

We were allowed another night's rest, with a sufficiency of food,— for just then provisions were plentiful in the place, or we should have been left by our masters to pick up what we could. We tried in vain to discover who the charitable female was who had brought us provisions on the previous evening. It confirmed my belief, however, that Woman is the same all the world over; and that in every place some are to be found who, according to the light within them, endeavour to do their duty in the sight of God, by affording sympathy and help to their fellow-creatures in distress.

Again we were on the road,—Ben being summoned to attend to his master, while we trudged wearily on foot. Having neither cattle, sheep, nor goats to impede us, our progress was more rapid than it had been across the Desert. The baggage was carried on camels and asses; while the more wealthy people rode, and the rest had to walk.

For several days we advanced, passing numerous ruins, which showed how thickly the country at one time had been populated. At last one afternoon we encamped on high ground, outside an ancient town or fortress, amid which palms and other trees had grown up, attesting its antiquity. The tents were pitched, and Boxall, Halliday, and I were sent out with the horses and camels to graze on the pastures surrounding the hill. Returning in the evening, we met Ben with his camel—beside which it was his duty to sleep close to his master's tent. Ours was not far off.

"I have a notion, Mr Blore," said Ben, "that if you could take my place for the evening, you would find out more of what these fellows are about than I can. Half-a-dozen or more are sure to be seated in front of the tent for a couple of hours or so after dark, talking away, and smoking their pipes; but for the life of me, though I listen, I cannot make out what they say. They will not know the difference between you and I, however, and the camel will be as quiet with you as he is with me."

I was very willing to take advantage of Ben's suggestion; so giving my horses into his keeping, I took his camel and led it up in front of Siddy Boo Cassem's tent, where, making it lie down, I threw myself on the ground near it. Its owner and several friends were seated, as Ben expected,—the hoods of their burnouses, drawn over their heads, making them look more like a party of old crones than stalwart Arabs habituated to war and the chase; or I might have taken them for the witches in "Macbeth" discussing their malevolent designs. On one side were the ruined walls of the Roman town, with a tall monument rising above them; in front were the tents, spread beneath a few sparsely scattered palm-trees; while beyond could be seen the boundless Desert, the crescent moon casting a pale light over the scene.

As Siddy Boo Cassem knew that Ben could not understand him, even had he been, as he supposed, near at hand, he and his friends spoke in loud tones; every now and then indulging in a chuckling laugh at each other's wit, or at the recollection of some scene in which they had been engaged. I listened attentively, endeavouring to catch all they said. Much of their conversation was not very edifying, but I became all attention when Siddy Boo Cassem began to talk of his famous camel, and to boast of his deads.

"Curses on the mother who bore them!" he exclaimed. "The rogues would like to have him again, if they knew how near he was to them; but I will take good care that none of their tribe scour again over the plain on his back. He is not likely to remember his old haunts, or the masters who owned him, or I should not have brought him so near them again."

"How did you obtain him, O friend of the Prophet?" asked one of the party.

"As wise men obtain what they desire and cannot otherwise get," answered Siddy Boo Cassem. "I stole him. I heard the report of his swiftness, and determined to become his master. At that time I possessed two fine black slaves, nimble of foot, and cunning in all their ways. Mounted on a fleet steed, of black hue, in case I should have to beat a retreat, and accompanied by my two slaves, I approached the camp an hour after midnight. One of the slaves had also visited the camp some days before, that he might ascertain where the Bu Saef was wont to be tethered; and I had promised him his liberty should we succeed. I remained behind a ruined wall, through which I had a view of the camp. Anxiously I watched, till in less than an hour I distinguished through the gloom the shadowy figure of the longed-for camel coming across the plain towards me. I already felt that he was mine, and could scarcely refrain from galloping forward to meet him. He reached the ruins, the faithful lad leading him; but just at the moment I was mounting on his back a party of horsemen were seen issuing from the camp. Alee threw himself upon my horse, while I gave Bu Saef the rein. Fleet as the wind he flew over the plain. A shriek reached my ears; my slave had received his death-blow. A shot followed; neither Alee nor my black horse did I ever see more. But I had obtained the object of my desire, at the price of a horse and two slaves, which was as nothing compared to his value. Ever since, for many a long year, have I ridden Bu Saef across the Desert in safety, distancing every foe when pursued, following up their traces when they have been attempting to escape, and ascertaining the whereabouts of their camp."

"Allah is great! you performed a fine stroke of business," exclaimed the company in chorus.

"Ho, ho! if you stole Bu Saef, we shall be justified in returning him to his former owners, Siddy Boo Cassem," I thought to myself. But how that was to be done, was the question. Bu Saef could not carry all five of us, that was certain; and probably would refuse to move unless mounted by his accustomed rider. I listened as eagerly as before to the conversation, which went on without cessation for some hours; for the Arabs are as good talkers as any people on the earth. I gathered from what I heard that our party had advanced nearly as far north as it was considered prudent to go, as the country beyond was held by the infidels, or by tribes on friendly terms with them; that the great chief, Abd-el-Kader, having been captured, his hordes were dispersed; and that the tribe from which the Bu Saef had been stolen was now encamped at no great distance from where we were. Of course, I knew that the infidels spoken of were the French; and I felt sure that, could we communicate with any outpost, the officer in command would do his utmost to obtain our liberation—though that might be a difficult matter to accomplish. The tribes of the Desert still entertained hostile feelings towards those who were on friendly terms with the French, and no intercourse was maintained between them. The exact object of our expedition I could not learn; but that was of little consequence. The great point to decide was the means of getting away; and that I did not despair of, difficult as it appeared.

AN EAVESDROPPER

I lay perfectly still, so that, should any of the Arabs look towards me, they might suppose I was asleep. My only fear was that Siddy Boo Cassem might summon Ben, when I should run a great risk of being discovered, and he might suspect that I had an object in taking his slave's place. I was relieved at length when the Arabs separated, some going into Siddy Boo Cassem's tent, and others elsewhere. At last, on hearing loud snoring from the tent, I crept slowly away, crouching down on the ground till I found Ben, who in like manner returned to his proper place.

After this, as may be supposed, we could talk of nothing else but the means of escape. The distance between us and the tribe we wished to reach was about thirty miles. On foot, it would be scarcely possible to accomplish that distance during the night, even were we to run the whole distance. We should also probably fall in with natives, who might take it into their heads to stop us, and perhaps put us to death; while, as soon as our flight was discovered, we should certainly be pursued.

Selim, who was as anxious to escape as we were, volunteered to go first, to try and find some place in which we might conceal ourselves should we be pursued, and where we might remain till the camp had broken up and returned southward. He believed that he would have time to make a search during the night for the sort of place which would answer our purpose, and to return before daybreak without being discovered.

If not pursued, we intended to push on as far as we could without stopping. We therefore hid away as large a stock of provisions as we could, so that, should we be obliged to lie concealed for any length of time, we might not be starved. From the information I gained, too, it seemed likely that we should soon be shifting our camp, and we could scarcely expect to reach a place from which we were so likely to make our escape as where we now were. Besides, the moon was nearly at its full, and though we might get out of the camp more easily during the dark, still we could not find our way unless with the light which it would afford us. We had already wandered over the country for some distance from the hill, and had carefully noted the road that it was evident we should take. We determined, therefore, no longer to put off our adventure.

Selim slipped out directly all around him were asleep, made his way down the hill without being seen, and was soon lost in the darkness. We resolved, should he return unobserved, and report favourably, to start the next night.

So anxious were we all, we could with difficulty go to sleep, though we did not expect him back for some hours. My eyes at length closed; and it seemed but a moment afterwards when I heard a voice whispering in my ear, and looking up, saw Selim seated by my side. "All right," he said; "I have discovered an old ruin, about a mile from this, some way off the highroad; and though I had no little fear of meeting with hyenas or other wild beasts, I explored it completely, and found within the walls a hollow space with a narrow entrance, in which we might remain concealed—even if the people are looking for us—by blocking up the passage with a few stones. The place I speak of will do even though we are pursued immediately on leaving the camp. After this I went on for two hours, when I found, amid a grove of palm-trees, a still larger ruin. One side had fallen down; and I thought that if I could climb up I might find some chambers or hollows in the heaps of ruins, in which we might conceal ourselves without much risk of being discovered. I was not disappointed; and if we can reach that spot without being seen, we may remain there in safety till our pursuers have returned."

This information greatly raised our spirits, and we resolved to leave the camp without further delay, and make our way to the tribe in alliance with the French.

We had of late performed our respective duties with such apparent cheerfulness that the Arabs supposed we were reconciled to our lot. Providence, too, just then favoured us in a way we little expected. Siddy Boo Cassem fell ill, and recollecting that Boxall was supposed to possess medical knowledge, he sent for him; directing me to come also, to act as interpreter. Boxall very conscientiously recommended a sudorific, and charged him to keep himself well covered up during the night, and on no account to leave his couch. We accordingly piled on the top of him all the cloaks and rugs we could find, and so wrapped him up that he could not well move had he wished it.

Unsuspicious of our designs, he promised to follow Boxall's injunctions.

The moon was now waning, and would not rise till some time after the occupants of the camp had gone to sleep. Selim, we agreed, was to start first; Boxall, Halliday, and I, should we not be interrupted, were to follow; while Ben, mounted on the camel, was to make his way down the hill, and place himself at our head, in order that, should he be seen, he might be taken for some traveller, with his attendants, leaving the camp on a night journey. As soon as we were out of sight of the camp, Ben was to start off at full speed to the northward; and as I had instructed him what to say, we hoped he would be able to make himself sufficiently understood to induce the tribe to move forward to our rescue.

Selim set off at the time agreed on, and soon disappeared in the darkness. We then crept out one by one, and made our way among the sleeping camels and horses, unobserved by any of their keepers. We next waited anxiously for the appearance of Ben; who, to our great satisfaction, at last came riding down the hill, and placed himself at our head,—when it was almost ludicrous to observe the air of unconcern he assumed as he rode forward at our head. The plain we had to pass was perfectly open, without a tree or shrub to conceal us, so that all we could hope for was that no suspicious eyes might be turned in the direction we were pursuing. On we went, wishing that Ben would hasten forward with the camel; but there he sat, letting the beast walk at its usual pace—which, when it was not obliged to put forth its powers, was unusually slow.

We had got round the hill, and were steering northward, when, as we looked over our shoulders, what was our dismay to see several Arabs mounted on camels coming down from the camp at full speed! It was evident that Ben had been seen, and his object suspected.

Boxall shouted to him to push on without thinking of us, and not to pull rein till he had reached those who might be induced to come to our assistance.

OUR ESCAPE

"Ay, ay, sir," he answered. "Trust me for that. I'll not drop anchor till Bu Saef has rejoined his old masters."

Saying this, off he went; and we felt very sure that, fleet as were the camels who were pursuing him, he would not be overtaken. In a few seconds he was out of sight.

Chapter Sixteen.

Hotly pursued—Ben gallops off on Bu Saef—We find
concealment in a ruin—Surrounded by our pursuers—A
fierce conflict—Ben appears—A friendly reception—How
Ben arrived at the French camp—Sail for Old England—
Conclusion.

We ran on as fast as our legs could carry us, hoping that the Arabs,
having their eyes fixed on Ben, had not perceived us. Bu Saef had a
long start, for the other camels while descending the hill could not
advance so rapidly as on the plain. We had thus also an advantage,
of which we were determined to make the best use: inured to long
tramps across the Desert, with but little flesh on our bones, and our
muscles well strung, we could run as fast as any ordinary camels over
the hard ground. We were in good wind, too, and had no fear of
getting tired; instead, therefore, of stopping at the first place Selim had
discovered, we pushed on for the ruined temple he had discovered in
the wood. I may formerly have run faster for a short distance, but
never had I gone over so many miles of ground at such a rate.

Almost before I thought it possible that we could have got so far,
Selim, who led the way, pointing to a wood, cried out, "There's the
place where we can hide ourselves!" We immediately darted into it,
he leading us amid the trees to the ruins he had described, and up
which we quickly scrambled. Now and again turning our heads
where the ground was more open, and where no trees or other
objects impeded the view, we caught glimpses of the shadowy forms
of our pursuers against the dark sky; but the sight only nerved us to
fresh exertions. Mounting up steps formed by the fallen walls, we
gained the top ledge, which had apparently once supported a floor;
and creeping along it, and through a narrow doorway, we found
ourselves in a small chamber some twenty feet or so above the
ground. Numbers of loose stones lay about, with which we instantly
set to work to block up the entrance, making as little noise in the
operation as we could. A small fracture in the wall would serve as a
window, too, on the side which commanded the road, and enable us

to look out. By piling up a few stones, I found I was able to reach it; so I took post there to watch our pursuers, while the rest were working as I have described.

BEN'S FLIGHT.

Scarcely had I begun to look out when I saw five men on camels, the moon shining on their arms, pushing along as fast as they could go to the northward, evidently supposing that we were before them. I had little fear of their overtaking Ben; indeed, they themselves could scarcely have expected to do so. Had we, however, continued on, they would certainly have come up with us.

Though I would gladly have thrown myself on the ground to rest, I continued looking out from my watchtower. But no other Arabs followed. Probably it was thought that the five armed men could easily master us. My fear was that, when they could not find us, they might suspect where we were hidden, and should come and search the ruins. No one appeared, however; and I had waited for upwards of an hour when I saw the five camels returning at a leisurely pace, the riders looking about them on every side. The trees in front of the building at length hid them from sight. Would they now venture to stop and search for us? As the Arabs have a notion that such places are inhabited by Jins or evil spirits, I was in hopes that they would, at all events, not attempt to explore it till daylight; but even if they did, we considered that we were so securely hidden that they were not likely to find us. At last their voices ceased; whatever might have been their suspicions, they continued their way back to the camp.

We now held a consultation whether we should at once push on to meet our expected friends, or remain in our secure hiding-place till their arrival.

Tired as we were with our long run, during which we had strained every muscle to the utmost, we settled to remain in the ruins till the afternoon; indeed, it was not likely that, even should Ben induce the allies of the French to come to our assistance, they could reach the place for some hours. He would not know, either, whether we had been captured or not; and as it must have seemed to him that there was every probability of our having again fallen into the hands of our task-masters, he might have advised the sheikh to wait till he could send forward a force able to cope with the party under Siddy Boo Cassem.

Our spirits were high, for we had accomplished far more than we expected, and we had every hope of escaping from the galling bondage we had for so long endured.

"Come, Charlie," said Boxall, "I'll take the look-out now." So gladly yielding up my place, I threw myself on the ground, and was asleep in a few moments.

When I awoke, daylight was streaming in through our narrow look-out hole, at which Selim was now stationed, while Boxall and Halliday were fast asleep, they having been in the interval on the watch. I did not wake them; but climbing up where Selim stood, I asked if he had seen anything.

"No," he answered; "not a single person has passed. The peasantry, I suspect, have fled from this part of the country, and we may possibly make our way to the camp of our friends without meeting any one. It would, however, be a long journey on foot; and should Siddy Boo Cassem send out an expedition, we might run the risk of being overtaken and recaptured."

Notwithstanding what he said, I could not help feeling a strong desire to push on, and I thought of proposing to Boxall and Halliday to do so. Still, while they slept so soundly, I did not like to awake them.

After some time I told Selim to lie down again, and I would keep watch.

Feeling very hungry, I munched some of the dates and barley-bread which we had brought with us. This made me thirsty, and reminded me that we must search for water before we could attempt to proceed. I was, therefore, on the point of awaking Selim and asking him to make his way out to look for some—he being more likely to succeed than any of us—when the sound of horses' hoofs on the hard ground reached my ear. Turning my head round, I saw, marching from behind the grove of trees which concealed the road abreast of us, a troop of horsemen, among whom I recognised a number of the chiefs and others whom I had seen at the camp. Several of them dashed into the wood, through which they passed quickly, and then, as I guessed from the sounds which reached me, came close up to the ruin. I fancied that some had dismounted, and were scrambling among the masses of stone searching for us, and I trembled lest we might have left some traces by which they should discover our retreat. I dared not move, for fear they might hear me; and I dreaded every moment that my companions would awake, and, unaware of our danger, utter some sound which might draw attention to us. I was almost afraid to breathe.

More horsemen now appeared on the road, and from the movements of the party there was no doubt that they were convinced we were hiding in the neighbourhood. I listened to the voices of those who were searching for us, and tried to make out what was said. They appeared to be stumbling among the masses of fallen ruins, looking into every hole, and poking their swords into every crevice.

"The cursed Nazarenes cannot be here," I at last heard one exclaim. "They must have gone on further, if they are not concealed nearer the camp."

"They may have fleet heels, but they could not have got further than this when we passed the place," exclaimed a second.

"May curses rest on them and their ancestors," growled another.

Still my companions slept. Even now I dreaded lest the slightest sound they might make should catch the ears of our pursuers, who at that moment were close under us. It did not occur to them that, like cats, we should have climbed up to such a height; nor, of course, were they aware of the existence of the secret chamber in which we lay hid. Perhaps hundreds of years had passed since it was entered by a human being, and it was next to a miracle that Selim should have discovered it.

How thankful I felt when, by the sounds made by the Arabs as they scrambled over the ruins, I knew that they were returning to their horses. Presently I caught sight of them, as they passed in front of my look-out hole on their way to join their comrades, who had gone on in advance. Not, however, till they were at a considerable distance, did I venture to arouse my companions. I then got Boxall to look out at them, for I suspected he might otherwise suppose that the account I had to give was a creation of my imagination.

He and the rest were all now convinced of the danger we had escaped. The question as to whether we should leave our place of concealment was settled, too, for the present; for, of course, we determined to remain where we were till the Arabs had left the neighbourhood.

I have not repeated one tenth part of the curses heaped on our heads, or the threats of vengeance uttered by our pursuers. Their chief cause of anger, however, was the loss of the famed Bu Saef. Among them I now recognised Siddy Boo Cassem, as well as several of his relatives and friends; and I had not the slightest doubt but that they would have put us to death in revenge for our having carried off the animal. Should they overtake Ben, his fate would be sealed; but we had little fear on his account, as he must, unless some accident had happened to him, be many leagues ahead of his pursuers.

None of us felt inclined to go to sleep again; but we judged it prudent to remain close in our lair, for fear any passer-by should catch sight of us, and inform our enemies on their return. At length we suffered so greatly from thirst, that we were induced to let Selim creep out to try and find water. Boxall had thoughtfully brought away a leathern bottle, such as Arabs always carry with them; but he had not filled it, on account of the weight. We charged Selim not to go far, however, and to conceal himself as much as possible, while he kept a sharp look-out on every side, as it would be far better to endure the severest thirst rather than run the risk of being discovered. Often before had we endured thirst, but on such occasions we had been unable to obtain water; now that it was possible to get it, we could not resist the temptation, notwithstanding the risk to be run.

Having removed a few of the stones, Selim crawled out, and scrambled down among the ruins; but we could not watch him without exposing ourselves, and had therefore to remain in anxious suspense during his absence. It seemed to us a terribly long time; and at length we began to fear that Siddy Boo Cassem's party would return before he got back to us. We waited and waited, our thirst increasing till we could scarcely bear it longer—one of us all the while keeping a look-out at the only aperture by which we could command a view of the road.

A couple of hours, at the least, must have passed, when we heard a slight noise beneath us; and the next instant Selim came crawling along the ledge, and entered by the hole we had made.

"Quick, quick!" he whispered, "stop it up. I was pursued, and must have been noticed entering the ruin."

He had brought the bottle full of water, and, in spite of our anxiety, we could not resist putting it in succession to our lips till we had drained it to the bottom.

While the rest sat down, I continued to look out; and we listened anxiously for the approach of the people Selim had seen. In a short time we heard people speaking beneath us. They were Arabs, and, from their style of speaking, natives of the place—who would probably be as ready to deliver us up to one party as the other, and would choose the one with whom they could make the best bargain. They were far more likely to discover us than Siddy Boo Cassem's followers, as they most probably were well acquainted with the ruin. Our anxiety was somewhat relieved, however, when we heard one of them remark—

"It must have been a Jin, though he looked like a black slave; and this is known to be the dwelling-place of Jins."

"Take care lest any of them rush out on us," cried another.

"Allah, Allah, Allah is great, and Mohammed is his Prophet!" they sang out in chorus, as a charm to keep the Jins at a distance.

Notwithstanding their fears, they continued to hunt about. We might possibly, by uttering some wild shrieks or other strange sounds, have put them to flight, but the risk was too great, as they were evidently climbing about among the stones, and making a more thorough search than the other party had done.

Just then I caught sight, in the distance, of a horseman galloping along the road at full speed. His turban was off, and his sword broken. Others followed, in even worse plight; and as they came nearer I saw that blood was streaming from the heads or sides of several of them.

Presently the sound of a dropping fire reached us. A larger body of those who had ridden by in such gallant trim in the morning now galloped past in an opposite direction, without turbans, their weapons broken or lost, their dresses torn, and covered with dust from head to foot. A still larger body followed, keeping close together, and firing as they advanced,—evidently in pursuit of the former.

The Arabs who were hunting for us rushed off on hearing the sounds, and we were left in safety, as far as they were concerned; but whether the pursuers of our late masters would prove friends or foes, we could not tell. They were just at the end of the wood when the fugitives rallied, and charged them with such fury that they were driven back, and we feared that the fortunes of the day would be changed. Several fell on both sides. Siddy Boo Cassem fought with the greatest bravery, and encouraging his followers to merit paradise, again and again charged his foes.

We looked in vain for Bu Saef. Had the camel appeared, our doubts as to Ben's safety, and the way we should be treated by the hitherto victorious party, would have been set at rest.

Just then, amid the clouds of dust which surrounded the combatants, we caught sight of a fresh body of horsemen coming from the northward. In a few minutes they had reached the scene of conflict, shouting, as they advanced, various battle-cries, some in Arabic, others in French. Presently a cry louder than all the rest reached our ears—a truly British Hurrah!—and at the same time I caught sight of Ben, sticking like wax to the back of a fiery steed, and flourishing a huge sabre, as he led on a party of dark-skinned Arabs, who had to urge forward their steeds to keep up with him. The front ranks, which had hitherto been hotly engaged and hard pressed, wheeled aside to let the new-comers pass. Siddy Boo Cassem saw them coming, and knowing that all hope of victory was lost, shouted to his people, wheeled round his horse, and galloped off as fast as the animal could put his feet to the ground. Ben and his followers then swept by like a whirlwind, and our only fear now was that the gallant fellow might lose his life by a chance shot from the flying enemy.

Having no longer any doubt as to the reception we would meet with, we were about to rush out and join the Algerines; but Boxall stopped us. "Stay," he exclaimed; "they may suppose we are a party of the enemy lying in ambush. Let one of us go forward and present himself."

I volunteered, and descending from our place of concealment, advanced outside the wood. Already a party of the Algerine forces had halted to attend to the wounded; while several of the Arabs levelled their rifles at me, and two or three bullets whistled near my head, before I could make them understand that I was a friend.

On reaching the main body, I found several persons dressed in half Oriental and half European costume, some of whom I guessed were French surgeons, from the way they were attending to the wounded Arabs. I quickly made myself known, and met with a cordial reception.

Going to a spot whence I could be seen from the tower, I made the signal agreed on to my friends within it, who at once descended and hurried to the spot. The French officers congratulated us warmly on our wonderful escape, they having heard from Ben of our long captivity. One of them — who was the officer in command — spoke English fairly, and gave us an account of the sailor's arrival among them, at which they, and even the Arabs, who guessed what we were talking about, laughed heartily.

The information of the approach of an enemy had a short time before been brought to them, and the French had just arrived at the Arab camp preparatory to commencing a march southward, when, by the light of the full moon, a camel, fleet as the wind, was seen approaching the camp. The animal, instead of being reined up by its rider, galloped forward, the assembled multitude making way on either side; when suddenly it stopped, and, as a natural consequence, off flew honest Ben from its back into their midst. Without being in the least disconcerted, as soon as he had picked himself up he began to shout out, in English and such Arabic as he could command —

"Come along, all of you, as fast as you can, and save my officers from being knocked on the head by the villainous crew from whom we have escaped, as we had a right to do."

How Ben might have been received by the Arabs, it is hard to say; but at that moment the sheikh, the former owner of Bu Saef, came forward and recognised his well-beloved and long-lost camel. In a moment Ben found himself treated with the greatest respect and attention. The French commandant coming up, quickly learned all about us; and finding that there was no time to be lost, he at once despatched the first party of Arab cavalry that was ready to start, following himself shortly afterwards with others, accompanied by Ben.

The French commandant having posted men in the wood and among the ruins, so as to attack the enemy on their flank, in the event of those who had gone in pursuit being compelled to retreat, we waited anxiously for their return. Presently we saw clouds of dust rising from the south, out of which the Algerine forces at length emerged. I looked out eagerly for Ben; and not seeing him, feared that he must have fallen. At length, to my great joy, I caught sight of him, with his huge sabre in his hand, alongside the sheikh; with whom he seemed to be on the most intimate terms. Ben's delight at seeing us was great in the extreme; and throwing himself from his horse, he ran up to us, shaking us all in succession warmly by the hand.

"Beg pardon, gentlemen, for the liberty I take," he exclaimed; "but I cannot help it—on my life, I cannot—I am so glad to see that you have got away all right from those cut-throat fellows! They will not dare to make slaves of English officers again in a hurry."

As the French commandant was doubtful of the strength of the enemy, who might possibly descend in force, he ordered his troops to return. The wounded were placed in panniers on the backs of mules, which were brought up for the purpose; and several of the enemy's horses being caught, we were soon all mounted, and on the way with our new friends to the northward. We reached the French outposts by nightfall, where we were most hospitably entertained by the commandant and his officers, who supplied us with clothing and other necessaries.

The sheikh, to show his gratitude to Ben for having brought him back Bu Saef, offered to receive him into his tribe, and to make him a chief.

"Please, Mr Blore, tell the old gentleman that I am much obliged to him," answered Ben; "but as I have not fallen quite into his style of living, I beg he will excuse me; and, to say the truth, I had rather serve on board a man-of-war till I can get a pension, and go and settle down with my Susan in Old England, than turn into an Arab sheikh with a dozen wives and a thousand blackamoor followers."

Having recruited our strength, we some days after left our kind French friends and set off for Algiers, where we arrived safely; and soon afterwards, accompanied by Selim, we embarked for England.

HOW BEN REACHED THE FRENCH CAMP

I need not say that we were welcomed there as if from the dead, by
our friends; and I trust that we were all thankful for the merciful
way in which we had been preserved from the numberless dangers

we had gone through. Andrew Spurling was delighted to see us. "I told you, Mr Blore, that you would find Arabic useful, though I little thought at the time how much service its acquirement would render you," he exclaimed as he shook me by the hand. "However, it proves, as I once observed to you, that the more knowledge we can pick up the better, as we can never tell how valuable it may become to us."

Lightning Source UK Ltd.
Milton Keynes UK
UKHW010852100921
390347UK00001B/93